"I can look at a man—one glance will do—and know instantly whether he's adequate," said the golden-haired lady.

"Thank you," I said.

"Save the compliments. Sometimes I'm wrong, of course," she said, poisonously sweet. "Not always, but sometimes."

"Sometimes I am, too."

"About women?"

"About anything. I have second sight, you know. The future is an open book to me."

"You sound serious," she said.

"I am. It's the way I earn my living. . . ."

THE STOCHASTIC MAN

Robert Silverberg

FAWCETT GOLD MEDAL • NEW YORK

It is remarkable that a science which began with the consideration of games of chance should have become the most important object of human knowledge. . . . The most important questions of life are, for the most part, really only problems of probability.

—LAPLACE, *Théorie Analytique des Probabilités*

Once a man learns to *see* he finds himself alone in the world with nothing but folly.

—CASTANEDA, *A Separate Reality*

THE STOCHASTIC MAN

THIS BOOK CONTAINS THE COMPLETE TEXT OF THE ORIGINAL HARDCOVER EDITION.

Published by Fawcett Gold Medal Books, a unit of CBS Publications, the Consumer Publishing Division of CBS Inc., by arrangement with Scott Meredith Literary Agency

Copyright © 1975 by Robert Silverberg

ISBN: 0-449-13570-5

Printed in the United States of America

12 11 10 9 8 7 6 5 4 3

1

We are born by accident into a purely random universe. Our lives are determined by entirely fortuitous combinations of genes. Whatever happens happens by chance. The concepts of cause and effect are fallacies. There are only *seeming* causes leading to *apparent* effects. Since nothing truly follows from anything else, we swim each day through seas of chaos, and nothing is predictable, not even the events of the very next instant.

Do you believe that?

If you do, I pity you, because yours must be a bleak and terrifying and comfortless life.

I think I once believed something very much like that, when I was about seventeen and the world seemed hostile and incomprehensible. I think I once believed that the universe is a gigantic dice game, without purpose or pattern, into which we foolish mortals interpose the comforting notion of causality for the sake of supporting our precarious, fragile sanity. I think I once felt that in this random, capricious cosmos we're lucky to survive from hour to hour, let alone from year to year, because at any moment, without warning or reason, the sun might go nova or the world turn into a great blob of petroleum jelly. Faith and good works are insufficient, indeed irrele-

vant; anything might befall anyone at any time; therefore
live for the moment and take no heed of tomorrow, for it
takes no heed of you.

A mighty cynical-sounding philosophy, and mighty
adolescent-sounding, too. Adolescent cynicism is mainly
a defense against fear. As I grew older I suppose I found
the world less frightening, and I became less cynical. I
regained some of the innocence of childhood and accepted, as any child accepts, the concept of causality.
Push the baby and the baby falls down. Cause and effect.
Let the begonia go a week without water and the begonia
starts to shrivel. Cause and effect. Kick the football hard
and it sails through the air. Cause and effect, cause and
effect. The universe, I conceded, may be without purpose,
but certainly not without pattern. Thus I took my first
steps on the road that led me to my career and thence into
politics and from there to the teachings of the all-seeing
Martin Carvajal, that dark and tortured man who now
rests in the peace he dreaded. It was Carvajal who brought
me to the place in space and time I occupy on this day.

2 My name is Lew Nichols. I have light sandy hair, dark eyes, no significant identifying scars, and I stand exactly two meters tall. I was married—two-group—to Sundara Shastri. We had no children and now we are separated, no decree. My current age is not quite thirty-five years. I was born in New York City on 1 January 1966 at 0216 hours. Earlier that evening two simultaneous events of historic magnitude were recorded in New York: the inauguration of the glamorous and famous Mayor John Lindsay and the onset of the great, catastrophic first New York subway strike. Do you believe in simultaneity? I do. There's no stochasticity without simultaneity, and no sanity either. If we try to see the universe as an aggregation of unrelated happenings, a sparkling pointillist canvas of noncausality, we're lost.

My mother was due to deliver in mid-January, but I arrived two weeks ahead of time, most inconveniently for my parents, who had to get to the hospital in the small hours of New Year's Eve in a city suddenly deprived of public transport. If their predictive techniques had been keener, they might have thought of renting a car that evening. If Mayor Lindsay had been using better pre-

7

dictive techniques, I suppose the poor bastard would have resigned at his own swearing-in and saved himself years of headaches.

3 Causality is a decent, honorable principle, but it doesn't have all the answers. If we want to make sense of things, we have to move on beyond it. We have to recognize that many important phenomena refuse to be packed into neat casual packages but can be interpreted only by stochastic methods.

A system in which events occur according to a law of probability but aren't individually determined in accordance with the principle of causality is a stochastic system. The daily rising of the sun isn't a stochastic event; it's inflexibly and invariably determined by the relative positions of the earth and the sun in the heavens, and once we understand the causal mechanism there's no risk in predicting that the sun will rise tomorrow and the next day and the next. We can even predict the exact time of sunrise, and we don't *guess* it, we *know it in advance*. The tendency of water to flow downhill isn't a stochastic event either; it's a function of gravitational attraction, which we hold to be a constant. But there are many areas where causality fails us and stochasticity must come to our rescue.

For instance we're unable to predict the movements of any one molecule in a liter of oxygen, but with some

9

understanding of kinetic theory we can confidently antici-
pate the behavior of the whole liter. We have no way of
foretelling when a particular uranium atom will undergo
radioactive decay, but we can calculate quite accurately
how many atoms in a block of U-235 will disintegrate in
the next ten thousand years. We don't know what the
next spin of the roulette wheel will bring, but the house
has a good idea of what its take is likely to be over the
course of a long evening. All sorts of processes, however
unpredictable they may seem on a minute-to-minute or
case-by-case basis, are predictable by stochastic techniques.

Stochastic. According to the Oxford English Dictionary
this word was coined in 1662 and is now *rare* or *obs*.
Don't believe it. It's the OED that's *obs*., not *stochastic*,
which gets less *obs*. every day. The word is from the
Greek, originally meaning "target" or "point of aim,"
from which the Greeks derived a word meaning "to aim
at a mark," and, by metaphorical extension, "to reflect,
to think." It came into English first as a fancy way of
saying "pertaining to guesswork," as in Whitefoot's remark about Sir Thomas Browne in 1712: "Tho' he were
no prophet . . . yet in that faculty which comes nearest it,
he excelled, i.e., the stochastick, wherein he was seldom
mistaken, as to future events."

In the immortal words of Ralph Cudworth (1617–
1688), "There is need and use of this stochastical judging
and opinion concerning truth and falsehood in human
life." Those whose way of life is truly governed by the
stochastic philosophy are prudent and judicious, and tend
never to generalize from a skimpy sample. As Jacques
Bernoulli demonstrated early in the eighteenth century,
an isolated event is no harbinger of anything, but the
greater your sampling the more likely you are to guess the
true distribution of phenomena within your sample.

So much for probability theory. I pass swiftly and
uneasily over Poisson distributions, the Central Limit
Theorem, the Kolmogorov axioms, Ehrenhaft games,
Markov chains, the Pascal triangle, and all the rest. I
mean to spare you such mathematical convolutions. ("Let

p be the probability of the happening of an event in a single trial, and let s be the number of times the event is observed to happen in n trials . . .") My point is only that the pure stochastician teaches himself to observe what we at the Center for Stochastic Processes have come to call the Bernoulli Interval, a pause during which we ask ourselves, *Do I really have enough data to draw a valid conclusion?*

I'm executive secretary of the Center, which was incorporated four months ago, in August, 2000. Carvajal's money pays our expenses. For now we occupy a five-room house in a rural section of northern New Jersey, and I don't care to be more specific about the location. Our aim is to find ways of reducing the Bernoulli Interval to zero: that is, to make guesses of ever-increasing accuracy on the basis of an ever-decreasing statistical sample, or, to put it another way, to move from probabilistic to absolute prediction, or, rephrasing it yet again, to replace guesswork with clairvoyance.

So we work toward post-stochastic abilities. What Carvajal taught me is that stochasticity isn't the end of the line: it's merely a phase, soon to pass, in our striving toward full revelation of the future, in our struggle to free ourselves from the tyranny of randomness. In the absolute universe all events can be regarded as absolutely deterministic, and if we can't perceive the greater structures, it's because our vision is faulty. If we had a real grasp of causality down to the molecular level, we wouldn't need to rely on mathematical approximations, on statistics and probabilities, in making predictions. If our perceptions of cause and effect were only good enough, we'd be able to attain absolute knowledge of what is to come. We would make ourselves all-seeing. So Carvajal said. I believe he was right. You probably don't. You tend to be skeptical about such things, don't you? That's all right. You'll change your mind. I know you will.

4   Carvajal is dead now; he died exactly when and as he knew he would. I am still here, and I think I know how I will die, too, but I'm not altogether sure of it, and in any case it doesn't seem to matter to me the way it did to him. He never had the strength that was necessary to sustain his visions. He was just a burned-out little man with tired eyes and a drained smile, who had a gift that was too big for his soul, and it was the gift that killed him as much as anything. If I truly have inherited that gift, I hope I make a better job of living with it than he did.

Carvajal is dead, but I'm alive and will be for some time to come. All about me flutter the indistinct towers of the New York of twenty years hence, glittering in the pale light of mornings not yet born. I look at the dull porcelain bowl of the winter sky and see images of my own face, grown much older. So I am not about to vanish. I have a considerable future. I know that the future is a place as fixed and intransient and accessible as the past. Because I know this I've abandoned the wife I loved, given up the profession that was making me rich, and acquired the enmity of Paul Quinn, potentially the most dangerous man in the world, Quinn who will be elected President of the

United States four years from now. I'm not afraid of
Quinn personally. He won't be able to harm me. He may
harm democracy and free speech, but he won't harm me.
I feel guilty because I will have helped put Quinn in the
White House, but at least I'll share that guilt with you
and you and you, with your blind mindless votes that
you'll live to wish you could call back. Never mind. We
can survive Quinn. I'll show the way. It will be my form
of atonement. I can save you all from chaos, even now,
even with Quinn astride the horizon and growing more
huge every day.

5 I was into probabilities for seven years, professionally, before I ever heard of Martin Carvajal. My business from the spring of 1992 onward was projections. I can look at the acorn and see the stack of firewood: it's a gift I have. For a fee, I would tell you whether I think particle chips will continue to be a growth industry, whether it's a good idea to open a tattooing parlor in Topeka, whether the fad for bare scalps is going to last long enough to make it worthwhile for you to expand your San Jose depilatory factory. And the odds are I'd be right.

My father liked to say, "A man doesn't choose his life. His life chooses him."

Maybe. I never expected to go into the prophecy trade. I never really expected to go into anything. My father feared I'd be a wastrel. Certainly it looked that way the day I collected my college diploma. (NYU '86.) I sailed through my three years of college not knowing at all what I wanted to do with my life, other than that it ought to be something communicative, creative, lucrative, and reasonably useful to society. I didn't want to be a novelist, a teacher, an actor, a lawyer, a stockbroker, a general, or a priest. Industry and finance didn't attract me, medicine was beyond my capabilities, politics seemed vulgar and blatant. I knew my skills, which are primarily verbal and conceptual, and I knew my needs, which are primarily security-oriented and privacy-oriented. I was and am bright, outgoing, alert, energetic, willing to work hard, and candidly opportunistic, though not, I hope, opportunistically candid. But I was missing a focus, a center, a defining point, when college turned me loose.

A man's life chooses him. I had always had an odd knack for uncanny hunches; by easy stages I turned that into my livelihood. As a summer fill-in job I did some part-time polltaking; one day in the office I happened to make a few astute comments about the pattern the raw data were showing, and my boss invited me to prepare a projective sampling template for the next step of the poll. That's a program that tells you what sort of questions you ought to ask in order to get the answers you need. The work was stimulating and my excellence at it had ego rewards. When one of my employer's big clients asked me to quit and do free-lance consulting work, I took the chance. From there to my own full-time consulting firm was only a matter of months.

When I was in the projection business many uninformed folk thought I was a pollster. No. Pollsters worked for *me*, a whole platoon of hired gallups. They were to me as millers are to a baker: they sorted the wheat from the chaff, I produced the seven-layer cakes. My work was a giant step beyond polltaking. Using data samples collected by the usual quasi-scientific methods, I derived far-ranging predictions, I made intuitive leaps, in short I guessed, and guessed well. There was money in it, but also I felt a kind of ecstasy. When I confronted a mound of raw samples from which I had to pull a major projection, I felt like a diver plunging off a high cliff into a sparkling blue sea, seeking a glittering gold doubloon hidden in the white sand far below the waves: my heart pounded, my mind whirled, my body and my spirit underwent a quantum kick into a higher, more intense energy state. Ecstasy.

What I did was sophisticated and highly technical, but

it was a species of witchcraft, too. I wallowed in harmonic means, positive skews, modal values, and parameters of dispersion. My office was a maze of display screens and graphs. I kept a battery of jumbo computers running around the clock, and what looked like a wristwatch on my wrong arm was actually a data terminal that rarely had time to cool. But the heavy math and the high-powered Hollywood technology were simply aspects of the preliminary phases of my work, the intake stage. When actual projections had to be made, IBM couldn't help me. I had to do my trick with nothing but my unaided mind. I would stand in a dreadful solitude on the edge of that cliff, and though sonar may have told me the configuration of the ocean bottom, though GE's finest transponders had registered the velocity of current flow and the water's temperature and turbidity index, I was altogether on my own in the crucial moment of realization. I would scan the water with narrowed eyes, flexing my knees, swinging my arms, filling my lungs with air, waiting until I *saw*, until I truly *saw*, and when I felt that beautiful confident dizziness back of my eyebrows I would jump at last, I would launch myself headlong into the surging sea in search of that doubloon, I would shoot naked and unprotected and unerring toward my goal.

6 From September of 1997 until March of 2000, nine months ago, I was obsessed with the idea of making Paul Quinn President of the United States.

Obsessed. That's a strong word. It smacks of Sacher-Masoch, Krafft-Ebing, ritual handwashing, rubber undergarments. Yet I think it precisely describes my involvement with Quinn and his ambitions.

Haig Mardikian introduced me to Quinn in the summer of '95. Haig and I went to private school together—the Dalton, circa 1980–82, where we played a lot of basketball—and we've kept in touch ever since. He's a slick lynx-eyed lawyer about three meters tall who wants to be, among many other things, the first United States Attorney General of Armenian ancestry, and probably will be.

(*Probably?* How can I doubt it?) On a sweltering August afternoon he phoned to say, "Sarkisian is having a big splash tonight. You're invited. I guarantee that something good will come out of it for you." Sarkisian is a real estate operator who, so it seems, owns both sides of the Hudson River for six or seven hundred kilometers.

"Who'll be there?" I asked. "Aside from Ephrikian, Missakian, Hagopian, Manoogian, Garabedian, and Boghosian."

"Berberian and Khatisian," he said. "Also—" And Mardikian ran off a brilliant, a dazzling, list of celebrities from the world of finance, politics, industry, science, and the arts, ending with "—and Paul Quinn." Meaningful emphasis on that final name.

"Should I know him, Haig?"

"You should, but right now you probably don't. At present he's the assemblyman from Riverdale. A man who'll be going places in public life."

I didn't particularly care to pass my Saturday night hearing some ambitious young Irish pol explain his plan for revamping the galaxy, but on the other hand I had done a few projective jobs for politicians before and there was money in it, and Mardikian probably knew what was good for me. And the guest list was irresistible. Besides, my wife was spending August as a guest of a temporarily shorthanded six-group in Oregon and I suppose I entertained some hopeful fantasy of going home that evening with a sultry dark-haired Armenian lady.

"What time?" I asked.

"Nine," Mardikian said.

So to Sarkisian's place: a triplex penthouse atop a ninety-story circular alabaster-and-onyx condo tower on a Lower West Side offshore platform. Blank-faced guards who might just as well have been constructs of metal and plastic checked my identity, scanned me for weapons, and admitted me. The air within was a blue haze. The sour, spicy odor of powdered bone dominated everything: we were smoking doped calcium that year. Crystalline oval windows like giant portholes ringed the entire apartment. In the eastward-facing rooms the view was blocked by the two monolithic slabs of the World Trade Center, but elsewhere Sarkisian did provide a decent 270-degree panorama of New York Harbor, New Jersey, the West Side Expressway, and maybe some of Pennsylvania. Only in one of the giant wedge-shaped rooms were the portholes opaqued, and when I went into an adjoining wedge and peered at a sharp angle I found out why: that side of the tower faced the still undemolished stump of the Statue of Liberty, and Sarkisian apparently didn't want the depressing sight to bring his guests down. (This was the summer of '95, remember, which was one of the more violent years of the decade, and the bombing still had everyone jittery.)

The guests! They were as promised, a spectacular swarm of contraltos and astronauts and quarterbacks and chairpersons of the board. Costumes ran to formal-flamboyant, with the expectable display of breasts and genitalia but also the first hints, from the avant-garde, of the *fin-de-siècle* love of concealment that now has taken over, high throats and tight bandeaus. Half a dozen of the men and several of the women affected clerical garb and there must have been fifteen pseudo generals bedecked with enough medals to shame an African dictator. I was dressed rather simply, I thought, in a pleatless radiation-green singlet and a three-strand bubble necklace. Though the rooms were crowded, the flow of the party was far from formless, for I saw eight or ten big swarthy outgoing men in subdued clothing, key members of Haig Mardikian's ubiquitous Armenian mafia, distributed equidistantly through the main room like cribbage pegs, like goalposts, like pylons, each occupying a preassigned fixed position and efficiently offering smokes and drinks, making introductions, directing people toward other people whose acquaintance it might be desirable for them to make. I was drawn easily into this subtle gridwork, had my hand mangled by Ara Garabedian or Jason Komurjian or perhaps George Missakian, and found myself inserted into orbit on a collision course with a sunny-faced golden-haired woman named Autumn, who wasn't Armenian and with whom I did in fact go home many hours later.

Long before Autumn and I came to that, though, I had been smoothly nudged through a long musical-chairs rotation of conversational partners, during the course of which I

—found myself talking to a female person who was black, witty, stunning-looking, and half a meter taller than I am, and whom I correctly guessed to be Ilene Mulamba, the head of Network Four, a meeting which led to my getting a fancy consulting contract for design of their split-signal ethnic-zone telecasts—

—gently deflected the playful advances of City Councilman Ronald Holbrecht, the self-styled Voice of the Gay Community and the first man outside California to win an election with Homophile Party endorsement—

—wandered into a conversation between two tall white-haired men who looked like bankers and discovered them to be bioenergetics specialists from Bellevue and Columbia-Presbyterian, swapping gossip about their current sonopuncture work, which involved ultrasonic treatment of advanced bone malignancies—

—listened to an executive from CBS Labs telling a goggle-eyed young man about their newly developed charisma-enhancement biofeedback-loop gadget—

—learned that the goggle-eyed young man was Lamont Friedman of the sinister and multifarious investment banking house of Asgard Equities—

—exchanged trifling chitchat with Nole MacIver of the Ganymede Expedition, Claude Parks of the Dope Patrol (who had brought his molecular sax, and didn't need much encouragement to play it), three pro basketball stars and some luminous right-fielder, an organizer for the new civil-service prostitutes' union, a municipal brothel inspector, an assortment of less trendy city officials, and the Brooklyn Museum's curator of transient arts, Mei-ling Pulvermacher—

—had my first encounter with a Transit Creed proctor, the petite but forceful Ms. Catalina Yarber, just arrived from San Francisco, whose attempt to convert me on the spot I declined with oblique excuses—

—and met Paul Quinn.

Quinn, yes. Sometimes I wake quivering and perspiring from a dreamed replay of that party in which I see myself swept by an irresistible current through a sea of yammering celebrities toward the golden, smiling figure of Paul Quinn, who waits for me like Charybdis, eyes agleam, jaws agape. Quinn was thirty-four then, five years my senior, a short powerful-looking man, blond, broad shoulders, wide-set blue eyes, a warm smile, conservative clothes, a rough masculine handshake, grabbing you by the inside of your biceps as well as by your hand, making eye contact with an almost audible snap, establishing instant rapport. All that was standard political technique, and I had seen it often enough before, but never with this degree of intensity and power. Quinn leaped across the person-person gap so quickly and so confidently that I began to suspect he must be wearing one of those CBS charisma-enhancement loops in his earlobe. Mardikian told him my name and right away he was into me with, "You're one of the people I was most eager to meet here tonight," and, "Call me Paul," and, "Let's go where it's a little quieter, Lew," and I knew I was being expertly conned and yet I was nailed despite myself.

He led me to a little salon a few rooms northwest of the main room. Pre-Columbian clay figurines, African masks, pulsar screens, splash stands—a nice mixture of old and new decorative notions. The wallpaper was *New York Times*, vintage 1980 or so. "Some party," Quinn said, grinning. He ran quickly down the guest list, sharing with me a small-boy awe at being among such celebrities.

Then he narrowed the focus and moved in on me.

He had been well briefed. He knew all about me, where I had gone to school, what my degree was in, what sort of work I did, where my office was. He asked if I had brought my wife—"Sundara, isn't that her name? Asian background?"

"Her family's from India."

"She's said to be quite beautiful."

"She's in Oregon this month."

"I hope I'll get a chance to meet her. Perhaps next time I'm out Richmond way I'll give you a call, yes? How do you like living on Staten Island, anyway?"

I had seen this before, too, the full Treatment, the politician's computerized mind at work, as though a nugget of microcircuitry were going click-click-click in there whenever facts were needed, and for a moment I suspected he might be some sort of robot. But Quinn was too good to be unreal. On one level he was simply feeding back everything he had been told about me, and making an impressive performance of it, but on another level he was communicating his amusement at the outrageous excessiveness of his own con job, as though inwardly winking and telling me, *I've got to pile it on, Lew, that's the way I'm supposed to play this dumb game.* Also he seemed to be picking up and reflecting the fact that I, too, was both amused and awed by his skill. He was good. He was frighteningly good. My mind went into automatic project and handed me a series of *Times* headlines that went something like this:

BRONX ASSEMBLYMAN QUINN
ATTACKS SLUM-CLEARANCE DELAYS

MAYOR QUINN CALLS FOR
CITY CHARTER REFORM

SENATOR QUINN SAYS
HE'LL SEEK WHITE HOUSE

QUINN LEADS NEW DEMOCRATS
TO NATIONWIDE LANDSLIDE

PRESIDENT QUINN'S FIRST TERM:
AN APPRAISAL

He went on talking, all the while smiling, maintaining eye contact, holding me impaled. He quizzed me about my profession, he pumped me for my political beliefs, he iterated his own. "They say you've got the best reliability index of any projector in the Northeast. . . . I'll bet not even you anticipated the Gottfried assassination, though. . . . You don't have to be much of a prophet to feel sorry for poor dopey DiLaurenzio, trying to run City Hall at a time like this. . . . This city can't be governed, it has to be juggled. . . . Are you as repelled by that phony Neighborhood Authority Act as I am? . . . What do you think of Con Ed's Twenty-third Street fusion project? . . . You ought to see the flow charts they

found in Gottfried's office safe. . . ." Deftly he plumbed
for common grounds in political philosophy, though he
had to be aware I shared most of his beliefs, for if he
knew so much about me he would know I was a registered New Democrat, that I had done the projections
for the Twenty-first Century Manifesto and its companion, the book *Toward a True Humanity*, that I felt
as he did about priorities and reforms and the whole
inane Puritan idea of trying to legislate morality. The
longer we spoke the more strongly I was drawn to him.

I began making quiet unsettling comparisons between
Quinn and some great politicians of the past—FDR,
Rockefeller, Johnson, the original Kennedy. They had all
had that warm beautiful doublethink knack of being able
to play out the rituals of political conquest and simultaneously to indicate to their more intelligent victims that
nobody's being fooled, we all know it's just a ritual, but
don't you think I'm good at it? Even then, even that first
night in 1995, when he was just a kid assemblyman unknown outside his own borough, I saw him heading into
political history alongside Roosevelt and JFK. Later I
began making more grandiose comparisons, between
Quinn and the likes of Napoleon, Alexander the Great,
even Jesus, and if such talk makes you snicker, please
remember that I am a master of the stochastic arts and
my vision is clearer than yours.

Quinn said nothing to me then about running for
higher office. As we returned to the party he simply remarked, "It's too early for me to be setting up a staff.
But when I do, I'll want you. Haig will be in touch."

"What did you think of him?" Mardikian asked me five
minutes later.

"He'll be mayor of New York City in 1998."

"And then?"

"You want to know more, man, you get in touch with
my office and make an appointment. Fifty an hour and
I'll give you the whole crystal-balling."

He jabbed my arm lightly and strode away laughing.

Ten minutes after that I was sharing a pipe with the
golden-haired lady named Autumn. Autumn Hawkes,

she was, the much-hailed new Met soprano. Quickly we negotiated an agreement, eyes only, the silent language of the body, concerning the rest of the night. She told me she had come to the party with Victor Schott—gaunt gigantic youngish Prussian type in somber medal-studded military outfit—who was due to conduct her in *Lulu* that winter, but Schott had apparently arranged a deal to go home with Councilman Holbrecht, leaving Autumn to shift for herself. Autumn shifted. I was undeceived about her real preference, though, for I saw her looking hungrily at Paul Quinn far across the room, and her eyes glowed. Quinn was here on business: no woman could bag him. (No man either!) "I wonder if he sings," Autumn said wistfully.

"You'd like to try some duets with him?"

"Isolde to his Tristan. Turandot to his Calaf. Aïda to his Radames."

"Salome to his Jokanaan?" I suggested.

"Don't tease."

"You admire his political ideas?"

"I could, if I knew what they were."

I said, "He's liberal and sane."

"Then I admire his political ideas. I also think he's overpoweringly masculine and superbly beautiful."

"Politicians on the make are said to be inadequate lovers."

She shrugged. "Hearsay evidence never impresses me. I can look at a man—one glance will do—and know instantly whether he's adequate."

"Thank you," I said.

"Save the compliments. Sometimes I'm wrong, of course," she said, poisonously sweet. "Not always, but sometimes."

"Sometimes I am, too."

"About women?"

"About anything. I have second sight, you know. The future is an open book to me."

"You sound serious," she said.

"I am. It's the way I earn my living. Projections."

"What do you see in my future?" she asked, half coy, half in earnest.

"Immediate or long range?"

"Either."

"Immediate," I said, "a night of wild revelry and a peaceful morning stroll in a light drizzle. Long range, triumph upon triumph, fame, a villa in Majorca, two divorces, happiness late in life."

"Are you a Gypsy fortuneteller, then?"

I shook my head. "Merely a stochastic technician, milady."

She glanced toward Quinn. "What do you see ahead for him?"

"Him? He's going to be President. At the very least."

7

In the morning, when we strolled hand in hand through the misty wooded groves of Securtiy Channel Six, it was drizzling. A cheap triumph: I tune in weather reports like anyone else. Autumn went off to rehearse, summer ended, Sundara came home exhausted and happy from Oregon, new clients picked my mind for lavish fees, and life went on.

There was no immediate follow-up to my meeting with Paul Quinn, but I hadn't expected one. New York City's political life was in wild flux just then. Only a few weeks before Sarkisian's party a disgruntled jobseeker had approached Mayor Gottfried at a Liberal Party banquet and, removing the half-eaten grapefruit from the astounded mayor's plate, had clapped a gram of Ascenseur, the new French political explosive, in its place. Exeunt His Honor, the assassin, four county chairmen, and a waiter, in one glorious boom. Which created a power vacuum in the city, for everyone had assumed the formidable mayor would be elected to another four or five terms, this being only his second, and suddenly the invincible Gottfried wasn't there, as though God had died one Sunday morning just as the cardinal was starting to serve the bread and wine. The new mayor, former City Council President DiLaurenzio, was a nonentity: Gottfried, like any true dictator, liked to surround himself with bland obliging ciphers. It was taken for granted that DiLaurenzio was an interim figure who could be pushed aside in the '97 mayoralty election by any reasonably strong candidate. And Quinn was waiting in the wings.

I heard nothing from or about him all fall. The Legislature was in session and Quinn was at his desk in Albany, which is like being on Mars so far as anybody in New York City cares. In the city the usual weird circus was going full blast, only more so than usual now that the potent Freudian force that was Mayor Gottfried, the Urban Allfather, dark of brow and long of nose, guardian of the weak and castrator of the unruly, had been removed from the scene. The 125th Street Militia, a new black self-determination force that had been boasting for months that it was buying tanks from Syria, not only unveiled three armored monsters at a noisy press conference but proceeded to send them across Columbus Avenue on a search-and-destroy mission into Hispano Manhattan, leaving four blocks in flames and dozens dead. In October, while the blacks were celebrating Marcus Garvey Day, the Puerto Ricans retaliated with a commando raid on Harlem, personally led by two of their three Israeli colonels. (The *barrio* boys had hired the Israelis to train their troops in '94, following the ratification of the anti-black "mutual defense" alliance put together by the Puerto Ricans and what was left of the city's Jewish population.) The commandos, in a lightning strike up Lenox Avenue, not only blew up the tank garage and all three tanks, but took out five liquor stores and the main numbers computer center, while a diversionary force slipped westward to firebomb the Apollo Theater.

A few weeks later at the site of the West Twenty-third Street Fusion Plant there was a shootout between the profusion group, Keep Our Cities Bright, and the anti-fusionists, Concerned Citizens Against Uncontrollable Technology. Four Con Edison security men were lynched and there were thirty-two fatalities among the demonstrators, twenty-one KOCB and eleven CCAUT, including a lot of politically involved young mothers on both sides and even a few babes in arms; this caused much horror and outcry (even in New York you can stir strong emotions by gunning babies during a demonstration), and Mayor DiLaurenzio found it expedient to appoint a study group to re-examine the whole question of building fusion plants within city limits. Since this amounted to a victory for CCAUT, a KOCB strike-force blockaded City Hall and began planting protest mines in the shrubbery, but they were driven off by a police tac squad strafing 'copter at a cost of nine more lives. The *Times* put the story on page 27.

Mayor DiLaurenzio, speaking from his Auxiliary City Hall somewhere in the East Bronx—he had set up seven offices in outlying boroughs, all in Italian neighborhoods, the exact locations being carefully guarded secrets—issued new lawnorder pleas. However, nobody in the city paid much attention to the mayor, partly because he was such a *nebbish* and partly as an overcompensating reaction to the removal of the brooding, sinister, overwhelming presence of Gottfried the Gauleiter. DiLaurenzio had staffed his administration, from police commissioner down to dogcatcher and clean-air administrator, with Italian cronies, which I suppose was reasonable enough, since the Italians were the only ones in town who showed any respect for him, and that merely because they were all his cousins or nephews. But that meant that the mayor's sole political support was drawn from an ethnic minority that grew more minor every day. (Even Little Italy was reduced to four blocks of Mulberry Street, with Chinese swarming on every side street and the new generation of *paisanos* holed up securely in Patchogue and New Rochelle.) An editorial in the *Wall Street Journal* suggested suspending the upcoming mayoralty election and placing New York City under a military administration, with a *cordon sanitaire* to keep infectious New Yorkism from contaminating the rest of the country.

"I think a UN peacekeeping force would be a better idea," Sundara said. This was early December, the night of the season's first blizzard. "This isn't a city, it's a staging ground for all the accumulated racial and ethnic hostilities of the last three thousand years."

"That's not so," I told her. "Old grudges don't mean crap here. Hindus sleep with Paks in New York, Turks and Armenians go into partnership and open restaurants. In this city we invent *new* ethnic hostilities. New York is nothing if it isn't avant-garde. You'd understand that if you'd lived here all your life the way I have."

"I feel as though I have."

"Six years doesn't make you a native."

"Six years in the middle of constant guerrilla warfare feels longer than thirty years anywhere else," she said.

Oh-oh. Her voice was playful, but her dark eyes held a malicious sparkle. She was daring me to parry, to contradict, to challenge. I felt the air about me glowing feverishly. Suddenly we were drifting into the I-hate-New-York conversation, always productive of rifts between us, and soon we would be quarreling in earnest. A native can hate New York with love; an outsider, and my Sundara would always be an outsider here, draws tense and heavy energy out of repudiating this lunatic place she has chosen to live in, and grows bloated and murderous with unearned fury.

Heading off trouble, I said, "Well, let's move to Arizona."

"Hey, that's my line!"

"I'm sorry. I must have missed my cue."

The tension was gone. "This *is* an awful city, Lew."

"Try Tucson, then. The winters are much better. You want to smoke, love?"

"Yes, but not that bone thing again."

"Plain old prehistoric dope?"

"Please," she said. I got the stash. The air between us was limpid and loving. We had been together four years, and, though some dissonances had appeared, we were still each other's best friend. As I rolled the smokes she stroked the muscles of my neck, cunningly hitting the pressure points and letting the twentieth century slide out of my ligaments and vertebrae. Her parents were from

Bombay but she had been born in Los Angeles, yet her supple fingers played Radha to my Krishna as though she were a *padmini* of the Hindu dawn, a lotus woman fully versed in the erotic shastras and the sutras of the flesh, which in truth she was, though self-taught and no graduate of the secret academies of Benares.

The terrors and traumas of New York City seemed indecently remote as we stood by our long crystalline window, close to each other, staring into the wintry moonbright night and seeing only our own reflections, tall fairhaired man and slender dark woman, side by side, side by side, allies against the darkness.

Actually neither of us found life in the city really burdensome. As members of the affluent minority we were insulated from much of the crazy stuff, sheltered at home in our maxsecure hilltop condo, protected by screens and filter mazes when we took the commuter pods across into Manhattan, guarded in our offices by more of the same. Whenever we yearned for an on-foot eyes-to-eyes nit-to-grit confront with urban reality we could have it, and when not there were watchful servocircuits to keep us from harm.

We passed the smoke back and forth, languidly letting fingers caress fingers at each interchange. She seemed perfect to me just then, my wife, my love, my other self, witty and graceful, mysterious and exotic, high forehead, blue-black hair, full-moon face—but a moon eclipsed, a moon empurpled by shadow; the perfect lotus woman of the sutras, skin fine and tender, eyes brilliant and beautiful as a fawn's, well defined and red at the corners, breasts hard and full and uplifted, neck elegant, nose straight and gracious. *Yoni* like an open lotus bud, voice as low and melodious as the kokila bird's, my prize, my love, my companion, my alien bride. Within twelve hours I would set myself on the path toward losing her, which perhaps is why I studied her with such intensity this snowy evening, and yet I knew nothing of what would happen, nothing, I knew nothing. Only I must have known.

Deliriously stoned, we sprawled snugly on the rough-skinned nubby yellow and red couch in front of our big window. The moon was full, a chilly white beacon splashing the city with ice-pure light. Snowflakes glittered beautifully on swirling updrafts outside. Our view was of the shining towers of downtown Brooklyn just across the harbor. Far-off exotic Brooklyn, darkest Brooklyn, Brooklyn red in fang and claw. What was going on over there tonight in the jungle of low grubby streets behind the glistening waterfront façade of high rises? What maimings, what garrotings, what gunplay, what profits and what losses? While we nestled our weedy heads in warm happy privacy, the less privileged were experiencing the true New York in that melancholy borough. Bands of marauding seven-year-olds were braving the fierce snow to harass weary homegoing widows on Flatbush Avenue, and boys armed with needle torches were gleefully cutting the bars on the lion cages in Prospect Park Zoo, and rival gangs of barely pubescent prostitutes, bare-thighed in gaudy thermal undershirts and aluminum coronets, were holding their vicious nightly territorial face-offs at Grand Army Plaza. Here's to you, good old New York. Here's to you, Mayor DiLaurenzio, benign and sanguine unexpected leader. And here's to you, Sundara, my love. This, too, is the true New York, the handsome young rich ones safe in their warm towers, the creators and devisers and shapers, the favorites of the gods. If we were not here it would not be New York but only a large and malevolent encampment of suffering maladjusted poor, casualties of the urban holocaust; crime and grime by themselves do not a New York make. There must also be glamour, and, for better, for worse, Sundara and I were part of that.

Zeus flung noisy handfuls of hail at our impervious window. We laughed. My hands slipped down over Sundara's smooth small hard-nippled flawless breasts, and with my toe I flicked the stud of our recorder, and from the speakers came her deep musical voice. A taped reading from the *Kama Sutra*. "Chapter Seven. The various ways to hit a woman and the accompanying sounds. Sexual intercourse can be compared to a lover's quarrel, because of the little annoyances so easily caused by love and the tendency on the part of two passionate individuals to change swiftly from love to anger. In the intensity of passion one often hits the lover on the body, and the parts of the body where these blows of love should be dealt are the shoulders—the head—the space between the breasts, the back—the *jaghana*—the sides. There are also four ways of hitting the loved one: with the back of the hand—with the fingers slightly contracted—with the fist —with the palm of the hand. These blows are painful and the person hit often emits a cry of pain. There are eight sounds of pleasurable anguish which correspond to the different kinds of blows. These are sounds: *hinn—phoutt—phatt—soutt—platt—*"

And as I touched her skin, as her skin touched mine, she smiled and whispered in unison with her own taped voice, her tone a bare sixth deeper now, *"Hinn . . . phoutt . . . soutt . . . platt . . ."*

8

I was at my office by half past eight the next morning and Haig Mardikian phoned exactly at nine.

"Do you really get fifty an hour?" he asked.

"I try to."

"I've got an interesting job for you, but the party in question can't go fifty."

"Who's the party? What's the job?"

"Paul Quinn. Needs a data-sampling director and campaign strategist."

"Quinn's running for mayor?"

"He figures it'll be easy to knock off DiLaurenzio in the primary, and the Republicans don't have anybody, so the moment is right to make his move."

"It sure is," I said. "The job is full time?"

"Very part time most of the year, then full time from the fall of '96 through to Election Day '97. Can you clear your long-range schedule for us?"

"This isn't just consulting work, Haig. It means going into politics."

"So?"

"What do I need it for?"

"Nobody needs anything except a little food and water now and then. The rest is preferences."

"I hate the political thing, Haig, especially local politics. I've seen enough of it just doing free-lance projections. You have to eat so much crap. You have to compromise yourself in so many ugly ways. You have to be willing to expose yourself to so much——"

"We're not asking you to be the candidate, boy. Only to help plan the campaign."

"Only. You want a year out of my life, and——"

"What makes you think Quinn will settle just for a year?"

"You make this terribly enticing."

Haig said after a bit, "There are powerful possibilities in it."

"Maybe."

"Not maybe. There are."

"I know what you mean. Still, power's not everything."

"Are you available, Lew?"

I let him dangle a moment. Or he let me dangle. Finally I said, "For you the price is forty."

"Quinn can go twenty-five now, thirty-five once the contributions start rolling in."

"And then a retroactive thirty-five for me?"

"Twenty-five now, thirty-five when we can afford it," Mardikian said. "No retroactive."

"Why should I take a pay cut? Less money for dirtier work?"

"For Quinn. For this goddamned city, Lew. He's the only man who can——"

"Sure. But am *I* the only man who can help him do it?"

"You're the best we can get. No, that sounds wrong. You're the best, Lew. Period. No con job."

"What's the staff going to be like?"

"All control centered in five key figures. You'd be one. I'd be another."

"As campaign manager?"

"Right. Missakian is coordinator of communications and media relations. Ephrikian is borough liaison."

"What does that mean?"

"Patronage man. And the finance coordinator is a

guy named Bob Lombroso, currently very big on Wall Street, who—"

"Lombroso? Is that Italian? No. Wait. What a stroke of genius! You managed to find a Wall Street Puerto to be your moneyman."

"He's a Jew," said Mardikian with a little dry laugh. "Lombroso is an old Jewish name, he tells me. We have a terrific team—Lombroso, Ephrikian, Missakian, Mardikian, and Nichols. You're our token WASP."

"How do you know I'm coming in with you, Haig?"

"I never doubted that you would."

"How do you *know*?"

"You think you're the only one who can see the future?"

9

So early in '96 we set up our headquarters on the ninth floor of an old weatherbeaten Park Avenue tower with a really spectacular view of the swollen midsection of the Pan Am Building, and we set about the job of making Paul Quinn mayor of this absurd city. It didn't look hard. All we had to do was assemble the proper number of qualifying petitions—a cinch, you can get New Yorkers to sign *anything*—and give our man enough citywide exposure to make him known throughout the five boroughs before the primary. The candidate was attractive, intelligent, dedicated, ambitious, self-evidently capable; therefore we had no image-making to do, no plastic-man cosmetic jobs.

The city had been dismissed as moribund so often, and so often had shown new twitches of unmistakable vitality, that the cliché concept of New York as a dying metropolis had finally gone out of fashion. Only fools or demagogues raised the point now. New York was supposed to have perished a generation ago, when the civil-service unions got hold of the town and began squeezing it mercilessly. But the long-legged go-getter Lindsay resurrected it into Fun City, only to have the fun turn into nightmare as skeletons armed with grenades began emerging from every closet. That was when New York found out what a *real* dying city was like; the previous period of decline started looking like a golden age. The white middle class split in a panicky exodus; taxes rose to repressive levels to keep essential services going in a city where half the people were too poor to pay the costs of upkeep; major businesses responded by whisking their headquarters off to leafy suburbs, further eroding the tax base. Byzantine ethnic rivalries exploded in every neighborhood. Muggers lurked behind every lamppost. How could such a plaguey city survive? The climate was hateful, the citizenry malign, the air foul, the architecture a disgrace, and a cluster of self-accelerating processes had whittled the economic base alarmingly.

But the city did survive, and even flourished. There was that harbor, there was the river, there was the happy geographical placement that made New York an indispensable neural nexus for the whole eastern coast, a ganglionic switchboard that couldn't be discarded. More: the city had attained, in its bizarre sweaty density, a kind of critical mass, a level of cultural activity that made it a breeder reactor for the soul, self-enriching, self-powering, for there was so much happening even in a moribund New York that the city simply could not die, it needs must go on throbbing and spewing forth the fevers of life, endlessly rekindling and renewing itself. An irrepressible lunatic energy ticked on and on at the city's heart and always would.

Not dying, then. But there were problems.

You could cope with the polluted air with masks and filters. You could deal with the crime the way you did with blizzards or summer heat, negatively by avoidance, positively by technological counterattack. Either you carried no valuables, moved with agility in the streets, and stayed indoors behind many locks as much as possible, or you equipped yourself with space-positive alarm systems, with anti-personnel batons, with security cones radiating from circuitry in the lining of your clothing, and went out to brave the yahoos. Coping. But the white middle class was gone, probably forever, and that caused difficulties that the electronics boys couldn't fix. The city by 1990 was largely black and Puerto Rican, dotted with two sorts of enclaves, one kind dwindling (the pockets of aging Jews and Italians and Irish) and one steadily expanding in size and power (the dazzling islands of the affluent, the managerial and creative classes). A city populated only by rich and by poor experiences certain nasty spiritual dislocations, and it will be a while before the emerging non-white bourgeoisie is a real force for social stability. Much of New York glitters as only Athens, Constantinople, Rome, Babylon, and Persepolis glittered in the past; the rest is a jungle, a literal jungle, fetid and squalid, where force is the only law. It is not so much a dying city as an ungovernable one, seven million souls moving in seven million orbits under spectacular centrifugal pressures that threaten at any moment to make hyperbolas of us all.

Welcome to City Hall, Mayor Quinn.

Who can govern the ungovernable? Someone always is willing to try, God help him. Out of our hundred-odd mayors some have been honest and many have been crooks, and about seven all told were competent and effective administrators. Two of those were crooks, but never mind their morals, for they knew how to make the city work as well as anybody. Some were stars, some were disasters, and they all, in the aggregate, helped to nudge the city toward its ultimate entropic debacle. And now Quinn. He promised greatness, combining, so it seemed, the force and vigor of a Gottfried, the glamour of a Lindsay, the humanity and compassion of a LaGuardia.

So we put him into the New Democratic primary against the feckless, helpless DiLaurenzio. Bob Lombroso milked the banking houses for millions, George Missakian put together a string of straightforward TV spots featuring many of the celebrities who had been at that party, Ara Ephrikian bartered commissionerships for support on the clubhouse level, and I dropped in at headquarters now and then with simple-minded projective reports that said nothing more profound than

play it safe

keep on truckin'
we've got it made.

Everybody expected Quinn to sweep the field, and in fact he took the primary with an absolute majority in a list of seven. The Republicans found a banker named Burgess to accept their nomination. He was unknown, a political novice, and I don't know if they were feeling suicidal or simply being realistic. A poll taken a month before the election gave Quinn 83 percent of the vote. That missing 17 percent bothered him. He wanted it all, and he vowed to take his campaign to the people. No candidate in twenty years had done the motorcade-and-handshake routine here, but he insisted on overruling a fretful assassination-minded Mardikian. "What are my chances of being gunned down if I go for a stroll in Times Square?" Quinn demanded of me.

I didn't pick up death vibes for him and I told him so.

I also said, "But I wish you wouldn't do it, Paul. I'm not infallible and you're not immortal."

"If it isn't safe in New York for a candidate to meet the voters," Quinn replied, "we might as well just use the place for a Z-bomb testing sight."

"A mayor was murdered here only two years ago."

"Everybody hated Gottfried. He was an Iron Cross fascist if anybody ever was. Why should someone feel like that about me, Lew? I'm going out."

Quinn went forth and pressed the flesh. Maybe it helped. He won the biggest election victory in New York history, an 88 percent plurality. On the first of January, 1998, an unseasonably mild, almost Floridian day, Haig Mardikian and Bob Lombroso and the rest of us in the inner circle clustered close on the steps of City Hall to watch our man take the oath of office. Vague disquiet churned inside me. What did I fear? I couldn't tell. A bomb, maybe. Yes, a shiny round black comic-strip bomb with a sizzling fuse whistling through the air to blow us all to mesons and quarks. No bomb was thrown. Why such a bird of ill omen Nichols? Rejoice! I remained edgy. Backs were slapped, cheeks were kissed. Paul Quinn was mayor of New York, and happy 1998 to all.

10   "If Quinn wins," Sundara said one night late in the summer of '97, "will he offer you a job in his administration?"

"Probably."

"Will you take it?"

"Not a chance," I told her. "Running a campaign is fun. Day-by-day municipal government is just a grubby bore. I'm going back to my regular clients as soon as the election's over."

Three days after the election Quinn sent for me and offered me the post of special administrative assistant and I accepted without hesitation, without one thought for my clients or my employees or my shiny office full of data-processing equipment.

Was I lying to Sundara on that summer night, then? No, the one I had been fooling was myself. My projection was faulty because my self-understanding had been imperfect. What I learned between August and November is that proximity to power becomes addictive. For more than a year I had been drawing vitality from Paul Quinn. When you spend so much time so close to so much power, you get hooked on the energy flow, you become a juice-junkie. You don't willingly walk away from the dynamo that's been nourishing you. When, as mayor-elect, Quinn hired me, he said he needed me, and I could buy that, but more truthfully I needed him. Quinn was poised for a huge surging leap, a brilliant cometlike passage through the dark night of American politics, and I yearned to be part of his train, to catch some of his fire and be warmed by it. It was that simple and that humiliating. I was free to pretend that by serving Quinn I was serving mankind, that I was participating in a grand exciting crusade to save the greatest of our cities, that I was helping to pull modern urban civilization back from the abyss and give it purpose and viability. It might even be true. But what drew me to Quinn was the attraction of power, power in the abstract, power for its own sake, the power to mold and shape and transform. Saving New York was incidental; riding the lines of force was what I craved.

Our whole campaign team went right into the new city administration. Quinn named Haig Mardikian his deputy mayor and Bob Lombroso his finance administrator. George Missakian became media coordinator and Ara Ephrikian was named head of the City Planning Commission. Then the five of us sat down with Quinn and handed out the rest of the jobs. Ephrikian proposed most of the names, Missakian and Lombroso and Mardikian evaluated qualifications, I made intuitive assessments, and Quinn passed final judgment. In this way we found the usual assortment of blacks, Puerto Ricans, Chinese, Italians, Irish, Jews, etc., to run the Human Resources Agency, the Housing and Redevelopment Board, the Environmental Protection Administration, the Cultural Resources Administration, and the other big numbers. Then we discreetly planted many of our friends, including an inordinate number of Armenians and Sephardic Jews and other exotics, high in the lower echelons. We kept the best people from the DiLaurenzio administration—there weren't very many—and resuscitated a few of Gottfried's hard-nosed but enlightened commissioners. It was a heady feeling to be picking a government for New York City, to drive out the hacks and timeservers and replace them with creative, adventurous men and women who happened, only *happened*, also to provide the ethnic and geographic mix that the cabinet of the mayor of New York must have.

My own job was amorphous, evanescent: I was private adviser, hunch maker, troubleshooter, the misty presence behind the throne. I was supposed to use my intuitive faculties to keep Quinn a couple of steps ahead of cataclysm, this in a city where the wolves descend on the mayor if the weather bureau lets an unexpected snowstorm slip into town. I took a pay cut amounting to about half the money I would have made as a private consultant. But my municipal salary was still more than I really needed. And there was another reward: the knowledge that as Paul Quinn climbed I would climb with him.

Right into the White House.

I had felt the imminence of Quinn's presidency that first night in '95, Sarkisian's party, and Haig Mardikian felt it long before that. The Italians have a word, *papabile*, to describe a cardinal who might plausibly become Pope. Quinn was presidentially *papabile*. He was young, personable, energetic, independent, a classic Kennedy figure, and for forty years Kennedy types had had a mystic hold on the electorate. He was unknown outside of New York, sure, but that scarcely mattered: with all urban crises running at an intensity 250 percent above the levels of a generation ago, anybody who shows he's capable of governing a major city automatically becomes a potential President, and if New York did not break Quinn the way it broke Lindsay in the 1960s he would have a national reputation in a year or two. And then—

And then—

By early autumn of '97, with the mayoralty already as good as won, I found myself becoming concerned, in what I soon recognized to be an obsessive way, with Quinn's chances for a presidential nomination. I *felt* him as President, if not in 2000 then four years later. But merely making the prediction wasn't enough. I played with Quinn's presidency the way a little boy plays with himself, exciting myself with the idea, manipulating pleasure for myself out of it, getting off on it.

Privately, secretly—for I felt abashed at such premature scheming; I didn't want cold-eyed pros like Mardikian and Lombroso to know I was already enmeshed in misty masturbatory fantasies of our hero's distant glowing future, though I suppose they must have been thinking similar thoughts themselves by then—I drew up endless lists of politicians worth cultivating in places like California and Florida and Texas, charted the dynamics of the national electoral blocs, concocted intricate schemas representing the power vortices of a national nominating convention, set up an infinity of simulated scenarios for the election itself. All this was, as I say, obsessive in nature, meaning that I returned again and again, eagerly, impatiently, unavoidably, in any free moment, to my projections and analyses.

Everyone has some controlling obsession, some fixation that becomes an armature for the construct that is his life: thus we make ourselves into stamp collectors, gardeners, skycyclists, marathon hikers, sniffers, fornicators. We all have the same kind of void within, and each of us fills that void in essentially the same way, no matter what kind of stuffing for the emptiness we choose. I mean we pick the cure we like best but we all have the same disease.

So I dreamed dreams of President Quinn. I thought he deserved the job, for one thing. Not only was he a compelling leader but he was humane, sincere, and responsive to the needs of the people. (That is, his political philosophy sounded much like mine.) But also I was finding in myself a need to involve myself in the advancement of other people's careers—to ascend vicariously, quietly placing my stochastic skills at the service of others. There was some subterranean kick in it for me, growing out of a complex hunger for power coupled with a wish for self-effacement, a feeling that I was most invulnerable when least visible. I couldn't become President myself; I wasn't willing to put myself through the turbulence, the exertion, the exposure, and that fierce gratuitous loathing that the public so readily bestows on those who seek its love. But by toiling to make Paul Quinn President I could slip into the White House anyway, by the back door, without laying myself bare, without taking the real risks. There's the root of the obsession most nakedly revealed. I meant to use Paul Quinn and let him think he was using me. I had identified myself, *au fond*, with him: he was, for me, my alter ego, my walking mask, my catspaw, my puppet, my front man. I wanted to rule. I wanted power. I wanted to be President, King, Emperor, Pope, Dalai Lama. Through Quinn I would get there in the only way I could. I would hold the reins of the man who held the reins. And thus I would be my own father and everybody else's big daddy too.

11 There was one frosty day late in March '99 that started like most of the other days since I had gone to work for Paul Quinn, but went off on an unexpected track before afternoon arrived. I was up at quarter past seven, as usual. Sundara and I showered together, the pretext being conservation of water and energy, but actually we both had this little soap fetish and loved lathering each other until we were slippery as seals. Quick breakfast, out of the house by eight, commuter pod to Manhattan. My first stop was my uptown office, my old Lew Nichols Associates office, which I was maintaining with a skeleton staff during my time on the city payroll. There I handled routine projective analysis of minor administrative hassles—the siting of a new school, the closing of an old hospital, zoning changes to allow a new wipe-out center for brain-injured sniffers in a residential district, all trivia but potentially explosive trivia in a city where every citizen's nerves are taut beyond hope of slackening and small disappointments quickly start looking like insupportable rebuffs. Then, about noon, I headed downtown to the Municipal Building for conference and lunch with Bob Lombroso.

"Mr. Lombroso has a visitor in his office," the receptionist told me, "but he'd like you to go on inside anyway."

Lombroso's office was a fitting stage for him. He is a tall well-set-up man in his late thirties, somewhat theatrical in appearance, a commanding figure with dark curling hair silvering at the temples, a coarse black close-cropped beard, a flashing smile, and the energetic, intense manner of a successful rug merchant. His office, redecorated from standard Early Bureaucrat at his own expense, was an ornate Levantine den, fragrant and warm, with dark shining leather-paneled walls, dense carpets, heavy brown velvet draperies, dim bronze Spanish lamps perforated in a thousand places, a gleaming desk made of several somber woods inlaid with plaques of tooled morocco, great white urnlike Chinese floor vases, and, in a baroque glass-fronted credenza, his cherished collection of medieval Judaica—silver headpieces, breastplates, and pointers for the scrolls of the Law, embroidered Torah curtains out of the synagogues of Tunisia or Iran, filigreed Sabbath lamps, candlesticks, spice boxes, candelabra. In this musky cloistered sanctuary Lombroso reigned over the municipal revenues like a prince of Zion: woe betide the foolish Gentile who disdained his counsel.

His visitor was a faded-looking little man, fifty-five or sixty years old, a slight, insignificant person with a narrow oval head sparsely thatched with short gray hair. He was dressed so plainly, in a shabby old brown suit out of the Eisenhower era, that he made Lombroso's nippy-dip sartorialism seem like the most extreme peacock extravagance and even made me feel like a dandy in my five-year-old copper-threaded maroon cape. He sat quietly, slouched, hands interlocked. He looked anonymous and close to invisible, one of nature's natural-born Smiths, and there was a leaden undertone to his skin, a wintry slackness to the flesh of his cheeks, that spoke of an exhaustion that was as much spiritual as physical. Time had emptied this man of any strength he might once have had.

"I want you to meet Martin Carvajal, Lew," Lombroso said.

Carvajal rose and clasped my hand. His was cold. "A pleasure at last to encounter you, Mr. Nichols," he said in a mild, numb voice that came to me from the far side of the universe.

The odd courtly phrasing of his greeting was strange. I wondered what he was doing here. He looked so juiceless, so much like an applicant for some very minor bureaucratic job, or, more plausibly, like some down-at-the-heel uncle of Lombroso's here to pick up his monthly stipend: but only the powerful were admitted to Finance Administrator Lombroso's lair.

But Carvajal was not the relict I took him to be. Already, in the moment of our handshake, he appeared to have an improbable access of strength; he stood taller, the lines of his face grew taut, a certain Mediterranean flush brightened his complexion. Only his eyes, bleak and lifeless, still betrayed some vital absence within.

Sententiously Lombroso said, "Mr. Carvajal was one of our most generous contributors to the mayor's campaign," giving me a suave Phoenician glance that told me, *Treat him kindly, Lew, we want more of his gold.*

That this drab, seedy stranger should be a wealthy campaign benefactor, a person to be flattered and curried and admitted to the sanctum of a busy official, shook me profoundly, for rarely had I misread someone so thoroughly. But I managed a bland grin and said, "What business are you in, Mr. Carvajal?"

"Investments."

"One of the shrewdest and most successful private speculators I've ever known," Lombroso offered.

Carvajal nodded complacently.

"You earn your living entirely from the stock market?" I asked.

"Entirely."

"I didn't think anyone actually was able to do that."

"Oh, yes, yes, it can be done," Carvajal said. His tone was thin and husky, a murmur out of the tomb. "All it takes is a decent understanding of trends and a little courage. Haven't you ever been in the market, Mr. Nichols?"

"A little. Just dabbling."

"Did you do well?"

"Well enough. I have a decent understanding of trends

myself. But I don't feel comfortable when the really wild fluctuations start. Up twenty, down thirty—no, thanks. I like sure things, I suppose."

"So do I," Carvajal replied, giving his statement a little propulsive twist, a hint of meaning beyond meaning, that left me baffled and uncomfortable.

Just then a sweet bell tinkled in Lombroso's inner office, which opened out of a short corridor to the left of his desk. I knew it meant the mayor was calling; the receptionist invariably relayed Quinn's calls to the back room when Lombroso had strangers out front. Lombroso excused himself and, with quick heavy strides that shook the carpeted floor, went to take the call. Finding myself alone with Carvajal was suddenly overwhelmingly disturbing; my skin tingled and there was pressure at my throat, as though some potent psychic emanation swept irresistibly from him to me the moment the neutral damping presence of Lombroso was removed. I was unable to stay. Excusing myself also, I hastily followed Lombroso to the other room, a narrow elbow-jointed cavern full of books from floor to ceiling, heavy ornate tomes that might have been Talmuds and might have been bound volumes of Moody's stock and bond manuals, and probably were a mixture of both. Lombroso, surprised and annoyed at my intrusion, angrily jabbed a finger toward his telephone screen, on which I could see the image of Mayor Quinn's head and shoulders. But instead of leaving I offered a pantomime of apology, a wild barrage of bobs and waves and shrugs and idiotic grimaces, that led Lombroso to ask the mayor to hold the line a moment. The screen went blank.

Lombroso glowered at me. "Well?" he demanded. "What's wrong?"

"Nothing. I don't know. I'm sorry. I couldn't stay in there. Who *is* he, Bob?"

"Just as I told you. Big money. Strong Quinn backer. We have to make nice for him. Look, I'm on the phone. The mayor has to know—"

"I don't want to be alone in there with him. He's like one of the walking dead. He gives me the creepies."

"What?"

"I'm serious. It's like some kind of cold deathly force coming from him, Bob. He makes me itch. He gives off scary vibes."

"Oh, Jesus, Lew."

"I can't help it. You know how I pick up things."

"He's a harmless little geezer who made a lot of money in the market and likes our man. That's *all*."

"Why is he here?"

"To meet you," Lombroso said.

"Just that? Just to meet me?"

"He wanted very much to talk to you. Said it was important for him to get together with you."

"What does he want with me?"

"I said that's all I know, Lew."

"Is my time for sale to anybody who's ever given five bucks to Quinn's campaign fund?"

Lombroso sighed. "If I told you how much Carvajal gave, you wouldn't believe it, and in any case, yes, I think you might be able to spare some time for him."

"But—"

"Look, Lew, if you want more answers you'll have to get them from Carvajal. Go on back to him now. Be a sweetheart and let me talk to the mayor. Go on. Carvajal won't hurt you. He's just a little puny thing." Lombroso swung away from me and reactivated the phone. The mayor reappeared on the telephone screen. Lombroso said, "I'm sorry, Paul. Lew had a bit of a nervous breakdown, but I think he's going to pull through. Now—"

I returned to Carvajal. He was sitting motionless, head bowed, arms limp, as if an icy blast had passed through the room while I was gone, leaving him parched and withered. Slowly, with obvious effort, he reconstituted himself, sitting up, filling his lungs, pretending to an animation that his eyes, his empty and frightening eyes, wholly betrayed. One of the walking dead, yes.

"Will you be joining us for lunch?" I asked him.

"No. No, I wouldn't impose. I wanted only a few words with you, Mr. Nichols."

"I'm at your service."

"Are you? How splendid." He smiled an ashen smile. "I've heard a good deal about you, you know. Even before you went into politics. In a way, we've both been in the same line of work."

"You mean the market?" I said, puzzled.

His smile grew brighter and more troubling. "Predictions," he said. "For me, the stock market. For you, consultant to business and politics. We've both lived by our wits and by our, ah, decent understanding of trends."

I was altogether unable to read him. He was opaque, a mystery, an enigma.

He said, "So now you stand at the mayor's elbow, telling him the shape of the road ahead. I admire people who have such clear vision. Tell me, what sort of career do you project for Mayor Quinn?"

"A splendid one," I said.

"A successful mayor, then."

"He'll be one of the finest this city's ever had."

Lombroso came back into the room. Carvajal said, "And afterward?"

I looked uncertainly at Lombroso, but his eyes were hooded. I was on my own.

"After his term as mayor?" I asked.

"Yes."

"He's still a young man, Mr. Carvajal. He might win three or four terms as mayor. I can't give you any sort of meaningful projection about events a dozen years from now."

"Twelve years in City Hall? Do you think he'll be content to stay there as long as that?"

Carvajal was playing with me. I felt I had been drawn unawares into some sort of duel. I gave him a long look and perceived something terrifying and indeterminable, something powerful and incomprehensible, that made me grasp the first available defensive move, I said, "What do *you* think, Mr. Carvajal?"

For the first time a flicker of life showed in his eyes. He was enjoying the game.

"That Mayor Quinn is headed for higher office," he said softly.

"Governor?"

"Higher."

I made no immediate answer, and then I was unable to answer, for an immense silence had seeped out of the leather-paneled walls to engulf us, and I feared being the one to puncture it. If only the phone would ring again, I thought, but all was still, as becalmed as the air on a freezing night, until Lombroso rescued us by saying, "We think he has a lot of potential, too."

"We have big plans for him," I blurted.

"I know," said Carvajal. "That's why I'm here. I want to offer my support."

Lombroso said, "Your financial aid has been tremendously helpful to us all along, and—"

"What I have in mind isn't only financial."

Now Lombroso looked to me for help. But I was lost. I said, "I don't think we're following you, Mr. Carvajal."

"If I could have a moment alone with you, then."

I glanced at Lombroso. If he was annoyed at being tossed out of his own office, he didn't show it. With characteristic grace he bowed and stepped into the back room. Once more I was alone with Carvajal, and once more I felt ill at ease, thrown awry by the peculiar threads of invulnerable steel that seemed to lace his shriveled and enfeebled soul. In a new tone, insinuating, confidential, Carvajal said, "As I remarked, you and I are in the same line of work. But I think our methods are rather different, Mr. Nichols. Your technique is intuitive and probabilistic, and mine— Well, mine is different. I believe perhaps some of my insights might supplement yours, is what I'm trying to say."

"Predictive insights?"

"Exactly. I don't wish to intrude on your area of responsibility. But I might be able to make a suggestion or two that I think would be of value."

I winced. Suddenly the enigma lay unraveled and what was revealed within was anticlimactically commonplace. Carvajal was nothing but a rich political amateur who, figuring that his money qualified him as a universal expert, hungered to meddle in the doings of the pros. A hobbyist.

An armchair politico. Jesus! Well, make nice for him, Lombroso had said. I would make nice. Groping for tact, I told him stiffly, "Of course. Mr. Quinn and his staff are always glad to hear helpful suggestions."

Carvajal's eyes searched for mine, but I avoided them. "Thank you," he whispered. "I've put down a few things to begin with." He offered me a folded slip of white paper. His hand trembled a little. I took the slip without looking at it. Suddenly all strength seemed to go from him, as if he had come to the last of his resources. His face turned gray, his joints visibly loosened. "Thank you," he murmured again. "Thank you very much. I think we'll be seeing each other soon." And he was gone. Bowing himself out the door like a Japanese ambassador.

You meet all kinds in this business. Shaking my head, I opened his slip of paper. Three things were written on it in a spidery handwriting:

1. *Keep an eye on Gilmartin.*
2. *Mandatory national oil gellation—come out for it soon.*
3. *Socorro for Leydecker before summer. Get to him early.*

I read them twice, got nothing from them, waited for the familiar clarifying leap of intuition, didn't get that either. Something about this Carvajal seemed to short my faculties completely. That ghostly smile, those burned-out eyes, these cryptic notations—every aspect of him left me baffled and disturbed. "He's gone," I called to Lombroso, who emerged at once from his inner room.

"Well?"

"I don't know. I absolutely don't know. He gave me this," I said, and passed the slip to him.

"Gilmartin. Gellation. Leydecker." Lombroso frowned. "All right, wizard. What does it mean?"

Gilmartin had to be State Controller Anthony Gilmartin, who had clashed with Quinn a couple of times already over city fiscal policy but who hadn't been in the news in months. "Carvajal thinks there'll be more trouble with Albany about money," I hazarded. "You'd know more about that than I do, though. Is Gilmartin grumbling about city spending again?"

"Not a word."

"Are we preparing a batch of new taxes he won't like?"

"We would have told you by now if we were, Lew."

"So there are no potential conflicts shaping up between Quinn and the controller's office?"

"I don't see any in the visible future," Lombroso said. "Do you?"

"Nothing. As for mandatory oil gellation—"

"W*e are* talking about pushing through a tough local law," he said. "No tankers entering New York Harbor carrying ungelled oil. Quinn isn't sure it's as good an idea as it sounds, and we were getting around to asking you for a projection. But national oil gellation? Quinn hasn't been speaking out much on matters of national policy."

"Not yet."

"Not yet, no. Maybe it's time. Maybe Carvajal is on to something there. And the third one—"

"Leydecker," I said. Leydecker, surely, was Governor Richard Leydecker of California, one of the most powerful men in the New Democratic Party and the early front runner for the presidential nomination in 2000. "*Socorro* is Spanish for 'help,' isn't it, Bob? Help Leydecker, who doesn't need any help? Why? How can Paul Quinn help Leydecker, anyway? By endorsing him for President? Aside from winning Leydecker's good will, I don't see how that's going to do Quinn any good, and it isn't likely to give Leydecker anything he doesn't already have in his pocket, so—"

"Socorro is lieutenant-governor of California," Lombroso said gently. "Carlos Socorro. It's a man's name, Lew."

"Carlos. Socorro." I closed my eyes. "Of course." My cheeks blazed. All my list-making, all my frantic compiling of power centers in the New Democratic Party, all my sweaty doodling of the past year and a half, and yet I had still managed to forget Leydecker's heir

apparent. Not *socorro* but Socorro, idiot! I said, "What'
he hinting at, then? That Leydecker will resign to see:
the nomination, making Socorro governor? Okay, tha
computes. But get to him early? Get to whom?" I fal
tered. "Socorro? Leydecker? It comes out all muddy
Bob. I'm not getting a reading that makes any sense."

"What's your reading of Carvajal?"

"A crank," I said. "A rich crank. A weird little mar
with a bad case of politics on the brain." I put the note
in my wallet. My head was throbbing. "Forget it. I hu-
mored him because you said I should humor him. I was
a very good boy today, wasn't I, Bob? But I'm not
required to take any of this stuff seriously, and I refuse
to try. Now let's go to lunch and smoke some good bone
and have some very shiny martinis and talk shop." Lombroso smiled his most radiant smile and patted my back
consolingly and led me out of the office. I banished
Carvajal from my mind. But I felt a chill, as though I had
entered a new season and the season wasn't spring, and
the chill lingered long after lunch was over.

12 In the next few weeks we got down in earnest to the job of planning Paul Quinn's ascent—and our own—to the White House. I no longer had to be coy about my desire, bordering on need, to make him President; by now everyone in the inner circle openly admitted to the same fervor I had found so embarrassing when I first felt it a year and a half earlier. We were all out of the closet now.

The process of creating Presidents hasn't changed much since the middle of the nineteenth century, though the techniques are a bit different in these days of data nets, stochastic forecasts, and media-intensive ego saturation. The starting point, of course, is a strong candidate, preferably one with a power base in a densely populated state. Your man has to be plausibly presidential; he must look and sound like a President. If that isn't his natural style, he'll have to be trained to create a sense of plausibility around himself. The best candidates have it naturally. McKinley, Lyndon Johnson, FDR, and Wilson all had that dramatic presidential look. So did Harding. No man ever looked more like a President than Harding; it was his only qualification for the job, but it was enough to get him there. Dewey, Al Smith, McGovern, and Humphrey didn't have it, and they lost. Stevenson and Willkie did, but they were up against men who had more of it. John F. Kennedy didn't conform to the 1960 ideal of what a President should look like—sage, paternal—but he had other things going for him, and by winning he altered the model to some degree, benefiting, among others, Paul Quinn, who was presidentially plausible because he was Kennedyesque. *Sounding* like a President is important, too. The would-be candidate has to come across as firm and serious and vigorous, yet charitable and flexible, with a tone communicating Lincoln's warmth and wisdom, Truman's spunk, FDR's serenity, JFK's wit. Quinn could hold his own in that department.

The man who wants to be President must assemble a team—someone to raise money (Lombroso), someone to charm the media (Missakian), someone to analyze trends and suggest the most profitable policies (me), someone to put together a nationwide alliance of political chieftains (Ephrikian), someone to direct and coordinate strategy (Mardikian). The team then goes forth with the product, makes the proper connections in the worlds of politics, journalism, and finance, and establishes in the public's mind the concept that this is the Right Man for the Job. By the time of the nominating convention enough delegates have to be rounded up, via open or covert pledges, to put the candidate over on the first ballot or at worst the third; if you can't get him the nomination by then, alliances crumble and dark horses stalk the night. Once he's nominated, you pick a running mate who is as much unlike the candidate in philosophy, looks, and geographical background as anyone can be who is still on speaking terms with him, and off you go to pound the esteemed opponent into the dust.

Early in April '99 we held our first formal strategy meeting in Deputy Mayor Mardikian's office in the west wing of City Hall—Haig Mardikian, Bob Lombroso, George Missakian, Ara Ephrikian, and me. Quinn wasn't there; Quinn was in Washington haggling with the Department of Health, Education and Welfare for an increased appropriation for the city under the Emotional Stability Act. There was an electric crackle in the room that had nothing to do with the purifying system's output of ozone. It was the crackle of power, real and potential. We had gathered to begin the business of shaping history.

The table was round, but I felt myself occupying a place at the center of the group. The four of them, already far better versed in the ways of might and influence than I, were looking to me for direction, for the future was a mist and they could only guess at the riddles of days undawned and they believed I *saw*, I *knew*. I was not about to explain the difference between *seeing* and merely being good at guessing. I savored that sense of dominance. Power is addictive, oh, yes, at whatever level we may attain it. There I sat among the millionaires, two lawyers and a stockbroker and a data-net tycoon, three swarthy Armenians and a swarthy Spanish Jew, each of them as hungry as I to feel the resonant triumph of a successful presidential bid, each as greedy as I for a share of vicarious glory, each already carving empires for himself within the government-to-come, and they waited for me to tell them how to go about what was in literal fact the conquest of the United States of America.

Mardikian said, "Let's begin with a reading, Lew. How do you rate Quinn's actual chances for getting the nomination next year?"

I made the appropriate seerlike pause, I looked as though I were grasping for the stochastic totems, I gazed into the vasty reaches of space, staring at dancing dust motes for auguries, I cloaked myself in vatic pomposity, I did the whole wicked impressive act, and after a moment I replied solemnly, "For the nomination, maybe one chance in eight. For election, one chance in fifty."

"Not so good."

"No."

"Not good at all," said Lombroso.

Mardikian, dismayed, tugging at the tip of his fleshy imperial nose, said, "Are you telling us we ought to skip it altogether? Is that your evaluation?"

"For next year, yes. Forget the presidency thing."

"We just quit?" Ephrikian said. "We just stick here in City Hall and drop the whole deal?"

"Wait," Mardikian murmured to him. He faced me again. "What about running in '04, Lew?"

"Better. Much better."

Ephrikian, a burly black-bearded man with a fashionably shaven scalp, looked impatient and bothered. He scowled and said, "The media is talking big right now about what Quinn has accomplished in his first year as mayor. I think this is the moment to grab for the next rung, Lew."

"I agree," I said amiably.

"But you tell us he'll be beaten in 2000."

"I say anybody the New Democrats put up will be beaten," I replied. "Anyone. Quinn, Leydecker, Keats, Kane, Pownell, anybody. This is the moment for Quinn to grab, all right, but the right next rung isn't necessarily the top one."

Missakian, squat, precise, thin-lipped, the communications expert, the man of clear vision, said, "Can you be more specific, Lew?"

"Yes," I said, and swung into it.

I set forth my not very chancy prediction that whoever went up against President Mortonson in 2000—Leydecker, most likely—would get beaten. Incumbent Presidents in this country don't lose elections unless their first term has been a disaster of Hooverian proportions, and Mortonson had done a nice clean dull unexceptionable sluggish job, the kind a lot of Americans like. Leydecker would mount a respectable challenge, but there were really no issues, and he would be defeated and might be defeated badly, even though he was of obvious presidential caliber. Best to stay out of Leydecker's path, then, I argued. Give him a free run. Any attempt by Quinn to wrest the nomination from him next year would probably fail, anyway, and would certainly make Leydecker Quinn's enemy, which wasn't desirable. Let Leydecker have the accolade, let him go on to destroy himself in the election trying to beat the invincible Mortonson. We would wait to put Quinn up—still young, untarnished by defeat—in 2004, when the Constitution prohibited Mortonson from running again.

"So Quinn comes out big for Leydecker in 2000 and then goes to sit on his hands?" Ephrikian asked.

"More than that," I said. I looked toward Bob Lombroso. He and I had already discussed strategy and come to an agreement, and now, hunching his powerful shoulders forward, sweeping the Armenian side of the table with an elegant heavy-lidded glance, Lombroso began to outline our plan.

Quinn would make an open bid for national prominence during the next few months, peaking in the early summer of '99 with a cross-country tour and major speeches in Memphis, Chicago, Denver, and San Francisco. With some solid attention-getting accomplishments in New York City behind him (enclave realignment, curriculum streamlining, deGottfriedizing of the police force, etc.), he would begin speaking out on larger issues like regional fusion-power interchange policy and reenactment of the repealed Privacy Laws of 1982 and—why not?—mandatory oil gellation. By autumn he would begin a direct attack on the Republicans, not so much Mortonson himself as selected cabinet members (especially Secretary of Energy Hospers, Secretary of Information Theiss, and Secretary of the Environment Perlman). Thus he would inch into contention, becoming a national figure, a rising young leader, a man to reckon with. People would start talking about his presidential possibilities, though the polls would rank him well behind Leydecker as a favorite for the nomination—we'd see to that—and he would never actually declare himself in the running. He'd let the media assume he preferred Leydecker to any of the other declared candidates, though he would be careful not to make any outright endorsement of Leydecker. At the New Democratic convention in San Francisco in 2000, once Leydecker had been nominated and had made the traditional free-choice speech declining to name his running mate, Quinn would launch a game and dramatic but ultimately unsuccessful bid for the *vice*-presidential nomination. Why vice-presidential? Because the floor fight would give him major media exposure without opening him, as a presidential bid would, to accusations of premature ambition, and without angering the powerful Leydecker. Why unsuccessful? Because Leydecker was going to lose the election to Mortonson anyway, and there was nothing for Quinn to gain in going down to defeat with him as his running mate. Better to be turned aside at the convention—thereby establishing the image of a brilliant newcomer of great promise thwarted by political hacks—than to be repudiated at the polls. "Our model," Lombroso concluded, "is John F. Kennedy, edged out for vice-president just this way in 1956, head of the ticket in 1960. Lew has run simulations showing the overlap of dynamics, one on one, and we can show you the profiles."

"Great," Ephrikian said. "When's the assassination due—2003?"

"Let's keep it serious," said Lombroso gently.

"Okay," said Ephrikian. "I'll give you serious, then. What if Leydecker decides he'd like to run again in 2004?"

"He'll be sixty-one years old then," Lombroso replied, "and he'll have a previous defeat on his record. Quinn will be forty-three and unbeaten. One man will be on the way down, the other obviously on the way up, and the party will be hungry for a winner after eight years out of power."

There was a long silence.

"I like it," Missakian announced finally.

I said, "What about you, Haig?"

Mardikian had not spoken for a while. Now he nodded. "Quinn's not ready to take over the country in 2000. He will be in 2004."

"And the country will be ready for Quinn," said Missakian.

13 One thing about politics, the man said, is that it makes strange bedfellows. But for politics, Sundara and I surely would never have wandered into an ad hoc four-group that spring with Catalina Yarber, the Transit Creed proctor, and Lamont Friedman, the highly ionized young financial genius. But for Catalina Yarber, Sundara might not have opted for Transit. But for Sundara's conversion, she would very likely still be my wife. And so, and so, the threads of causation, everything leading back to the same point in time.

What happened is that as a member of Paul Quinn's entourage I received two free tickets to the $500-a-plate Nicholas Roswell Day dinner that the New York State New Democratic Party holds every year in the middle of April. This is not only a memorial tribute to the assassinated governor but also, indeed primarily, a fund-raising affair and a showcase for the party's current superstar. The main speaker this time, of course, was Quinn.

"It's about time I went to one of your political dinners," Sundara said.

"They're pure formaldehyde."

"Nevertheless."

"You'll hate it, love."

"Are you going?" she asked.

"I have to."

"Then I think I'll use the other ticket. If I fall asleep, nudge me when the mayor gets up to talk. He turns me on."

So on a mild rainy night she and I podded out to the Harbor Hilton, that great pyramid all agleam on its pliable pontoon platform half a kilometer off Manhattan's tip, and foregathered with the cream of the eastern liberal establishment in the sparkling Summit Room, from which I had a view of—among other things— Sarkisian's condo tower on the other side of the bay, where nearly four years earlier I had first met Paul Quinn. A good many alumni of that gaudy party would be at tonight's dinner. Sundara and I drew seats at the same table as two of them, Friedman and Ms. Yarber.

During the preliminary session of bone-doping and cocktails Sundara drew more attention than any of the senators, governors, and mayors present, Quinn included. This was partly a matter of curiosity, since everybody in New York politics had heard about my exotic wife but few had met her, and partly because she was surely the most beautiful woman in the room. Sundara was neither surprised nor annoyed. She has been beautiful all her life, after all, and has had time to grow accustomed to the effects her looks evoke. Nor had she dressed like one who minds being stared at. She had chosen a sheer harem suit, dark and loose and flowing, that covered her body from toes to throat; beneath it she was bare and when she passed before a source of light she was devastating. She glowed like a radiant moth in the middle of the gigantic ballroom, supple and elegant somber and mysterious, highlights sparkling in her ebon hair, hints of breast and flank tantalizing the onlookers. Oh, she was having a glorious time! Quinn came over to greet us, and he and Sundara transformed a chaste kiss-and-hug into an elaborate pas de deux of sexual charisma that made some of our elder statesmen gasp and redden and loosen their collars. Even Quinn's wife, Laraine, famous for her Gioconda smile, looked shaken a bit, though she has the most secure marriage of any politician I know. (Or was she merely amused by Quinn's ardor? That opaque smirk!)

Sundara was still emanating pure *Kama Sutra* when we took our seats. Lamont Friedman, sitting halfway around the circular table from her, jerked and quivered when her eyes met his, and stared at her with ferocious intensity while muscles twitched wildly in his long narrow neck. Meanwhile, in a more restrained but no less intense way, Friedman's companion of the evening, Ms. Yarber, was also giving Sundara the stare.

Friedman. He was about twenty-nine, weirdly thin, maybe 2.3 meters tall, with a bulging Adam's apple and crazy exophthalmic eyes; a dense mass of kinky brown hair engulfed his head like some woolly creature from another planet that was attacking him. He had come out of Harvard with a reputation for monetary sorcery and, after going to Wall Street when he was nineteen, had become the head magus of a band of spaced-out financiers calling themselves Asgard Equities, which through a series of lightning coups—option-pumping, feigned tenders, double straddles, and a lot of other techniques I but dimly comprehend—had within five years gained control of a billion-dollar corporate empire with extensive holdings on every continent but Antarctica. (And it would not amaze me to learn that Asgard held the customs-collection franchise for McMurdo Sound.)

Ms. Yarber was a small blond person, thirty or so, lean and a trifle hard-faced, energetic, quick-eyed, thin-lipped. Her hair, boyishly short, fell in sparse bangs over her high inquisitive forehead. She wore not much face makeup, only a faint line of blue around her mouth, and her clothes were austere—a straw-colored jerkin and a straight, simple brown knee-length skirt. The effect was restrained and even ascetic, but, I had noticed as we sat down, she had neatly balanced her prevailingly asexual image with one stunning erotic touch: her skirt was entirely open from hip to hem for a span of perhaps twenty centimeters down the left side, exposing as she moved a sleek muscular leg, a smooth tawny thigh, a glimpse of buttock. At mid-thigh, fastened by an encircling chain, she wore the little abstract medallion of the Transit Creed.

And so to dinner. The usual banquet fare: fruit salad, consommé, protosoy filet, steam-table peas and carrots, flagons of California Burgundy, lumpy baked Alaska, everything served with maximum clatter and minimum grace by stony-faced members of downtrodden minority groups. Neither the food nor the decor had any taste, but no one minded that; we were all so doped that the menu was ambrosia and the hotel was Valhalla. As we chattered and ate, an assortment of small-time political pros circulated from table to table, slapping backs and gladding hands, and also we endured a procession of self-important political wives, mainly sixtyish, dumpy, and grotesquely garbed in the latest nippy-dip styles, wandering about digging their proximity to the mighty and famous. The noise level was 20 db up from Niagara. Geysers of ferocious laughter came splashing from this table or that as some silver-maned jurist or revered legislator told his or her favorite scabrous Republican / gay / black / Puerto / Jew / Irish / Italian / doctor / lawyer / rabbi / priest / female politician / Mafioso joke in the finest 1965 style. I felt, as I had always felt at these functions, like a visitor from Mongolia hurled without phrasebook into some unknown American tribal ritual. It might have been unendurable if tubes of high-quality bone had not kept coming around; the New Democratic Party may stint on the wine but it knows how to buy dope.

By the time the speechmaking began, about half past nine, a ritual within the ritual was unfolding: Lamont Friedman was flashing almost desperate signals of desire at Sundara, and Catalina Yarber, though she was obviously also drawn to Sundara, had in a cool unemotional nonverbal way offered herself to me.

As the master of ceremonies—Lombroso, managing brilliantly to be elegant and coarse at the same time—went into the core of his routine, alternating derisive pokes at the most distinguished members of the party present in the room with obligatory threnodies to the traditional martyrs Roosevelt, Kennedy, Kennedy, King,

Roswell, and Gottfried, Sundara leaned toward me and whispered. "Have you been watching Friedman?"

"He has a bad case of horn, I'd say."

"I thought geniuses were supposed to be more subtle."

"Perhaps he thinks the least subtle approach is the most subtle approach," I suggested.

"Well, I think he's being adolescent."

"Too bad for him, then."

"Oh, no," Sundara said. "I find him attractive. Weird but not repellent, you know? Almost fascinating."

"Then the direct approach is working for him. See? He *is* a genius."

Sundara laughed. "Yarber's after you. Is she a genius, too?"

"I think it's really you she wants, love. It's called the indirect approach."

"What do you want to do?"

I shrugged. "It's up to you."

"I'm for it. How do you feel about Yarber?"

"Much energy there, is my guess."

"Mine too. Four-group tonight, then?"

"Why not," I said, just as Lombroso sent the audience into deafening merriment with an elaborately polyethnic-perverse climax to his introduction to Paul Quinn.

We gave the mayor a standing ovation, neatly choreographed by Haig Mardikian from the dais. Resuming my seat, I sent Catalina Yarber a body-language telegram that brought dots of color to her pale cheeks. She grinned. Small sharp even teeth, set close together. Message received. Done and done. Sundara and I would have an adventure with these two tonight, then. We were more monogamous than most couples, hence our two-group basic license: not for us the brawling multiheaded households, the squabbles over private property, the communal broods of kiddies. But monogamy is one thing and chastity is another, and if the former still exists, however metamorphosed by the evolutions of the era, the latter is one with the dodo and the trilobite. I welcomed the prospect of a passage at arms with the vigorous little Ms. Yarber. Yet I found myself envying Friedman, as I always envied

Sundara's partner of the night: for he would have the unique Sundara, who was to me still the most desirable woman in the world, and I must settle for someone I desired but desired less than she. A measure of love, I suppose, is what that was, love within the context of exofidelity. Lucky Friedman! One can come to a woman like Sundara for the first time only once.

Quinn spoke. He is no comic, and he made only a few perfunctory jokes, to which his listeners tactfully over-reacted; then it was down to serious business, the future of New York City, the future of the United States, the future of humanity in the coming century. The year 2000, he told us, holds immense symbolic value: it is literally the coming of the millennium. As the digit shifts, let us wipe clean the slate and begin afresh, remembering but not re-enacting the errors of the past. We have, he said, been through the ordeal by fire in the twentieth century, enduring vast dislocations and transformations and in-juries; we have several times come close to the destruc-tion of all life on earth; we have confronted ourselves with the likelihood of universal famine and universal poverty; we have plunged ourselves foolishly and avoid-ably into decades of political instability; we have been the victims of our own greed, fear, hatred, and ignorance: but now, with the energy of the solar reaction itself in our control, with population growth stable, with a workable balance reached between economic expansion and protec-tion of the environment, the time has come to build the ultimate society, a world in which reason prevails and right is triumphant, a world in which the full flowing of human potential can be realized.

And so on, a splendid vision of the era ahead. Noble rhetoric, especially from a mayor of New York, tradi-tionally more concerned with the problems of the school system and the agitation of the civil-service unions than with the destiny of mankind. It would have been easy to dismiss the speech as mere pretty bombast; but no, im-possible, it held significance beyond its theme, for what we were hearing was the first trumpet call of a would-be world leader. There he stood, looking half a meter taller than he was, face flushed, eyes bright, arms folded in that characteristic pose of force in repose, hitting us with those clarion phrases:

"—as the digit shifts, let us wipe clean the slate—"

"—we have been through the ordeal by fire—"

"—the time has come to build the ultimate society—"

The Ultimate Society. I heard the click and the whirr, and the sound was not so much the shifting of the digit as the extrusion of a new political slogan, and I didn't need great stochastic gifts to guess that we would all hear much, much more about the Ultimate Society before Paul Quinn was done with us.

Damn, but he was compelling! I was eager to be off and into the night's exploits, and still I sat motionless, rapt, and so did this whole audience of boozy pols and stoned celebrities, and even the waiters halted their eternal clashing of trays as Quinn's magnificent voice rolled through the hall. Since that first night at Sarkisian's I had watched him grow steadily stronger, more solid, as though his rise to prominence had confirmed in him his own self-appraisal and burned away whatever shred of diffidence was in him. Now, glittering in the spotlights, he seemed a vehicle for cosmic energies; there played through him and out from him an irresistible power that shook me profoundly. A new Roosevelt? A new Kennedy? I trembled. A new Charlemagne, a new Mohammed, maybe a new Genghis Khan.

He finished with a flourish and we were up and screaming, no need of Mardikian's choreography now, and the media folk were running to claim their cassettes and the hard-eyed clubhouse boys were slapping palms and talking about the White House and women were weeping and Quinn, sweating, arms outspread, accepted our homage with quiet satisfaction, and I sensed the first rumblings of the juggernaut through these United States.

It was an hour more before Sundara and Friedman and Catalina and I got out of the hotel. To the pod, quickly home. Odd self-conscious silences; all four of us eager to get to it, but the social conventions temporarily prevail, and we pretend to coolness; and, besides, Quinn has overwhelmed us. We are so full of him, his resonant phrases, his vital presence, that we are all four of us made ciphers, numb, selfless, stunned. No one can initiate the first move. We chatter. Brandy, bone; a tour of the apartment; Sundara and I show off our paintings, our sculptures, our primitive artifacts, our view of the Brooklyn skyline; we become less ill at ease with one another, but still there is no sexual tension; that mood of erotic anticipation that had been building so excitingly three hours earlier has been wholly dissipated by the impact of Quinn's speech. Was Hitler an orgasmic experience? Was Caesar? We sprawl on the thick white carpet. More brandy. More bone. Quinn, Quinn, Quinn: instead of sexing we talk politics. Friedman, finally, most unspontaneously, slides his hand along Sundara's ankle and up over her calf. It is a signal. We will force the intensity. "He *has* to run next year," says Catalina Yarber, ostentatiously maneuvering herself so that the slit in her skirt flops open, displaying flat belly, golden curls. "Leydecker's got the nomination wrapped up," Friedman opines, growing bolder, caressing Sundara's breasts. I touch the dimmer switch, kicking in the altered-light rheostat, and the room takes on a shining psychedelic texture. About, about, in reel and rout, the witchfires dance. Yarber offers a fresh tube of bone. "From Sikkim," she declares. "The best stuff going." To Friedman she says, "I know Leydecker's ahead, but Quinn can push him aside if he tries. We can't wait four more years for him." I draw deep on the tube and the Sikkimese dope sets up a breeder reaction in my brain. "Next year is too soon," I tell them. "Quinn looked incredible tonight, but we don't have enough time to hit the whole country with him between here and a year from November. Mortonson's a cinch for reelection anyway. Let Leydecker use himself up next year and we move Quinn into position in '04." I would have gone on to outline the whole feigned-vice-presidential-bid strategy but Sundara and Friedman had vanished into the shadows, and Cataline was no longer interested in politics.

Our clothes fell away. Her body was trim, athletic, boyishly smooth and muscular, breasts heavier than I had expected, hips narrower. She kept her Transit Creed emblem chained to her thigh. Her eyes gleamed but her skin was cool and dry and her nipples weren't erect; whatever she might be feeling, it didn't currently include strong physical desire for Lew Nichols. What I felt for her was curiosity and a certain remote willingness to fornicate; no doubt she felt no more for me. We entangled our bodies, stroked each other's skins, made our mouths meet and our tongues tickle. It was such an impersonal thing that I was afraid I'd never get it up, but the familiar reflexes took hold, the old reliable hydraulic mechanisms began shunting blood toward my loins, and I felt the proper throb, the proper stiffening. "Come," she said, "be born to me now." A strange phrase. Transit stuff, I learned later. I hovered above her and her slim strong thighs gripped me and I went into her.

Our bodies moved, up and down, back and forth. We rolled into this position and that one, joylessly running through the standard repertoire. Her skills were formidable, but there was a contagious chillness about her manner of doing it that rendered me a mere screwing machine, a restless piston endlessly ramming a cylinder, so that I copulated without pleasure and almost without sensation. What could she be getting out of it? Not much, I supposed. It's because she's really after Sundara, I thought, and is putting up with me merely to get a chance at *her*. I was right but I was wrong, for, I would learn eventually, Ms. Yarber's steely passionless technique was not so much a reflection of a lack of interest in me as it was a result of Transit teaching. Sexuality, say the good proctors, traps one in the here and now and delays transitions, and transition is all: the steady state is death. Therefore engage in coition if you must, or if there is some greater goal to be gained by it, but be not dissolved by ecstasy lest you mire yourself wrongfully in the intransitive condition.

Even so. We indulged in our icy ballet for what seemed like weeks, and then she came, or allowed herself to come, in a quiet quick quiver, and with silent relief I nudged myself across the boundary into completion, and we rolled apart, hardly breathing hard.

"I'd like more brandy," she said after a bit.

I reached for the cognac. From far away came the groans and gasps of more orthodox pleasure: Sundara and Freidman going at it.

Catalina said, "You're very competent."

"Thank you," I replied uncertainly. No one had ever said quite that to me before. I wondered how to respond and decided to make no attempt at reciprocity. Cognac for two. She sat up, crossed her legs, smoothed her hair, sipped her drink. She looked unsweaty, unruffled, unfucked, in fact. Yet, strangely, she glowed with sexual energy; she seemed genuinely pleased with what we had done and genuinely pleased, as well, with me. "I mean that," she said. "You're superb. You do it with power and detachment."

"Detachment?"

"Non-attachment, I should say. We value that. In Transit, non-attachment is what we seek. All Transit processes work toward creating flux, toward constant evolutionary change, and if we allow ourselves to become attached to any aspect of the here and now, to become attached to erotic pleasure, for example, to become attached to getting rich, to become attached to any ego aspect that ties us to intransient states—"

"Catalina—"

"Yes?"

"I'm very looped. I can't handle theology now."

She grinned. "To become attached to non-attachment," she said, "is one of the worst follies of all. I'll have mercy. No more Transit talk."

"I'm grateful."

"Some other time, perhaps? You and Sundara both. I'd love to explain our teachings, if—"

"Of course," I said. "Not now."

We drank, we smoked, eventually we found ourselves fornicating again—it was my defense against her yearning to convert me—and this time she must have had her tenets less firmly to the fore of her consciousness, for our interchange was less of a copulation, more a making of love. Toward dawn Sundara and Friedman appeared, she looking sleek and glorious, he bony and drained and even a bit dazed. She kissed me across a gulf of twelve meters, a pucker of air: Hello, love, hello, I love you most of all. I went to her and she pressed tight against me and I nibbled her earlobe and said, "Have fun?" She nodded dreamily. Friedman must have his skills, too, not all of them financial. "Did he talk Transit to you?" I wanted to know. Sundara shook her head. Friedman wasn't into Transit yet, she murmured, though Catalina had been working on him.

"She's working on me, too," I said.

Friedman was slumped on the couch, glassy-eyed, staring dully at the sunrise over Brooklyn. Sundara, steeped in classical Hindu erotology, was a heavy trip for any man.

—when a woman clasps her lover as closely as a serpent twines around a tree, and pulls his head towards her waiting lips, if she then kisses him making a light hissing sound "soutt soutt" and looks at him long and tenderly —her pupils dilated with desire—this posture is known as the Clasp of the Serpent—

"Anyone for breakfast?" I asked.

Catalina smiled obliquely. Sundara merely inclined her head. Friedman looked unenthusiastic. "Later," he said, voice barely rising above a whisper. A burned-out husk of a man.

—when a woman places one foot on the foot of her lover, and the other around his thigh, when she puts one arm around his neck and the other around his loins, and softly croons her desire, as if she wished to climb the firm stem of his body and capture a kiss—it is known as the Tree Climber—

I left them sprawled in their various parts of the living room and went off to shower. I had had no sleep but my mind was alert and active. A strange night, a busy night:

I felt more alive than in weeks, and I sensed a stochastic tickle, a tremor of clairvoyance, that warned me I was moving to the threshold of some new transformation. I took the shower full force, punching for maximum vibratory enhancement, waves of ultrasound keying into my throbbing outreaching nervous system, and emerged looking for new worlds to conquer.

No one was in the living room but Friedman, still naked, still glazed of eye, still supine on the couch.

"Where'd they go?" I asked.

Languidly he waved a finger toward the master bedroom. So Catalina had scored her goal after all.

Was I expected to extend similar hospitality to Friedman now? My bisexuality quotient is low and he inspired not a shred of gaiety in me just then. But no, Sundara had dismantled his libido; he flashed no signs except exhaustion. "You're a lucky man," he murmured after a while. "What a marvelous woman. . . . What . . . a . . . marvelous . . ." I thought he had dozed. ". . . woman. Is she for sale?"

"Sale?"

He sounded almost serious.

"Your Oriental slave girl is who I'm talking about."

"My wife?"

"You bought her in the market in Baghdad. Five hundred dinars for her, Nichols."

"No deal."

"A thousand."

"Not for two empires," I said.

He laughed. "Where'd you find her?"

"California."

"Are there any more like that out there?"

"She's unique," I told him. "So am I, so are you, so is Catalina. People don't come in standard models, Friedman. Are you interested in breakfast yet?"

He yawned. "If we want to be reborn on the proper level we must learn to purify ourselves of the needs of the meat. That's Transit. I'll mortify my meat by renouncing breakfast as a start." His eyes closed and he went away.

I had breakfast alone and watched morning come rushing out of the Atlantic at us. I took the morning *Times* out of its door slot and was pleased to see that Quinn's speech had made the front page, below the fold but with a two-column photo. MAYOR CALLS FOR FULL HUMAN POTENTIAL. That was the headline, a bit below the *Times'* usual standard of incisiveness. The story used his Ultimate Society tag as its lead and quoted half a dozen glittering phrases in the first twenty lines. The story then jumped to page 21, and the complete text was in a box accompanying the jump. I found myself reading it, and as I read I found myself wondering why I had been so stirred, for the printed speech seemed to lack any real content; it was purely a verbal object, a collection of catchy lines, offering no program, making no concrete suggestions. And to me last night it had sounded like a blueprint for Utopia. I shivered. Quinn had provided nothing more than an armature; I myself had hung the trimmings on, all my vague fantasies of social reform and millennial transformation. Quinn's performance had been pure charisma in action, an elemental force working us over from the dais. So it is with all the great leaders: the commodity they have to sell is personality. Mere ideas can be left to lesser men.

The phone began ringing a little after eight. Mardikian wanted to distribute a thousand videotapes of the speech to New Democratic organizations all over the country; what did I think? Lombroso reported pledges of half a million to the as yet nonexistent Quinn-for-President campaign kitty in the aftermath of the speech. Missakian . . . Ephrikian . . . Sarkisian . . .

When I finally had a quiet moment, I came out and found Catalina Yarber, wearing her blouse and her thigh chain, prodding Lamont Friedman into wakefulness. She gave me a foxy grin. "We'll be seeing more of each other, I know," she said throatily.

They left. Sundara slept on. There were no more phone calls. Quinn's speech was making waves everywhere. Eventually she emerged, naked, delicious, sleepy, but perfect in her beauty, not even puffy-eyed.

"I think I want to know more about Transit," she said.

14

Three days later I came home and was startled to find Sundara and Catalina, both nude, kneeling side by side on the living-room carpet. How beautiful they looked, the pale body beside the chocolate one, the short yellow hair and the long black cascade, the dark nipples and the pink. It was not the prelude to a pasha's orgy, though. The air was rich with incense and they were running through litanies. "Everything passes," Yarber intoned, and Sundara repeated, "Everything passes." A golden chain constricted the dusky satin of my wife's left thigh and the Transit Creed medallion was mounted on it.

She and Catalina displayed a courteous don't-mind-us attitude toward me and went on with what they were doing, which evidently was an extended catechism. I thought they would rise at some point and disappear into the bedroom, but no, the nudity was purely ritual, and when they were done with the teachings they donned their clothes and brewed tea and gossiped like old friends. That night, when I reached for Sundara, she said gently that she couldn't make love just now. Not *wouldn't*, not *didn't want to*, but *couldn't*. As if she had entered into a state of purity that must not at the moment be defiled by lust.

So it began, Sundara's passage into Transit. At first there was only the morning meditation, ten minutes in silence; then there were the evening readings, out of mysterious paperbound books poorly printed on cheap paper; in the second week she announced there would be a meeting in the city every Tuesday night, and could I manage without her? Tuesdays became nights of sexual abstinence for us also; she was apologetic but firm about that. She seemed distant, preoccupied, engrossed with her conversion. Even her work, the art gallery she ran so shrewdly, seemed unimportant to her. I suspected she was seeing Catalina often in the city during the day, and I was right, though in my naïve Western materialist way I imagined they were merely having a love affair, meeting in hotel rooms for interludes of slippery grapplings and tonguings, when in fact it was Sundara's soul far more than her body that had been seduced. Old friends had warned me long ago: marry a Hindu and you'll be twirling prayer wheels with her from dusk to dawn, you'll turn into a vegetarian, she'll have you singing hymns to Krishna. I laughed at them. Sundara was American, Western, earthy. But now I saw her Sanskrit genes taking their revenge.

Transit, of course, wasn't Hindu—more a mixture of Buddhism and fascism, actually, a stew of Zen and Tantra and Platonism and Gestalt therapy and Poundian economics and what-all else, and neither Krishna nor Allah nor Jehovah nor any other divinity figured in its beliefs. It had come out of California, naturally, six or seven years ago, a characteristic product of the Wild '90s that had succeeded the Goofy '80s that had followed the Horrid '70s, and, diligently proselytized by an ever-expanding horde of dedicated proctors, it had spread rapidly through such less enlightened places as the eastern United States. Until Sundara's conversion I had paid little attention to it; it was not so much repugnant as irrelevant to me. But as it began to absorb more and more of my wife's energies, I started to take a closer look.

Catalina Yarber had been able to express most of the basic tenets in five minutes, the night she and I bedded. This world is unimportant, the Transit folk assert, and our passage through it is brief, a quick trifling trip. We go through, we are reborn into it, we go through again, we keep on going through until at last we are freed from the wheel of karma and pass onward to the blissful annihilation that is nirvana, when we become one with the cosmos. What holds us to the wheel is ego attachment: we become hooked on things and needs and pleasures, on self-gratification, and so long as we retain a self that requires gratification we will be born again and again into this dreary meaningless little mud-ball. If we want to move to a higher plane and ultimately to reach the Highest, we must refine our souls in the crucible of renunciation.

All that is fairly orthodox Eastern theology. The special kicker of Transit is its emphasis on volatility and mutability. Transition is all; change is essential; stasis kills; rigid consistency is the road to undesirable rebirths. Transit processes work toward constant evolution, toward perpetual quicksilver flow of the spirit, and encourage unpredictable, even eccentric, behavior. That's the appeal: the sanctification of craziness. The universe, the proctors say, is in perpetual flux; we never can step twice into the same river; we must flow and yield; we must be supple, protean, kaleidoscopic, mercurial; we must accept the knowledge that permanence is an ugly delusion and everything, ourselves included, is in a state of giddy unending transition. But although the universe is fluid and wayward, we are not therefore condemned to blow haphazardly in its breezes. No, they tell us: *because* nothing is deterministic, *because* nothing is unbendingly foreordained, everything is within our individual control. We are the existential shapers of our destinies, and we are free to grasp the Truth and act on it. What is the Truth? That we must freely choose not to be ourselves, that we must discard our rigidly conceived self-images, for only through the unimpeded flow of the Transit processes can we abolish the ego attachments that tie us to intransient low-plane states.

These teachings were threatening to me. I am not comfortable with chaos. I believe in order and predictability. My gift of second sight, my innate stochasticity, is founded on the notion that patterns exist, that probabilities are real. I prefer to believe that while it is not certain that tea over a flame will boil or that a rock thrown in the air will fall, these events are highly likely. The Transit people, it seemed to me, were striving toward abolition of that likelihood: to produce iced tea on a stove was their aim.

Coming home was an adventure now.

One day the furniture was rearranged. *Everything.* All our carefully calculated effects were destroyed. Three days later I found the furniture in yet another pattern, even more clumsy. I made no comment either time and after about a week Sundara put things back the way they had been at first.

Sundara dyed her hair red. The effect was ghastly.

She kept a white cross-eyed cat for six days.

She begged me to accompany her to a Tuesday night process session, but when I agreed she canceled my appointment an hour before we were due to set out, and went alone, explaining nothing.

She was in the hands of the apostles of chaos. Love breeds patience; therefore I was patient with her. Whatever way she chose to wage her war on stasis, I was patient. This is only a phase, I told myself. Only a phase.

15 On the 9th day of May, 1999, between the hours of four and five in the morning, I dreamed that State Controller Gilmartin was being executed by a firing squad.

I can be so precise about the date and the time because it was a dream so vivid, so much like the eleven o'clock news unreeling on the screen of my mind, that it awakened me, and I mumbled a memo about it into my bedside recorder. I learned long ago to make notes on dreams of such intensity, because they often turn out to be premonitions. In dreams comes truth. Joseph's Pharaoh dreamed he stood by a river out of which came seven plump cattle and seven scrawny ones—fourteen omens. Calpurnia saw the statue of her husband Caesar spouting blood the night before the ides of March. Abe Lincoln dreamed of hearing the subdued sobs of invisible mourners and beheld himself going downstairs to find a catafalque in the East Room of the White House, an honor guard of soldiers, a body in funeral vestments on the bier, a throng of weeping citizens. Who is dead in the White House? the dreaming President asks, and they tell him that the dead man is the President, slain by an assassin. Long before Carvajal entered my life I knew that the future's moorings are weak, that floes of time break loose and drift back across the great sea to our sleeping minds. So I paid heed to my Gilmartin dream.

I saw him, plump, pale, sweating, a tall round-faced man with cold blue eyes, hauled into a bare dusty court-yard, a place of fierce sunlight and harsh sharp shadows, by a squad of scowling soldiers in black uniforms. I saw him struggling at his bonds, snuffling, twisting, beseech-ing, protesting his innocence. The soldiers standing shoulder to shoulder, lifting their rifles, an infinitely long moment of silent aiming. Gilmartin moaning, praying, whining, at the very end finding a scrap of dignity, pull-ing himself erect, squaring his shoulders, facing his killers defiantly. The order to fire, the crack of guns, the body jerking and writhing hideously, slumping against the ropes . . .

Now what to make of this? The promise of trouble for Gilmartin, who had made financial troubles for the Quinn administration and whom I didn't like, or merely the hope of it? An assassination brewing, perhaps? Assassinations had been a big thing in the early '90s, bigger even than in the bloody Kennedy years, but I thought the fad had gone out of fashion again. Who would assassinate a drab hack like Gilmartin, anyway? Maybe what I was picking up was a premonition that Gilmartin would die of natural causes. Gilmartin boasted of his good health, though. An accident, then? Or maybe just metaphorical death—a lawsuit, a political squabble, a scandal, an impeachment?

I didn't know how to interpret my dream or what to do about it, and ultimately I decided not to do anything. And so we missed the boat on the Gilmartin scandal, which indeed was what I was perceiving—no firing squad, no assassination for the controller, but shame, resignation, jail. Quinn could have made tremendous political capital out of it if it had been city investigators who exposed Gilmartin's manipulations, if the mayor had risen in righteous wrath to say that the city was being short-changed and an audit was needed. But I failed to see the larger pattern, and it was a state accountant, not one of our people, who eventually blew the story open—how

Gilmartin had been systematically diverting millions of dollars of state funds intended for New York City into the treasuries of a few small upstate towns, and thence into his own pockets and those of a couple of rural officials. Too late I realized that I had had *two* chances at knocking Gilmartin down, and I had fumbled both of them. A month before my dream Carvajal had given me that mysterious note. Keep an eye on Gilmartin, he had suggested. Gilmartin, oil gellation, Leydecker. Well?

"Talk to me about Carvajal," I said to Lombroso.

"What do you want to know?"

"How well has he actually done in the market?"

"So well it's uncanny. He's cleared nine or ten million that I know of, just since '93. Maybe a lot more. I'm sure he works through several brokerage firms. Numbered accounts, dummy nominees, all sorts of tricks to hide how much he's really been taking out of the Street."

"He earns all of it from trading?"

"All of it. He gets in, rides a stock straight up, gets out. There were people in my office who made fortunes just by following his picks."

"Is it possible," I asked, "for anybody to outguess the market that consistently over so many years?"

Lombroso shrugged. "I suppose a few people have done it. We have our legends of great traders all the way back to Bet-a-Million Gates. Nobody I know has been as consistent as Carvajal."

"Does he have inside information?"

"He can't have. Not on so many different companies. It has to be pure intuition. He just buys and sells, buys and sells, and reaps his profits. Came in cold one day, opened an account, no bank references, no Wall Street connections. Always cash transactions, never margin. Spooky."

"Yes," I said.

"Quiet little man. Sat watching the tape, put in his orders. No fuss, no chatter, no excitement."

"Is he ever wrong?"

"He's taken some losses, yes. Small ones. Small losses, big winnings."

"I wonder why."

"Why what?" Lombroso asked.

"Why any losses at all?"

"Even Carvajal has to be fallible."

"Really?" I said. "Maybe he takes the losses for strategic effect. Calculated setbacks, to encourage people to believe he's human. Or to keep others from automatically backing his picks and distorting the fluctuations."

"Dont you think he's human, Lew?"

"I think he's human, yes."

"But—?"

"But with a very special gift."

"For picking stocks that are going to go up. Very special."

"More than that."

"More how?"

"I'm not ready to say."

"Why are you afraid of him, Lew?" Lombroso said.

"Did I say I was? When?"

"The day he came here, you told me he made you feel creepy, that he gives off scary vibes. Remember?"

"I suppose I did."

"You think he's practicing witchcraft? You think he's some kind of magician?"

"I know probability theory, Bob. If there's one thing I do know, it's probability theory. Carvajal's done a couple of things that go beyond normal probability curves. One is his stockmarket performance. Another is this Gilmartin thing."

"Perhaps Carvajal gets his newspapers delivered a month in advance," Lombroso said.

He laughed. I didn't.

I said, "I have no hypotheses at all. I only know that Carvajal and I operate in the same kind of business, and that he's so much better at it than I am there's no comparison. What I tell you now is that I'm baffled and a little frightened."

Lombroso, calm to the point of seeming patronizing, drifted easily across his majestic office and stared a moment into his showcase of medieval treasures. At length he said, speaking with his back turned, "You're being excessively melodramatic, Lew. The world is full of people who frequently make lucky guesses. You're one yourself. He's luckier than most, sure, but that doesn't mean he can see the future."

"All right, Bob."

"Does it? When you come to me and say the probability of an unfavorable public response to this or that piece of legislation is thus-and-such, are you seeing into the future, or just taking a guess? I never heard you claim clairvoyance, Lew. And Carvajal—"

"All right!"

"Easy, man."

"I'm sorry."

"Can I get you a drink?"

"I'd like to change the subject," I said.

"What would you like to talk about next?"

"Oil gellation policy."

He nodded blandly. "The City Council," he said, "has had a bill in committee all spring that calls for gellation of all oil aboard tankers coming into New York Harbor. Environmentalists are for it, naturally, and, naturally, the oil companies are against it. Consumer groups aren't too happy about it because the bill is bound to push up refining costs, which means retail price increases. And—"

"Don't tankers carry gelling equipment already?"

"They do, yes. Been a federal regulation since, oh, '83 or so. The year they first began the heavy offshore pumping in the Atlantic. Whenever a tanker has an accident that causes structural rupture and there's a chance of an oil spill, a nozzle system sprays all the crude in the damaged section with gelling agents that turn the oil into a solid glob, right? Which keeps the oil inside the tank, and even if the ship breaks up altogether the gelled oil floats in big chunks that can easily be scooped up. Then they simply have to heat the gel to—what is it, 130 degrees Fahrenheit?—and it turns back into oil. But it takes three or four hours just to spray the stuff into one of those huge tanks, and another seven or eight for the oil to gel, so we have a period of maybe twelve hours following the onset of gellation in which the oil is still fluid, and a lot of oil can escape in twelve hours. So City Councilman Ladrone has this plan requiring oil to be gelled as a routine step in transporting it by sea to refineries, not just as an emergency response in case a tanker cracks open. But the political problems are—"

"Do it," I said.

"I have a stack of pro and con position papers that I'd like you to see before—"

"Forget them. Do it, Bob. Get that bill out of committee and into law this week. Effective, say, June first. Let the oil companies scream all they want. Have the bill enacted and have Quinn sign it with a very visible flourish."

"The big problem," Lombroso said, "is that if New York enacts a law like that and the other Eastern Seaboard cities don't, then New York will simply cease to serve as a port of entry for crude oil heading toward metropolitan-area refineries, and the revenue that we lose will be—"

"Don't worry about it. Pioneers have to take a few risks. Get the bill rammed through, and when Quinn signs it have him call upon President Mortonson to put a similar bill before Congress. Let Quinn stress that New York City is going to protect its beaches and harbors no matter what, but that he hopes the rest of the country won't be too far behind. Got it?"

"Aren't you pushing ahead too fast with this, Lew? It's not like you just to issue *ex cathedra* instructions like this when you haven't even studied the—"

"Maybe I can see the future, too," I said.

I laughed. He didn't.

Bothered as he was by my insistence on haste, Lombroso did the needful. We conferred with Mardikian, Mardikian spoke with Quinn, Quinn passed the word to the City Council, and the bill became law. The day Quinn was due to sign it, a delegation of oil-company lawyers showed up at his office to threaten, in their politely oily way, a harrowing court fight if he didn't veto the measure. Quinn sent for me and we had a two-minute discussion.

"Do I really want this law?" he asked, and I said, "You really do," and he sent the oil lawyers away. At the signing he delivered an impromptu and impassioned ten-minute speech in favor of national mandatory gellation. It was a slow day for the networks, and the heart of Quinn's speech, a lively two-and-a-half-minute segment about the rape of the environment and man's determination not to acquiesce passively, made it into the night's news programs from coast to coast.

The timing was perfect. Two days later the Japanese supertanker *Exxon Maru* was rammed off California and broke apart in a really spectacular way; the gelling system malfunctioned and millions of barrels of crude oil fouled the shoreline from Mendocino to Big Sur. That evening a Venezuelan tanker heading for Port Arthur, Texas, experienced some mysterious calamity in the Gulf of Mexico that spilled a load of ungelled oil on the shores of the whooping crane wildlife refuge near Corpus Christi. The next day there was a bad spill somewhere off Alaska, and, just as though these three awful spills were the first the world had ever known, suddenly everybody in Congress was deploring pollution and talking about mandatory gellation—with Paul Quinn's brand-new New York City legislation frequently being mentioned as the prototype for the proposed federal law.

Gilmartin.

Gellation.

One tip remained: *Socorro for Leydecker before summer. Get to him early.*

Cryptic and opaque, like most oracular pronouncements. I was entirely stopped by it. No stochastic technique at my command yielded a useful projection. I doodled a dozen scenarios and they all came out bewildering and meaningless. What kind of professional prophet was I when I was handed three solid clues to future events and I could turn a trick on but one out of the three?

I began to think I ought to pay a call on Carvajal.

Before I could do anything, though, stunning news rolled out of the West. Richard Leydecker, governor of

California, titular leader of the New Democratic Party, front-running candidate for the next presidential nomination, dropped dead on a Palm Springs golf course on Memorial Day at the age of fifty-seven, and his office and power descended to Lieutenant-Governor Carlos Socorro, who thereby became a mighty political force in the land by virtue of his control of the country's wealthiest and most influential state.

Socorro, who now would command the huge California delegation at next year's national New Democratic convention, began making king-making noises at his very first press conferences, two days after Leydecker's death. He managed to suggest, apropos of practically nothing, that he regarded Senator Eli Kane of Illinois as the most promising choice for next year's New Democratic nomination—thereby setting instantly into motion a Kane-for-President boom that would become overwhelming in the next few weeks.

I had been thinking about Kane myself. When the news of Leydecker's death came in, my immediate calculation was that Quinn should now make a play for the top nomination instead of the vice-presidency—why not grab the extra publicity now that we no longer needed to fear a murderous struggle with the omnipotent Leydecker?—but that we still should contrive things so that Quinn lost out on the convention floor to some older and less glamorous man, who then would go on to be trounced by President Mortonson in November. Quinn thus would inherit the fragments of the party to rebuild for 2004. Somebody like Kane, a distinguished-looking but hollow party-line politician, would be an ideal man for the role of the villain who deprives the dashing young mayor of the nomination.

For Quinn to move into serious contention against Kane, though, we would need Socorro's support. Quinn was still an obscure figure to much of the country, and Kane was famous and beloved in the vast mid-American heartland. Backing from California, giving Quinn the delegates from the two biggest states if not much else, would enable him to make a decent losing fight against

Kane. I figured that we would let a tasteful interval go by, perhaps a week, and then start making overtures to Governor Socorro. But Socorro's instant endorsement of Kane changed everything overnight and undercut Quinn completely. Suddenly there was Senator Kane touring California at the side of the new governor and emitting orotund bleats of praise for Socorro's administrative skills.

The fix was in and Quinn was out. A Kane-Socorro ticket was obviously in the making, and they would steamroller into next year's convention with a first-ballot nomination locked up. Quinn would merely look quixotic and ingenuous, or, worse, disingenuous, if he tried to mount a floor fight. We had failed to get to Socorro in time, despite Carvajal's tip, and Quinn had lost a chance to acquire a potent ally. No fatal damage had been done to Quinn's 2004 presidential chances, but our tardiness had been costly all the same.

Oh, the chagrin, the same, the obloquy! Oh, the bitter onus, Nichols! Here, says the strange little man, here is a piece of paper with three pieces of the future written on it. Take such action as your own prophetic skills tell you is desirable. Fine, you say, thanks a million, and your skills tell you nothing, and nothing is what you do. And the future slides down around your ears to become the present, and you see quite clearly the things you should have done, and you look foolish in your own eyes.

I felt humble. I felt worthless.

I felt that I had failed some sort of test.

I needed guidance. I went to Carvajal.

16

This is a place where a millionaire gifted with second sight lives? A small grimy flat in a squat dilapidated ninety-year-old apartment house just off Flatbush Avenue in deepest Godforsaken Brooklyn? Going there was an experiment in foolhardiness. I knew—anybody in the municipal administration quickly gets to know—which areas of the city had been written off as out of bounds, beyond hope of redemption, outside the rule of law. This was one of them. Beneath the veil of time and decay I could see the bones of old residential respectability here; it had been a district of lower-middle-class Jews once, a neighborhood of kosher butchers and unsuccessful lawyers, and then lower-middle-class black, and then slum black, probably with Puerto enclaves, and now it was just a jungle, a corroding wasteland of crumbling little red-brick semidetached two-family houses and soot-filmed six-story apartment buildings, inhabited by drifters, sniffers, muggers, muggers of muggers, feral cat packs, short-pants gangs, elephant rats, and Martin Carvajal. *"There?"* I blurted when, having suggested a meeting to Carvajal, he suggested we hold it at his home. I suppose it was tactless to be so astonished at where he lived. He replied mildly that no harm would come to me. "I think

I'll arrange for a police escort anyway," I said, and he laughed and said that was the surest way to invite trouble, and he told me again, firmly, to have no fear, that I would be in no peril if I came alone.

The inner voice whose promptings I always obey told me to have faith, so I went to Carvajal without a police escort, though not without fear.

No cab would go into that part of Brooklyn and pod service, of course, does not reach places like that. I borrowed an unmarked car from the municipal pool and drove it myself, not having the gall to risk a chauffeur's life out there. Like most New Yorkers, I drive infrequently and poorly, and the ride had perils of its own. But in time I came, undented if not undaunted, to Carvajal's street. Filth I had expected, yes, and rotting mounds of garbage in the street, and the rubble-strewn sites of demolished buildings looking like the gaps left by knocked-out teeth; but not the dry blackened corpses of beasts in the streets—dogs, goats, pigs?—and not the woody-stemmed weeds cracking through the pavement as if this were some ghost town, and not the reek of human dung and urine, and not the ankle-deep swirls of sand. A blast of oven heat hit me when I emerged, timidly and with misgivings, from the coolness of my car. Though this was only early June, a terrible late-August heat baked these miserable ruins. This is New York City? This might have been an outpost in the Mexican desert a century ago.

I left the car set on full alarm. Myself, I was carrying a top-strength anti-personnel baton and wearing a hip-hugging security cone warranted to knock any malefactor a dozen meters. Still I felt hideously exposed as I crossed the dreary pavement, knowing I had no defense against a casual sniper pot-shotting from above. But though a few sallow-faced inhabitants of this horrendous village eyed me sourly from the darkness behind their cracked and jagged windows, though a few lean-hipped street cowboys gave me long bleak glances, no one approached me, no one spoke to me, there were no fourth-floor fusillades. Entering the sagging building where Carvajal lived, I felt almost relaxed: maybe the neighborhood had been much maligned, maybe its dark reputation was a product of middle-class paranoia. Later I learned I would never have lasted sixty seconds outside my automobile if Carvajal hadn't given orders insuring my safety. In this parched jungle he had immense authority; to his fierce neighbors he was a sort of warlock, a sacred totem, a holy fool, respected and feared and obeyed. His gift of vision, no doubt, used judiciously and with overwhelming impact, had made him invulnerable here—in the jungle no one trifles with a shaman—and today he had spread his mantle over me.

His apartment was on the fifth floor. There was no elevator. Each flight of stairs was a grim adventure. I heard the scurrying of giant rats, I choked and retched at foul unfamiliar odors, I imagined seven-year-old murderers lurking in every pool of shadow. Without incident I reached his door. He opened before I could find the bell. Even in this heat he wore a white shirt with buttoned collar, a gray tweed jacket, a brown necktie. He looked like a schoolmaster waiting to hear me recite my Latin conjugations and declensions. "You see?" he said. "Safe and sound. I knew. No harm."

Carvajal lived in three rooms: a bedroom, a living room, a kitchen. The ceilings were low, the plaster was cracking, the faded green walls looked as if they had last been painted in the days of Tricky Dick Nixon. The furniture was even older, with a Truman-era look to it, floppy and overstuffed, floral slipcovers and sturdy rhinocerous legs. The air was unconditioned and stifling; the illumination was incandescent and dim; the TV was an archaic table model; the kitchen sink had running water, not ultrasonics. When I was growing up in the mid-1970s, one of my closest friends was a boy whose father had died in Vietnam. He lived with his grandparents, and their place looked exactly like this one. Carvajal's apartment eerily recaptured the texture of mid-century America; it was like a movie set, or a period room at the Smithsonian.

With remote, absentminded hospitality he settled me on the battered living-room sofa and apologized for having neither drink nor drug to offer me. He was not an indulger, he explained, and very little was sold in this neighborhood. "It doesn't matter," I said grandly. "A glass of water will be fine."

The water was tepid and faintly rusty. That's fine, too, I told myself. I sat unnaturally upright, spine rigid, legs tense. Carvajal, perching on the cushion of the armchair to my right, observed, "You look uncomfortable, Mr. Nichols."

"I'll unwind in a minute or two. The trip out here—"

"Of course."

"But no one bothered me in the street. I have to confess I was expecting trouble, but—"

"I told you no harm would come."

"Still—"

"But I told you," he said mildly. "Didn't you believe me? You should have believed me, Mr. Nichols. You know that."

"I suppose you're right," I said, thinking, *Gilmartin, gellation, Leydecker.* Carvajal offered me more water. I smiled mechanically and shook my head. There was a sticky silence. After a moment I said, "This is a strange part of town for a person like you to choose."

"Strange? Why?"

"A man of your means could live anywhere in the city."

"I know."

"Why here, then?"

"I've always lived here," he said softly. "This is the only home I've ever known. These furnishings belonged to my mother, and some to *her* mother. I hear the echoes of familiar voices in these rooms, Mr. Nichols. I feel the living presence of the past. Is that so odd, to go on living where one has always lived?"

"But the neighborhood—"

"Has deteriorated, yes. Sixty years bring great changes. But the changes haven't been perceptible to me in any important way. A gentle decline, year by year, then perhaps a steeper decline, but I make allowances, I make adjustments, I grow accustomed to what is new and make it part of what has always been. And everything is so familiar to me, Mr. Nichols—the names written in the wet cement when the pavement was new long ago, the great ailanthus tree in the schoolyard, the weatherbeaten gargoyles over the doorway of the building across the street. Do you understand what I'm saying? Why should I leave these things for a sleek Staten Island condo?"

"The danger, for one."

"There's no danger. Not for me. These people regard me as the little man who's always been here, the symbol of stability, the one constant in a universe of entropic flow. I have a ritualistic value for them. I'm some sort of good-luck token, perhaps. At any rate no one who lives here has ever molested me. No one ever will."

"Can you be sure of that?"

"Yes," he said, with monolithic assurance, looking straight into my eyes, and I felt that chill again, that sense of standing on the rim of an abyss beyond my fathoming. There was another long silence. There was force flowing from him—a power altogether at odds with his drab appearance, his mild manner, his numb, burned-out expression—and that force immobilized me. I might have been sitting frozen for an hour. At length he said, "You wanted to ask me some questions, Mr. Nichols."

I nodded. Taking a deep breath, I plunged in. "You knew Leydecker was going to die this spring, didn't you? I mean, you didn't just guess he'd die. You knew."

"Yes." That same final, uncontestable *yes*.

"You knew that Gilmartin would get into trouble. You knew that oil tankers would spill ungelled oil."

"Yes. Yes."

"You know what the stock market is going to do tomorrow and the day after tomorrow, and you've made millions of dollars by using that knowledge."

"That's also true."

"Therefore it's fair to say that you see future events with extraordinary clarity, with supernatural clarity, Mr. Carvajal."

"As do you."

"Wrong," I said. "I don't see future events at all. I've got no vision whatsoever of things to come. I'm merely very very good at guessing, at weighing probabilities and coming up with the most likely pattern, but I don't really *see*. I can't ever be certain that I'm right, just reasonably confident. Because all I'm doing is guessing. You *see*. You told me almost as much when we met in Bob Lombroso's office: I guess; you *see*. The future is like a movie playing inside your mind. Am I right?"

"You know you are, Mr. Nichols."

"Yes. I know I am. There can't be any doubt of it. I'm aware of what can be accomplished by stochastic methods, and the things you do go beyond the possibilities of guesswork. Maybe I could have predicted the likelihood of a couple of oil-tanker breakups, but not that Leydecker would drop dead or that Gilmartin would be exposed as a crook. I might have guessed that *some* key political figure would die this spring, but never which one. I might have guessed that *some* state politician would get busted, but not by name. Your predictions were exact and specific. That's not probabilistic forecasting. That's more like sorcery, Mr. Carvajal. By definition, the future is unknowable. But you seem to know a great deal about the future."

"About the immediate future, yes. Yes, I do, Mr. Nichols."

"Only the immediate future?"

He laughed. "Do you think my mind penetrates all of space and time?"

"At this point I have no idea what your mind penetrates. I wish I knew. I wish I had some notion of how it works and what its limits are."

"It works as you described it," Carvajal replied. "When I want to, I *see*. A vision of things to come plays within me like a film." His voice was utterly matter-of-fact. He sounded almost bored. "Is that the only thing you came here to find out?"

"Don't you know? Surely you've seen the film of this conversation already."

"Of course I have."

"But you've forgotten some of the details?"

"I rarely forget anything," Carvajal said, sighing.

"Then you must know what else I'm going to ask."

"Yes," he admitted.

"Even so, you won't answer it unless I ask it."

"Yes."

"Suppose I don't," I said. "Suppose I just leave right now, without doing what I'm supposed to have done."

"That won't be possible," said Carvajal evenly. "I remember the course this conversation must take, and you don't leave before asking your next question. There's only one way for things to happen. You have no choice but to say and do the things I *saw* you say and do."

"Are you a god, decreeing the events of my life?"

He smiled wanly and shook his head. "Very much mortal, Mr. Nichols. Decreeing nothing. I tell you, though, the future's immutable. What you think of as the future. We're both actors in a script that can't be rewritten. Come, now. Let's play out our script. Ask me—"

"No. I'm going to break the pattern and walk out of here."

"—about Paul Quinn's future," he said.

I was already at the door. But when he spoke Quinn's name I halted, slack-jawed, stunned, and I turned. That was, of course, the question I had been going to ask, the question I had come here to ask, the question I had determined not to ask when I began to play my little game with immutable destiny. How poorly I had played! How sweetly Carvajal had maneuvered me! Because I was helpless, defeated, immobilized. You may think I was still free to walk out, but no, but no, not once he had invoked Quinn's name, not now that he had tantalized me with the promise of desired knowledge, not now that Carvajal had demonstrated once more, crushingly, conclusively, the precision of his oracular gift.

"You say it," I muttered. "You ask the question."

He sighed. "If you wish."

"I insist."

"You mean to ask if Paul Quinn is going to become President."

"That's it," I said hollowly.

"The answer is that I think he will."

"You *think?* That's the best you can tell me. You *think* he will?"

"I don't know."

"You know everything!"

"No," Carvajal said. "Not everything. There are limits, and your question lies beyond them. The only answer I can give you is a mere guess, based on the same sort of factors anyone interested in politics would consider. Considering those factors, I think Quinn is likely to become President."

"But you don't know for sure. You can't *see* him becoming President."

"Exactly."

"It's beyond your range? Not in the immediate future?"

"Beyond my range, yes."

"Therefore you're telling me that Quinn won't be elected in 2000, but you think he's a good bet for 2004, although you aren't capable of *seeing* as far as 2004."

"Did you ever believe Quinn would be elected in 2000?" Carvajal asked.

"Never. Mortonson's unbeatable. That is, unless Mortonson happens to drop dead the way Leydecker did, in which case it's anybody's election, and Quinn—" I paused. "What do you see in store for Mortonson? Is he going to live as long as the election of 2000?"

"I don't know," said Carvajal quietly.

"You don't know that either? The election's seventeen months away. Your range of clairvoyance is less than seventeen months, is that it?"

"At present, yes."

"Has it ever been greater than that?"

"Oh, yes," he said. "Much greater. I've seen thirty or forty years ahead, at times. But not now."

I felt Carvajal was playing with me again. Exasperated, I said, "Is there any chance your long-range vision will return? And give you, say, a vision of the 2004 election? Or even of the election of 2000?"

"Not really?"

Sweat was pouring down my body. "Help me. It's

extremely important for me to know whether Quinn's going to make it into the White House."

"Why?"

"Why, because I—" I stopped, astonished to realize I had no real answer beyond mere curiosity. I was committed to working for Quinn's election; presumably that commitment wasn't conditional on knowing I was working for a winner. Yet in the moments when I thought Carvajal was able to tell me. I had been desperate to know. Clumsily I said, "Because I'm, well, very much involved in his career, and I'd feel better knowing the direction it's likely to take, especially if I knew all our effort on his behalf wasn't going to go to waste. I—ah—" I halted, feeling inane.

Carvajal said, "I've given you the best answer I can. My guess is that your man will become President."

"Next year or in 2004?"

"Unless something happens to Mortonson, it looks to me as though Quinn has no chance until 2004."

"But you don't know whether something's going to happen to Mortonson?" I persisted.

"I've told you: I don't have any way of knowing that. Please believe that I can't *see* as far as the next election. And, as you yourself pointed out a few minutes ago, probabilistic techniques are worthless in predicting the date of death of any one person. Probabilities are all I'm going on in this. My guess isn't even as good as yours. In stochastic matters, Mr. Nichols, you're the expert, not I."

"What you're saying is that your support of Quinn isn't based on absolute knowledge, only a hunch."

"What support of Quinn?"

His question, so innocent in tone, took me aback. "You thought he'd make a good mayor. You want him to become President," I said.

"I did? I do?"

"You gave huge sums to his campaign treasury when he was running for mayor. What is that if it isn't support? In March you showed up at the office of one of his chief strategists and offered to do everything you could to help Quinn attain higher office. That isn't support?"

"It's of no concern to me at all whether Paul Quinn ever wins another election," Carvajal said.

"Really?"

"His career means nothing to me. It never has."

"Then why are you willing to contribute so heavily to his election kitty? Why are you willing to offer handy tips about the future to his campaign managers? Why are you willing—"

"Willing?"

"Willing, yes. Did I use the wrong word?"

"Will has nothing to do with it, Mr. Nichols."

"The more I talk with you, the less I understand."

"Will implies choice, freedom, volition. There are no such concepts in my life. I give to Quinn because I know I must, not because I prefer him to other politicians. I came to Lombroso's office in March because I *saw* myself, months ago, going there, and knew that I had to go that day, no matter what I'd rather be doing. I live in this crumbling neighborhood because I've never been granted a view of myself living anywhere else, and so I know this is where I belong. I tell you what I've been telling you today because this conversation is already as familiar to me as a movie I've seen fifty times, and so I know I must tell you things I've never told to another human being. I never ask why. My life is without surprises, Mr. Nichols, and it is without decisions, and it is without volition. I do what I know I must do, and I know I must do it because I've *seen* myself doing it."

His placid words terrified me more than any of the real or imagined horrors of the dark staircase outside. Never before had I looked into a universe from which free will, chance, the unexpected, the random, had all been banished. I saw Carvajal as a man dragged helpless but uncomplaining through the present by his inflexible vision of the immutable future. It frightened me, but after a moment the dizzying terror was gone, never to return; for after the first appalling perception of Carvajal as tragic victim came another, more exalting, of Carvajal as one whose gift was the ultimate refinement of my own, one who has moved beyond the vagaries of chance into a realm of utter predictability. I was drawn irresistibly to him by that insight. I felt our souls interpenetrate and knew I would never be free of him again. It was as though that cold force emanating from him, that chilly radiance born of his strangeness that had made him so repellent to me, had now reversed its sign and pulled me toward him.

I said, "You always act out the scenes you *see?*"

"Always."

"You never try to change the script?"

"Never."

"Because you're afraid of what might happen if you do?"

He shook his head. "How could I possibly be afraid of anything? What we fear is the unknown, isn't it? No: I obediently read the lines of the script because I know there's no alternative. What looks to you like the future is to me more like the past, something already experienced, something it would be futile to attempt to alter. I give money to Quinn, you see, because *I have already done so* and have perceived that giving. How could I *see* myself having given, if I fail in fact to give when the moment of my vision intersects the moment of my 'present'?"

"Do you ever worry about forgetting the script and doing the wrong thing when the moment comes?"

Carvajal chuckled. "If you could ever for an instant *see* as I *see,* you'd know how empty that question is. There's no way to do 'the wrong thing.' There's only 'the right thing,' that which happens, that which is real. I perceive what will happen; eventually it takes place; I am an actor in a drama that allows for no improvisations, as are you, as are we all."

"And you've never even once attempted to rewrite the script? In some small detail? Not even once?"

"Oh, yes, more than once, Mr. Nichols, and not only small details. When I was younger, much younger, before I understood. I would have a vision of some calamity, say a child running in front of a truck or a house on fire, and I would decide to play God, to prevent the calamity from occurring."

"And?"

"No way. However I planned things, when the moment came the event invariably happened as I had *seen* it happen. Always. Circumstances prevented me from preventing anything. Many times I experimented with changing the predestined course of events, and I never succeeded, and eventually I stopped trying. Since then I've simply played my part, reciting my lines as I know they must be recited."

"And you accept this fully?" I asked. I paced the room, restless, agitated, overheated. "To you the book of time is written and sealed and unalterable? Kismet and no arguments?"

"Kismet and no arguments," he said.

"Isn't that a pretty forlorn philosophy?"

He seemed faintly amused. "It's not a philosophy, Mr. Nichols. It's an accommodation to the nature of reality. Look, do you 'accept' the present?"

"What?"

"As things happen to you, do you recognize them as valid events? Or do you see them as conditional and mutable, do you have the feeling that you could change them in the moment they're happening?"

"Of course not. How could anybody change—"

"Precisely. One can try to redirect the course of one's future, one can even edit and reconstruct one's memories of the past, but nothing can be done about the moment itself as it flows into being and assumes existence."

"So?"

"To others the future looks alterable because it's inaccessible. One has the illusion of being able to create one's own future, to carve it out of the matrix of time yet unborn. But what I perceive when I *see*," he said, "is the 'future' only in terms of my temporary position in the time flow. In truth it's also the 'present,' the unalterable immediate present, of myself at a different position in the time flow. Or perhaps at the same position in a different time flow. Oh, I have many clever theories, Mr. Nichols. But they all come to the same conclusion: that what I witness isn't a hypothetical and conditional future, subject to modification through rearrangement of antecedent factors, but rather a real and unalterable event, as fixed as the present or the past. I can no more change it than you can change a motion picture as you sit watching it in a theater. I came to understand this a long time ago. And to accept. And to accept."

"How long have you had the power to *see?*"

Shrugging, Carvajal said, "All my life, I suppose. When I was a child I couldn't comprehend it; it was like a fever that came over me, a vivid dream, a delirium. I didn't know I was experiencing—shall we say, flashforwards? But then I found myself living through episodes I had previously 'dreamed.' That *déjà vu* sensation, Mr. Nichols, that I'm sure you've experienced now and then —it was my daily companion. There were times when I felt like a puppet jerking about on strings while someone spoke my lines out of the sky. Gradually I discovered that no one else experienced the *déjà vu* feeling as often or as intensely as I. I think I must have been twenty before I fully understood what I was, and close to thirty before I really came to terms with it. Of course I never revealed myself to anyone else, not until today, in fact."

"Because there was no one you trusted?"

"Because it wasn't in the script," he said with maddening smugness.

"You never married?"

"No."

"How could I want to? How could I want what I had obviously not wanted? I never *saw* a wife for myself."

"And therefore you must never have been meant to have one."

"Never have been meant?" His eyes flashed strangely. "I don't like that phrase, Mr. Nichols. It implies that there's some conscious design in the universe, an author for the great script. I don't think there is. There's no need to introduce such   complication. The script writes itself, moment by moment, and the script showed that I lived alone. One doesn't need to say I was *meant* to be single. Sufficient to say that I *saw* myself to be single, and so I *would* be single, and so I *was* single, and so I *am* single."

"The language lacks the proper tenses for a case like yours," I said.

"But you follow my meaning?"

"I think so. Would it be right to say that 'future' and 'present' are merely different names for the same events seen from different points of view?"

"Not a bad approximation," said Carvajal. "I prefer to think of all events as simultaneous, and what is in motion is our perception of them, that moving point of consciousness, not the events themselves."

"And sometimes it's given to someone to perceive events from several viewpoints at the same time, is that it?"

"I have many theories," he said vaguely. "Perhaps one of them is correct. What matters is the vision itself, not the explanation. And I have the vision."

"You could have used it to make millions," I said, gesturing at the shabby apartment.

"I did."

"No, I mean a really gigantic fortune. Rockefeller plus Getty plus Croesus, a financial empire on a scale the world's never seen. Power. Ultimate luxury. Pleasure. Women. Control of whole continents."

"It wasn't in the script," Carvajal said.

"And you accepted the script."

"The script admits of nothing other than acceptance. I thought you understood that point."

"So you made money, a lot of money but nothing like what you could have made, and it was all meaningless to you? You just let it pile up around you like falling autumn leaves?"

"I had no need of it. My needs are simple and my tastes are plain. I accumulated it because I *saw* myself playing the market and growing rich. What I *see* myself do, I do."

"Following the script. No questions asked about why."

"Millions of dollars. What have you done with it all?"

"I used it as I *saw* myself using it. I gave some of it away, to charities, to universities, to politicians."

"According to your own preferences or to the design you *saw* unfolding?"

"I have no preferences," he said calmly.

"And the rest of the money?"

"I kept it. In banks. What would I have done with it? It's never had any importance to me. As you say, meaningless. A million dollars, five million, ten million—just words." An odd wistful note crept into his voice. "What does have meaning? What does *meaning* mean? We merely play out the script, Mr. Nichols. Would you like another glass of water?"

"Please," I said, and the millionaire filled my glass.

My mind was whirling. I had come for answers, and I had had them, dozens of them, yet each had raised a cluster of new questions. Which he was willing to answer, evidently, for no reason other than that he *had* already answered them in his visions of this day. Talking to Carvajal, I found myself slipping between past and future tenses, lost in a grammatical maze of jumbled time and disordered sequences. And he was altogether placid, sitting almost motionless, his voice flat and sometimes nearly inaudible, his face without expression other than that peculiarly *destroyed* look. Destroyed, yes. He might have been a zombie, or perhaps a robot. Living a rigid preordained fully programmed life, never questioning the motives for any of his actions, simply going on and on, a puppet dangling from his own inevitable future, drifting in a deterministic existential passivity that I found bewildering and alien. For a moment I found myself pitying them. Then I wondered whether my compassion might not be misplaced. I felt the temptation of that existential passivity, and it was a powerful tug. How comforting it might be, I thought, to live in a world free of all uncertainty!

He said suddenly, "I think you should go now. I'm not accustomed to long conversations and I'm afraid this has tired me."

"I'm sorry. I didn't mean to stay so long."

"No need to apologize. All that happened today was as I *saw* it would be. So all is well."

"I'm grateful that you were willing to talk so openly about yourself," I said.

"Willing?" he said, laughing. "*Willing* again?"

"That word isn't in your working vocabulary?"

"No. And I hope to wipe it from yours." He moved toward the door in a gesture of dismissal. "We'll talk again soon."

"I'd like that."

"I regret I couldn't help you as much as you wished. Your question about what Paul Quinn will become—I'm sorry. The answer lies beyond my limits and I have no information to give. I can perceive only what I *will* perceive, do you see? Do you understand? I perceive only my own future perceptions, as though I look at the future through a periscope, and my periscope shows me nothing about next year's election. Many of the events leading up to the election, yes. The outcome itself, no. I'm sorry."

He took my hand a moment. I felt a current flowing between us, a distinct and almost tangible river of connection. I sensed great strain in him, not merely the strain of the conversation but something deeper, a struggle to maintain and extend that contact between us, to reach me on some profound level of being. The sensation disturbed and unsettled me. It lasted only an instant; then it snapped, and I fell back into aloneness with a perceptible impact of separation, and he smiled, gave me a courtly little nod of the head, wished me a safe journey home, showed me into the dark dank hallway.

Only as I was getting into my car a few minutes later did all the pieces slip into place and I come to comprehend what Carvajal had been telling me as we stood by the door. Only then did I understand the nature of the ultimate limit that governed his vision, that had turned him into the passive puppet he was, that had stripped all meaning from his actions. Carvajal had *seen* the moment of his own death. That was why he was unable to tell me who the next President was, yes, but the effect of that knowledge ran deeper than that. It explained why he drifted through life in the peculiarly unquestioning, uncaring way. For decades Carvajal must have lived with the awareness of how and where and when he would die, the absolute and indubitable knowledge of it, and that terrible knowledge had paralyzed his will in a fashion hard for ordinary people to grasp. That was my intuitive interpretation of his condition; and I trust my intuitions. Now the time of his end was less than seventeen months away; and he was drifting aimlessly toward it, accepting, playing out the script, not caring, not caring at all.

17   My head was whirling as I drove home, and it went on whirling for days. I felt stoned, drunk, intoxicated with a sense of infinite possibilities, of limitless openings. It was as though I was about to tap into some incredible source of energy toward which I had been moving, unknowingly, all my life.

That source of energy was Carvajal's visionary power.

I had gone to him suspecting he was what he was, and he had confirmed it; but he had done more than that. He had poured his story out to me so readily, once we were past the game-playing and the testing, that he seemed almost to be trying to lure me into some sort of relationship based on that gift of presentiment that we so unequally shared. After all, this was a man who for decades had lived secretively, furtively, a recluse quietly piling up his millions, celibate, friendless; and he had made a point of seeking me out at Lombroso's office, he had baited a trap for me with his three enigmatic tantalizing hints, he had snared me and drawn me to his hovel, he had freely answered my questions, he had expressed the hope that we would meet again.

What did Carvajal want from me? What role did he

have in mind for me? Friend? Appreciative one-man audience? Partner? Disciple?

Heir?

All of those suggested themselves to me. I was dizzied by a wild rush of options. But there was also the possibility that I was altogether deluded, that Carvajal had no role in mind for me at all. Roles are created by playwrights; and Carvajal was an actor, not a playwright. He simply picked up his cues and followed the script. And maybe to Carvajal I was merely a new character who had wandered onto the stage to engage him in conversation, who had appeared for reasons unknown to him and irrelevant to him, for reasons that mattered, if at all, only to the invisible and perhaps nonexistent author of the grand drama of the universe.

That was an aspect of Carvajal that bothered me profoundly, in a way that drunks have always bothered me. The boozer—or doper, or sniffer, or what have you— is in the most literal sense a person who is out of his right mind. Which means you can't take his words or his actions seriously. Let him say he loves you, let him say he hates you, let him tell you how much he admires your work or respects your integrity or shares your beliefs, and you can't ever know how sincere he is, because the booze or dope may be putting the words in his mouth. Let him propose a deal and you don't know how much he'll remember when his head is straight again. So your transaction with him while he's under the influence is essentially hollow and unreal. I'm an orderly and rational person and when I deal with someone I want to feel I'm having a real interaction with him. Not so, when I think I'm genuinely interacting and the other one is just saying whatever comes into his chemically altered head.

With Carvajal I felt many of the uncertainties. Nothing he said was necessarily kosher. Nothing necessarily made sense. He didn't act out of what I thought of as rational motives, such as self-interest or the general welfare; everything, even his own survival, seemed irrelevant to him. Thus his actions sidestepped stochasticity and common sense itself: he was unpredictable because he didn't follow discernible patterns, only the script, the sacred and unalterable script, and the script was revealed to him in bursts of non-logical non-sequential insight. "What I *see* myself do, I do." he had said. Never asking why. Fine. He *sees* himself giving all his money to the poor, so he gives all his money to the poor. He *sees* himself crossing the George Washington Bridge on a pogo stick, so he goes jumping away. He *sees* himself putting H_2SO_4 in his guest's water glass, so he pops the old sulphuric in without hesitating. He answers questions with the pre-ordained answers, whether what is preordained makes sense or not. And so on. Having surrendered totally to the dictates of the revealed future, he has no need to examine motives or consequences. Worse than a drunk, in fact. At least a boozer still has some shred of rational consciousness operating, however fuzzily, at the core.

A paradox, then. From Carvajal's point of view his every action was guided by rigid deterministic criteria; but from the point of view of those around him, his behavior was as irresponsibly random as that of any lunatic. (Or of any really dedicated Transit Creed flow-and-yielder.) In his own eyes he was obeying the supreme inflexibility of the stream of events; from the outside it looked as though he was blowing in every breeze. By doing as he *saw* he also raised uncomfortable chicken-and-egg questions about the underlying motives for his actions. Were there any at all? Or were his visions self-generating prophecies, entirely divorced from causality, devoid altogether from reason and logic? He *sees* himself crossing the bridge on a pogo stick next Fourth of July; therefore, when the Fourth of July comes he does it, for no other reason than that he has *seen* it. What purpose in fact was served by his crossing the bridge, other than the neat closing of the visionary circuit? The pogo-stick business was self-generating and pointless. How could one carry on dealings with such a man? He was a wild card in the flow of time.

Perhaps I was being too harsh, though. Maybe there were patterns I failed to see. It was possible that Carvajal's interest in me was real, that he had some genuine use for me in his lonely life. To be my guide, to be a father-surrogate to me, to pour into me, in the remaining months of his time, such knowledge as he was able to impart.

In any event I had real use for him. I was going to have him help me make Paul Quinn President.

Knowing that Carvajal couldn't *see* as far as next year's election was a drawback, but not necessarily a major one. Events as big as the presidential succession have deep roots; decisions taken now would govern the political twists and turns of the years ahead. Carvajal might already be in possession of sufficient data about the coming year to enable Quinn to construct alliances that would sweep him to the 2004 nomination. Such was my obsession that I intended to manipulate Carvajal for Quinn's benefit. By cunning question and answer I might be able to pry vital information out of the little man.

18 It was a troublesome week. On the political front the news was all bad. New Democrats everywhere were falling all over themselves to pledge their support to Senator Kane, and Kane, instead of keeping his vice-presidential options open in the traditional manner of front-running politicians, felt so secure that he cheerfully told a press conference that he would like to see Socorro share the ticket with him. Quinn, who had begun to gain a national following after the oil-gellation thing, abruptly ceased to matter to party leaders west of the Hudson River. Invitations to speak stopped coming in, the requests for autographed photos dried to a trickle—trifling signs, but significant ones. Quinn knew what was going on, and he wasn't happy about it.

"How did it happen so fast, this Kane-Socorro tie-up?" he demanded. "One day I was the great white hope of the party, the next all the clubhouse doors were slamming in my face." He gave us the famous intense Quinn stare, eyes clicking from one man to another, searching out the one who somehow had failed him. His presence was as overwhelming as ever; the presence of his disappointment was almost intolerably painful.

Mardikian had no answers for him. Neither did Lombroso. What could I say? That I had had the clues and had fumbled them? I took refuge behind a shrug and a "that's politics" alibi. I was being paid to come up with reasonable hunches, not to function as an all-out psychic. "Wait," I promised him. "New patterns are shaping up. Give me a month and I'll have all of next year mapped out for you."

"I'll settle for the next six weeks," Quinn said grumpily.

His annoyance subsided after a couple of tense days. He was too busy with local problems, of which there were suddenly a great many—the traditional hot-weather social unrest that hits New York every summer like a cloud of mosquitoes—to fret very long about a nomination he hadn't actually wanted to win.

It was a week of domestic problems, too. Sundara's ever-deepening involvement with the Transit Creed was beginning to get to me. Her behavior now was as wild, as unpredictable, as motiveless as Carvajal's; but they were coming to their crazy randomness from opposite directions, Carvajal's behavior governed by blind obedience to an inexplicable revelation, Sundara's by the desire to break free of all pattern and structure.

Whim reigned. The day I went to see Carvajal, she quietly went over to the Municipal Building to apply for a prostitute's license. It took her the better part of the afternoon, what with the medical exam, the union interview, the photography and fingerprinting, and all the rest of the bureaucratic intricacies. When I came home, my head full of Carvajal, she triumphantly flourished the little laminated card that made it legal for her to sell her body anywhere in the five boroughs.

"My God," I said.

"Is something wrong?"

"You just stood there in line like any twenty-dollar hooker out of Vegas?"

"Should I have used political influence to get my card?"

"What if some reporter had seen you down there, though?"

"So?"

"The wife of Lew Nichols, special administrative assistant to Mayor Quinn, joining the whores' union?"

"Do you think I'm the only married woman in that union?"

"I don't mean that. I'm thinking in terms of potential scandal, Sundara."

"Prostitution is a legal activity, and regulated prostitution is generally recognized as having social benefits which—"

"It's legal in New York City," I said. "Not in Kankakee. Not in Tallahassee. Not in Sioux City. One of these days Quinn's going to be looking for votes in those places and others like them, maybe, and some wise guy will dig up the information that one of Quinn's closest advisers is married to a woman who sells her body in a public brothel, and—"

"Am I supposed to govern my life by Quinn's need to conform to the morality of small-town voters?" she asked, dark eyes blazing, color glowing under the darkness of her cheeks.

"Do you *want* to be a whore, Sundara?"

"*Prostitute* is the term that the union leadership prefers to use."

"*Prostitute* isn't any prettier than whore. Aren't you satisfied with the arrangements we've been making? Why do you want to sell yourself?"

"What I want to be," she said icily, "is a free human being, released from all constricting ego attachments."

"And you'll get there through prostitution?"

"Prostitutes learn to dismantle their egos. Prostitutes exist only to serve the needs of others. A week or two in a city brothel will teach me how to subordinate the demands of my ego to the needs of those who come to me."

"You could become a nurse. You could become a masseuse. You could—"

"I chose what I chose."

"And that's what you're going to do? Spend the next week or two in a city brothel?"

"Probably."

"Did Catalina Yarber suggest this?"

"I thought of it myself," said Sundara solemnly. Her eyes flashed fire. We were at the edge of the worst quarrel of our life together, a straight I-forbid-this/don't-you-give-me-orders clash. I trembled. I pictured Sundara, sleek and elegant, Sundara whom all men and many women desired, punching the timeclock in one of those grim sterile municipal cubicles, Sundara standing at a sink swabbing her loins with antiseptic lotions, Sundara on her narrow cot with her knees pulled up to her breasts, servicing some stubble-faced sweat-stinking clod while an endless line waited, tickets in hand, at her door. No. I couldn't swallow it. Four-group, six-group, ten-group, whatever kind of communal sex she liked, yes, but not n-group, not infinity-group, not offering her precious tender body to every hideous misfit in New York City who had the price of admission. For an instant I really was tempted to rise up in old-fashioned husbandly wrath and tell her to drop all this foolishness, or else. But of course that was impossible. So I said nothing, while chasms opened between us. We were on separate islands in a stormy sea, borne away from each other by mighty surging currents, and I was unable even to shout across the widening strait, unable even to reach toward her with futile hands. Where had it gone, the oneness that had been ours for a few years? Why was the strait growing wider?

"Go to your whorehouse, then," I muttered, and left the apartment in a blind wild unstochastic frenzy of anger and fear.

Instead of registering at a brothel, though, Sundara podded to JFK airport and boarded a rocket bound for India. She bathed in the Ganges at one of the Benares ghats, spent an hour unsuccessfully searching for her family's ancestral neighborhood in Bombay, had a curry dinner at Green's Hotel, and caught the next rocket home. Her pilgrimage covered forty hours *in toto* and cost her exactly forty dollars an hour, a symmetry that failed to lighten my mood. I had the good sense not to make an issue of it. In any case I was helpless; Sundara was a free being and growing more free every day, and it was her privilege to consume her own money on anything she chose, even crazy overnight excursions to India. I was careful not to ask her, in the days following her return, whether she planned actually to use her new prostitute's license. Perhaps she already had. I preferred not to know.

19

A week after my visit to Carvajal he phoned to ask if I cared to have lunch with him the next day. So I met him, at his suggestion, at the Merchants and Shippers Club down in the financial district.

The venue surprised me. Merchants and Shippers is one of those venerable Wall Street watering holes populated exclusively by high-echelon brokers and bankers on a members-only basis, and when I say exclusively I mean that even Bob Lombroso, who is a tenth-generation American and very much a power on the Street, is tacitly barred from membership by his Judaism and chooses not to make a fuss about it. As in all such places, wealth alone isn't enough to get you in: you must be clubbable, a congenial and decorous man of the right ancestry who went to the right schools and belongs to the right firm. So far as I could see, Carvajal had nothing going for him along those lines. His *richesse* was *nouveau* and he was by nature an outsider, with none of the required prep-school background and high corporate affiliations. How had he managed to wangle a membership?

"I inherited it," he told me smugly as we settled into cozy, resilient well-upholstered chairs beside a window sixty floors above the turbulent street. "One of my fore-

113

fathers was a founding member, in 1823. The charter provides that the eleven founding memberships descend automatically to the eldest sons of eldest sons, world without end. Some very disreputable sorts have marred the sanctity of the organization because of that clause." He flashed a sudden and surprisingly wicked grin. "I come here about once every five years. You'll notice I've worn my best suit."

Indeed he had—a pleated gold and green herringbone doublet that was perhaps a decade past its prime but still had far more glitter and dash than the rest of his dim and fusty wardrobe. Carvajal, in fact, seemed considerably transformed today, more animated, more vigorous, even playful, distinctly younger than the bleak and ashen man I had come to know.

I said, "I didn't realize you had ancestors."

"There were Carvajals in the New World long before the *Mayflower* set out for Plymouth. We were very important in Florida in the early eighteenth century. When the English annexed Florida in 1763, one branch of the family moved to New York, and I think there was a time when we owned half the waterfront and most of the Upper West Side. But we were wiped out in the Panic of 1837 and I'm the first member of the family in a century and a half who's risen above genteel poverty. But even in the worst times we kept up our hereditary membership in the club." He gestured at the splendid redwood-paneled walls, the gleaming chrome-trimmed windows, the discreet recessed lighting. All about us sat titans of industry and finance, making and unmaking empires between drinks. Carvajal said, "I'll never forget the first time my father brought me here for cocktails. I was about eighteen, so that would be, say, 1957. The club hadn't moved into this building yet—it was still over on Broad Street in a cobwebbed nineteenth-century place—and we came in, my father and I, in our twenty-dollar suits and our wool neckties, and everyone looked like a senator to me, even the waiters, but no one sneered at us, no one patronized us. I had my first martini and my first filet mignon, and it was like an excursion to Vahalla, you know, or to Versailles, to Xanadu. A visit to a strange dazzling world where everyone was rich and powerful and magnificent. And as I sat at the huge old oak table across from my father a vision came to me, I began to *see,* I *saw* myself as an old man, the man I am today, dried out, with a fringe of gray hair here and there, the elderly self that I had already come to know and recognize, and that older me was sitting in a room that was truly opulent, a room of sleek lines and brilliantly imaginative furnishings, in fact this very room where we are now, and I was sharing a table with a much younger man, a tall, strongly built, dark-haired man, who leaned forward, staring at me in a tense and uncertain way, listening to my every word as if he were trying to memorize it. Then the vision passed and I was with my father again, and he was asking me if I was all right, and I tried to pretend it was the martini hitting me all at once that had made my eyes glaze over and my face go slack, for I wasn't much of a drinker even then. And I wondered if what I had *seen* was a kind of resonant counterimage of my father and me at the club, that is, I had *seen* my older self bringing my own son to the Merchants and Shippers Club of the distant future. For several years I speculated about who my wife would be and what my son would be like, and then I came to know that there would be no wife and no son. And the years went by and here we are, and there you sit opposite me, leaning forward, staring at me in a tense and uncertain way—"

A shiver rippled along my backbone. "You *saw* me here with you, more than forty years ago?"

He nodded nonchalantly and in the same gesture swung around to summon a waiter, stabbing the air with his forefinger as imperiously as though he were J. P. Morgan. The waiter hurried to Carvajal's side and greeted him obsequiously by name. Carvajal ordered a martini for me —because he had *seen* it long ago?—and dry sherry for himself.

"They treat you courteously here," I remarked.

"It's a point of honor for them to treat every member as if he's the Czar's cousin," Carvajal said. "What they say about me in private is probably less flattering. My membership is going to die with me, and I imagine the club will be relieved that no more shabby little Carvajals will deface the premises."

The drinks arrived almost at once. Solemnly we dipped glasses at each other in a perfunctory vestigial toast.

"To the future," Carvajal said, "the radiant, beckoning future," and broke into hoarse laughter.

"You're in lively spirits today."

"Yes, I feel bouncier than I have in years. A second springtime for the old man, eh? Waiter! *Waiter!*"

Again the waiter hustled over. To my astonishment Carvajal now ordered cigars, selecting two of the most costly from the tray the cigar girl brought. Once more the wicked grin. To me he said, "Are you supposed to save these things for after the meal? I think I want mine right away."

"Go ahead. Who'll stop you?"

He lit up, and I joined him. His ebullience was disconcerting and almost frightening. At our other two meetings Carvajal had appeared to be drawing on reservoirs of strength long since overdrawn, but today he seemed speedy, frantic, full of a wild energy obtained from some hideous source: I speculated about mysterious drugs, transfusions of bull's blood, illicit transplants of organs ripped from unwilling young victims.

He said suddenly, "Tell me, Lew, have you ever had moments of second sight?"

"I think so. Nothing as vivid as what you must experience, of course. But I think many of my hunches are based on flickers of real vision—subliminal flickers that come and go so fast I don't acknowledge them."

"Very likely."

"And dreams," I said. "Often in dreams I have premonitions and presentiments that turn out to be correct. As though the future is floating toward me, knocking at the gates of my slumbering consciousness."

"The sleeping mind is much more receptive to things of that sort, yes."

"But what I perceive in dreams comes to me in symbolic form, a metaphor rather than a movie. Just before Gilmartin was caught I dreamed he was being hauled before a firing squad, for example. As though the right information was reaching me, but not in literal one-to-one terms."

"No," Carvajal said. "The message came accurately and literally, but your mind scrambled and coded it, because you were asleep and unable to operate your receptors properly. Only the waking rational mind can process and integrate such messages reliably. But most people who are awake reject the messages altogether, and when they are asleep their minds do mischief to what comes in."

"You think many people get messages from the future?"

"I think everyone does," Carvajal said vehemently. "The future isn't the inaccessible, intangible realm it's thought to be. But so few admit its existence except as an abstract concept. So few let its messages reach them!" A weird intensity had come into his expression. He lowered his voice and said, "The future isn't a verbal construct. It's a place with an existence of its own. Right now, as we sit here, we are also *there, there plus one, there plus two, there plus n*—an infinity of *theres,* all of them at once, both previous to and later than our current position along our time line. Those other positions are neither more nor less 'real' than this one. They're merely in a place that happens not to be the place where the seat of our perceptions is currently located."

"But occasionally our perceptions—"

"Cross over," Carvajal said. "Wander into other segments of the time line. Pick up events or moods or scraps of conversation that don't belong to 'now.' "

"Do our perceptions wander," I asked, "or is it the events themselves that are insecurely anchored in their own 'now'?"

He shrugged. "Does that matter? There's no way of knowing."

You don't care how it works? Your whole life has been shaped by this and you simply don't—"

"I told you," Carvajal said, "that I have many theories.

So many, indeed, that they tend to cancel one another out. Lew, Lew, do you think I don't care? I've spent all my life trying to understand my gift, my power, and I can answer any of your questions with a dozen answers, each as plausible as the next. The two-times-lines theory, for example. Have I told you about that?"

"No."

"Well, then." Coolly he produced a pen and drew two firm lines parellel to each other across the tablecloth. He labeled the ends of one line X and Y, the other X′ and Y′. "This line that runs from X to Y is the course of history as we know it. It begins with the creation of the universe at X and ends with thermodynamic equilibrium at Y, all right? And these are some significant dates along its path." With fussy little strokes he sketched in crossbars, beginning at the side of the table closer to himself and proceeding toward me. "This is the era of Neanderthal man. This is the time of Jesus. This is 1939, the start of World War Two. Also the start of Martin Carvajal, by the way. When were you born? Around 1970?"

"1966."

"1966. All right. This is you, 1966. And this is the present year, 1999. Let's say you're going to live to be ninety. This is the year of your death, then, 2056. So much for line X–Y. Now this other line, X′–Y′—that's also the course of history in this universe, the very same course of history denoted by the other line. *Only it runs the other way.*"

"What?"

"Why not? Suppose there are many universes, each independent of all the others, each containing its unique set of suns and planets on which events occur unique to that universe. An infinity of universes, Lew. Is there any logical reason why time has to flow in the same direction in all of them?"

"Entropy," I mumbled. "The laws of thermodynamics. Time's arrow. Cause and effect."

"I won't quarrel with any of those ideas. So far as I know they're all valid within a closed system," said Carvajal. "But one closed system has no entropic responsibilities relative to another closed system, does it? Time can tick from A to Z in one universe and from Z to A in another, but only an observer outside both universes is going to know that, so long as within each universe the daily flow runs from cause to effect and not the other way. Will you admit the logic of that?"

I shut my eyes a moment. "All right. We have an infinity of universes all separate from one another, and the direction of time-flow in any of them may seem topsy-turvy relative to all the others. So?"

"In an infinity of anything, all possible cases exist, yes?"

"Yes. By definition."

"Then you'll also agree," Carvajal said, "that out of that infinity of unconnected universes there may be one that's identical to ours in all particulars, except only the direction of its flow of time relative to the flow of time here."

"I'm not sure I grasp—"

"Look," he said impatiently, pointing to the line that ran across the tablecloth from X' to Y'. "Here's another universe, side by side with our own. Everything that happens in it is something that also happens in ours, down to the most minute detail. But in this one the creation is at Y' instead of X and the heat death of the universe is at X' instead of Y. Down here"—he sketched a crossbar across the second line near my end of the table—"is the era of Neanderthal man. Here's the Crucifixion. Here's 1939, 1966, 1999, 2056. The same events, the same key dates, but running back to front. That is, they look back to front if you happen to live in this universe and can manage to get a peek into the other one. Over there, naturally, everything seems to be running in the right direction." Carvajal extended the 1939 and 1999 crossbars on the X–Y line until they intersected the X'–Y' line, and did the same for the 1999 and 1939 crossbars on the second line. Then he bracketed both sets of crossbars by connecting their ends, to form a pattern like this:

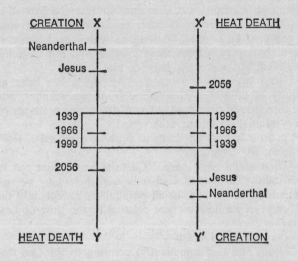

A waiter passing by glanced at what Carvajal was doing to the tablecloth and, coughing slightly, moved on, saying nothing, keeping his face rigid. Carvajal didn't seem to notice. He continued, "Let's suppose, now, that a person is born in the X to Y universe who is able, God knows why, to see occasionally into the X'–Y' universe. Me. Here I am, going from 1939 to 1999 in X-Y, peeking across now and then into X'–Y' and observing the events of their years 1939 to 1999, which are the same as ours except that they're flowing by in the reverse order, so at the time of my birth here everything in my entire X–Y lifetime has already happened in X'–Y'. When my consciousness connects with the consciousness of my other self over there, I catch him reminiscing about his past, which coincidentally is my future."

"Very neat."

"Yes. The ordinary person confined to a single universe can roam his memory at will, wandering around freely in his own past. But I have access to the memory of someone who's living in the opposite direction, which allows me to 'remember' the future as well as the past. That is, if the two-time-lines theory is correct."

"And is it?"

"How would I know?" Carvajal asked. "It's only a plausible operational hypothesis to explain what happens when I *see*. But how could I confirm it?"

I said, after a time, "The things you *see*—do they come to you in reverse chronological order? The future unrolling in a continuous scroll, that sort of thing?"

"No. Never. No more than your memories form a single continuous scroll. I get fitful glimpses, fragments of scenes, sometimes extended passages that have an apparent duration of ten or fifteen minutes or more, but always a random jumble, never any linear sequence, never anything at all consecutive. I learned to find the larger pattern myself, to remember sequences and hook them together in a likely order. It was like learning to read Babylonian poetry by deciphering cuneiform inscriptions on broken, scrambled bricks. Gradually I worked out clues to guide me in my reconstructions of the future: this is how my face will look when I'm forty, when I'm fifty, when I'm sixty, these are clothes I wore from 1965 to 1973, this is the period when I had a mustache, when my hair was dark, oh, a whole host of little references and associations and footnotes, which eventually became so familiar to me that I could *see* any scene, even the most brief, and place it within a matter of weeks or even days. Not easy at first, but second nature by this time."

"Are you *seeing* right now?"

"No," he said. "It takes effort to induce the state. It's rather like a trance." A wintry look swept his face. "At its most powerful it's a kind of double vision, one world overlying the other, so that I can't be entirely sure which world I'm inhabiting and which is the world I *see*. Even after all these years I haven't fully adjusted to that disorientation, that confusion." He may have shuddered then. "Usually it's not so intense. For which I'm grateful."

"Could you show me what it's like?"

"Here? Now?"

"If you would."

He studied me a long moment. He moistened his lips, compressed them, frowned, considered. Then abruptly his expression changed, his eyes becoming glazed and fixed as though he were watching a motion picture from the last row of a huge theater, or perhaps as if he were entering deep meditation. His pupils dilated and the aperture, once widened, remained constant regardless of the fluctuations of light as people walked past our table. His face showed evidence of great strain. His breathing was slow, hoarse, and regular. He sat perfectly still; he seemed altogether absent. A minute, maybe, elapsed; for me it was unendurably long. Then his fixity shattered like a falling icicle. He relaxed, shoulders slumping forward; color came to his cheeks in a quick pumping burst; his eyes watered and grew dull; he reached with a shaky hand for his water glass and gulped its contents. He said nothing. I dared not speak.

At length Carvajal said, "How long was I gone?"

"Only a few moments. It seemed a much longer time than it actually was."

"It was half an hour for me. At least."

"What did you *see?*"

He shrugged. "Nothing I haven't *seen* before. The same scenes recur, you know, five, ten, two dozen times. As they do in memory. But memory alters things. The scenes I *see* never change."

"Do you want to talk about it?"

"It was nothing," he said offhandedly. "Something that's going to happen next spring. You were there. That's not surprising, is it? We're going to spend a lot of time together, you and I, in the months to come."

"What was I doing?"

"Watching."

"Watching what?"

"Watching me," Carvajal said. He smiled, and it was a skeletal smile, a terrible bleak smile, a smile like all the smiles he had smiled that first day in Lombroso's office. All the unexpected buoyancy of twenty minutes ago had gone out of him. I wished I hadn't asked for the demonstration; I felt as though I'd talked a dying man

into dancing a jig. But after a brief interval of embarrassing silence he appeared to recover. He took a swaggering
pull at his cigar, he finished his sherry, he sat straight
again. "That's better," he said. "It can be exhausting
sometimes. Suppose we ask for the menu now, eh?"

"Are you really all right?"

"Perfectly."

"I'm sorry I asked you to—"

"Don't worry about it," he said. "It wasn't as bad as
it must have looked to you."

"Was it frightening, the thing you *saw?*"

"Frightening? No, no, not frightening. I told you, it
was nothing I haven't *seen* before. I'll tell you about it
one of these days." He summoned the waiter. "I think it's
time to have lunch," he said.

My menu bore no prices, a sign of class. The list of
offerings was incredible: baked salmon steak, Maine lob-
ster, roast sirloin, filet of sole, a whole roster of unob-
tainables, none of your dreary latter-day soybean clever-
nesses and seaweed confections. Any first-class New York
restaurant might be serving one kind of fresh fish and
one sort of meat, but to find nine or ten rarities on the
same menu was overwhelming testimony to the power and
wealth of the Merchants and Shippers Club's membership
and the high connections of its chef. It would hardly have
been more amazing to find the menu listing filet of uni-
corn and broiled sphinx chop. Having no idea what anything cost, I ordered blithely, cherrystone clams and the
sirloin. Carvajal opted for shrimp cocktail and the salmon. He declined wine but urged me to get a half bottle
for myself. The wine list likewise was priceless; I picked
a '91 Latour, probably twenty-five bucks. No sense being
stingy on Carvajal's behalf. I was his guest and he could
afford it.

Carvajal was watching me closely. He was more of a
puzzle than ever. Certainly he wanted something from
me; certainly he had some use for me. He seemed almost
to be courting me, in his remote, inarticulate, secretive
way. But he was giving no hints. I felt like a man playing

poker blindfolded against an opponent who could see my hand.

The demonstration of *seeing* that I had extracted from him had been so disturbing a punctuation of our conversation that I hesitated to return to the subject, and for a time we talked aimlessly and amiably about wine, food, the stock market, the national economy, politics, and similar neutral themes. Unavoidably we came around to the topic of Paul Quinn, and the air seemed to grow perceptibly heavier.

He said, "Quinn's doing a good job, isn't he?"

"I think so."

"He must be the city's most popular mayor in decades. He does have charm, eh? And tremendous energy. Too much, sometimes, yes? He often seems impatient, unwilling to go through the usual political channels to get things done."

"I suppose," I said. "He's impetuous, sure. A fault of youth. He isn't even forty years old, remember."

"He should go easier. There are times when his impatience makes him high-handed. Mayor Gottfried was high-handed, and you recall what happened to him."

"Gottfried was an out-and-out dictator. He tried to turn New York City into a police state and—" I halted, dismayed. "Wait a second. Are you hinting that Quinn's in real danger of assassination?"

"Not really. No more than any other major political figure."

"Have you *seen* anything that—"

"No. Nothing."

"I have to know. If you're in possession of any sort of data concerning an attempt on the mayor's life, don't play games with it. I want to hear about it."

Carvajal looked amused. "You misunderstand. Quinn's in no personal danger that I'm aware of, and I chose my words badly if I implied that he is. What I meant is that Gottfried's tactics were gaining enemies for him. If he hadn't been murdered he might, just might, have begun running into problems getting re-elected. Quinn's making

nemies lately, too. As he bypasses the City Council more
nd more, he's upsetting certain blocs of voters."

"The blacks, yes, but—"

"Not only the blacks. The Jews in particular are getting
nhappy about him."

"I wasn't aware of that. The polls don't—"

"Not yet, no. But it'll begin to surface in a few months.
Iis stand on that religious-instruction business in the
chools, for example, has apparently already hurt him in
he Jewish neighborhoods. And his comments about
srael at the dedication of the new Bank of Kuwait
ower on Lexington Avenue—"

"That dedication doesn't take place for another three
veeks," I pointed out.

Carvajal laughed. "It doesn't? Oh, I've mixed up again,
aven't I! I did see his speech on television, I thought,
ut perhaps—"

"You didn't see it. You *saw* it."

"No doubt. No doubt."

"What is he going to say about Israel?"

"Just a few light quips. But the Jewish people here
re extremely sensitive to such remarks, and the reac-
ion wasn't—isn't going to be—good. New York's Jews,
ou know, traditionally mistrust Irish politicians. Es-
ecially Irish mayors, but they weren't even all that fond
f the Kennedys before the assassinations."

"Quinn's no more of an Irishman than you are a Span-
rd," I said.

"To a Jew anybody named Quinn *is* an Irishman, and
is descendants unto the fiftieth generation will be Irish-
en, and I'm a Spaniard. They don't like Quinn's ag-
ressiveness. Soon they'll start to think he doesn't have
e right ideas about Israel. And they'll be grumbling
ut loud."

"When?"

"By autumn. The *Times* will do a front-page feature on
e alienation of the Jewish electorate."

"No," I said. "I'll send Lombroso to do the Kuwait
edication in Quinn's place. That'll shut Quinn up and

also remind everybody that we've got a Jew right at the highest level of the municipal administration."

"Oh, no, you can't do that," said Carvajal.

"Why not?"

"Because Quinn is going to speak. I *saw* him there."

"What if I arrange to have Quinn go to Alaska that week?"

"Please, Lew. Believe me, it's impossible for Quinn to be anywhere but at the Kuwait Bank Building on the day of the dedication. Impossible."

"And impossible, too, I guess, for him to avoid making wisecracks about Israel, even if he's warned not to do it?"

"Yes."

"I don't believe this. I think if I go to him tomorrow and say, Hey, Paul, my reading is the Jewish voters are getting restless, so maybe skip the Kuwait thing, he'll skip it. Or else tone down his remarks."

"He'll go," said Carvajal quietly.

"No matter what I say or do?"

"No matter what you say or do, Lew."

I shook my head. "The future isn't as inflexible as you think. We *do* have some say about events yet to come. I'll talk to Quinn about the Kuwait ceremony."

"Please don't."

"Why not?" I asked roughly. "Because you have some need to make the future turn out the right way?"

He seemed wounded by that. Gently he said, "Because I know the future always *does* turn out the right way. Do you insist on testing that?"

"Quinn's interests are my interests. If you've *seen* him do something damaging to those interests, how can I sit still and let him go ahead and do it?"

"There's no choice."

"I don't know that yet."

Carvajal sighed. "If you raise the matter of the Kuwait ceremony with the mayor," he said ponderously, "you will have had your last access to the things I *see*."

"Is that a threat?"

"A statement of fact."

"A statement that tends to make your prophency self-fulfilling. You know I want your help, so you seal my lips with your threat, so of course the ceremony comes off the way you *saw* it. But what's the good of your telling me things if I'm not allowed to act on them? Why don't you risk giving me free rein? Are you so unsure of the strength of your visions that you have to take this way of guaranteeing that they'll come out right?"

"Very well," Carvajal said mildly, without malice. "You have free rein. Do as you please. We'll see what happens."

"And if I speak to Quinn, will that mean a break between you and me?"

"We'll see what happens," he said.

He had me. Once again he had outplayed me; for how did I dare risk losing access to his vision, and how could I predict what his reaction to my treachery would be? I would have to let Quinn alienate the Jews next month, and hope to repair the damage later, unless I could find some way around Carvajal's insistence on silence. Maybe I ought to discuss this with Lombroso.

I said, "How badly disenchanted are the Jews going to be with him?"

"Enough to cost him a lot of votes. He's planning to run for re-election in '01, isn't he?"

"If he isn't elected President next year."

"He won't be," Carvajal said. "We both know that. He won't even run. But he'll need to be re-elected mayor in 2001 if he wants to try for the White House three years later."

"Definitely."

"Then he ought not to alienate the New York City Jewish vote. That's all I can tell you."

I made a mental note to advise Quinn to start repairing his ties with the city's Jews—visit some kosher delicatessens, drop in at a few synagogues on Friday night.

"Are you angry with me for what I said a little while back?" I asked.

"I never get angry," Carvajal said.

"Hurt, then. You looked hurt when I said you need to make the future turn out the right way."

"I suppose I was. Because it shows how little you've

understood me, Lew. As if you really do think I'm under some neurotic compulsion to fulfill my own visions. As if you think I'd use psychological blackmail to keep you from upsetting the patterns. No, Lew. The patterns *can't* be upset, and until you accept that, there can't be any real kinship of thought between us, no sharing of vision. What you said saddened me because it revealed to me how far away from me you really are. But no, no, I'm not angry with you. Is it a good steak?"

"Magnificent," I told him, and he smiled.

We finished the meal in virtual silence and left without waiting for the check. The club would bill him, I supposed. The tab must have run well over a hundred fifty dollars.

Outside, as we parted, Carvajal said, "Someday, when you *see* things yourself, you'll understand why Quinn has to say what I know he's going to say at the Kuwait Bank dedication."

"When I *see* things myself?"

"You will."

"I don't have the gift."

"Everyone has the gift," he said. "Very few know how to use it." He gave my forearm a quick squeeze and disappeared into the crowd on Wall Street.

20 I didn't put through an immediate call to Quinn, but I came close to it. As soon as Carvajal was out of sight I found myself wondering why I should hesitate. Carvajal's insights into things to come were demonstrably accurate; he had given me information important to Quinn's career; my responsibility to Quinn overrode all other considerations. Besides, Carvajal's concept of an inflexible, unchangeable future still seemed an absurdity to me. Anything that hadn't happened yet had to be subject to change; I could change it and I would, for Quinn's sake.

But I didn't put through the call.

Carvajal had asked me—ordered me, threatened me, warned me—not to intervene in this thing. If Quinn failed to keep his date with the Kuwaitis, Carvajal would know why, and that might be the end of my fragile, tantalizing relationship with the strangely potent little man. But *could* Quinn skip the Kuwait dedication, even if I intervened? According to Carvajal, that was impossible. On the other hand, perhaps Carvajal was playing games within games, and what he really foresaw was a future in which Quinn didn't attend the Kuwait function. In that case the script might call for me to be the agent of change, the one who prevented Quinn from keeping his date, and then Carvajal would be counting on me to be just contrary enough to help things work out the right way. That didn't sound very plausible, but I had to take the possibility into account. I was lost in a maze of blind alleys. My sense of stochasticity would not hold. I no longer knew what I believed about the future or even the present, and the past itself was starting to look uncertain. I think that luncheon with Carvajal began the process of stripping me of what I once regarded as sanity.

I pondered for a couple of days. Then I went to Bob Lombroso's celebrated office and dumped the whole business on him.

"I have a problem of political tactics," I said.

"Why come to me instead of Haig Mardikian? He's the strategist."

"Because my problem involves concealing confidential information about Quinn. I know something that Quinn might want to know, and I'm not able to tell him. Mardikian's such a gung-ho Quinn man that he's likely to get the story out of me under a pledge of secrecy and then head straight to Quinn with it."

"I'm a gung-ho Quinn man, too," Lombroso said. "*You're* a gung-ho Quinn man."

"Yes," I said. "But you're not so gung-ho that you'd breach a friend's confidence for Quinn's sake."

"Whereas you think Haig would?"

"He might."

"Haig would be upset if he knew you felt like that about him."

"I know you aren't going to report any of this to him," I said. "I *know* you aren't."

Lombroso made no reply, merely stood there against the magnificent backdrop of his collection of medieval treasures, digging his fingers deep into his dense black beard and studying me with those piercing eyes. There was a long worrisome silence. Yet I felt I had been right in coming to him rather than to Mardikian. Of the entire Quinn team Lombroso was the most reasonable, the most reliable, a splendidly sane, well-balanced man, centered and incorruptible, wholly independent of mind. If my judgment of him were wrong, I would be finished.

I said eventually, "Is it a deal? You won't repeat anything I tell you today?"

"Depends."

"On what?"

"On whether I agree with you that it's best to conceal the thing you want concealed."

"I tell you, and then you decide?"

"Yes."

"I can't do that, Bob."

"That means you don't trust me either, right?"

I considered for a moment. Intuition said go ahead, tell him everything. Caution said there was at least a chance he might override me and take the story to Quinn.

"All right," I said "I'll tell you the story. I hope that whatever I say remains between you and me."

"Go ahead," Lombroso said.

I took a deep breath. "I had lunch with Carvajal a few days ago. He told me that Quinn is going to make some wisecracks about Israel when he speaks at the Bank of Kuwait dedication early next month, and that the wisecracks are going to offend a lot of Jewish voters here, aggravating local Jewish disaffection with Quinn that I didn't know exists, but which Carvajal says is already severe and likely to get much worse."

Lombroso stared. "Are you out of your mind, Lew?"

"I might be. Why?"

"You really do believe that Carvajal can see the future?"

"He plays the stock market as though he can read next month's newspapers, Bob. He tipped us about Leydecker dying and Socorro taking over. He told us about Gilmartin. He—"

"Oil gellation, too, yes. So he guesses well. I think we've already had this conversation at least once, Lew."

"He doesn't guess. I guess. He *sees*."

Lombroso contemplated me. He was trying to look patient and tolerant, but he seemed troubled. He is above all else a man of reason; and I was talking madness to him. "You think he can predict the content of an off-the-cuff speech that isn't due to be delivered for three weeks?"

"I do."

"How is such a thing possible?"

I thought of Carvajal's tablecloth diagram, of the two streams of time flowing in opposite directions. I couldn't try to sell that to Lombroso. I said, "I don't know. I don't know at all. I take it on faith. He's shown me enough evidence so that I'm convinced he can do it, Bob."

Lombroso looked unconvinced.

"This is the first I've heard that Quinn is in trouble with the Jewish voters," he said. "Where's the evidence for that? What do your polls show?"

"Nothing. Not yet."

"Not *yet*? When does it start to turn up?"

"In a few months, Bob. Carvajal says the *Times* will run a feature this fall on the way Quinn is losing Jewish support."

"Don't you think I'd know it pretty quickly if Quinn were getting in trouble with the Jews, Lew? But from everything I hear, he's the most popular mayor with them since Beame, maybe since LaGuardia."

"You're a millionaire. So are your friends," I told him. "You can't get a representative sampling of popular opinion hanging out with millionaires. You aren't even a representative Jew, Bob. You said so yourself: you're a Sephardic, you're Latin, and Sephardim are an elite, a minority, an aristocratic little caste that has very little in common with Mrs. Goldstein and Mr. Rosenblum. Quinn might be losing the support of a hundred Rosenblums a day and the news wouldn't reach your crowd of Spinozas and Cardozos until they read about it in the *Times*. Am I right?"

Shrugging, Lombroso said, "I'll admit there's some truth in that. But we're getting off the track, aren't we? What's your actual problem, Lew?"

"I want to warn Quinn not to make that Kuwait speech, or else to lay off the wisecracks. Carvajal won't let me say a word to him."

"Won't *let* you?"

"He says the speech is destined to occur as he perceived it, and he insists I simply let it take place. If I do anything to prevent Quinn from doing what the script calls for for that day, Carvajal threatens to sever relations with me."

Lombroso, looking perturbed and mournful, walked in slow circles around his office. "I don't know which is crazier," he said finally. "Believing that Carvajal can see the future, or fearing that he'll get even with you if you transmit his hunch to Quinn."

"It's not a hunch. It's a true vision."

"So you say."

"Bob, more than anything else I want to see Paul Quinn go on to higher office in this country I've got no right to hold back data from him, especially when I've found a unique source like Carvajal."

"Carvajal may be just—"

"I have complete faith in him!" I said, with a passion that surprised me, for until that moment I still had had lingering uncertainties about Carvajal's power, and now I was fully committed to its validity. "That's why I can't risk a break with him."

"So tell Quinn about the Kuwait speech, then. If Quinn doesn't deliver it, how will Carvajal know you're responsible?"

"He'll know."

"We can announce that Quinn is ill. We can even check him into Bellevue for the day and give him a complete medical exam. We—"

"He'll know."

"We can hint to Quinn that he ought to go soft on any remarks that might be construed as anti-Israeli, then."

"Carvajal will know I did it," I said.

"He really has you by the throat, doesn't he?"

"What shall I do, Bob? Carvajal's going to be fantastically useful to us, whatever you may think at the moment I don't want to take the chance of spoiling things with him."

"Then don't. Let the Kuwaiti speech happen as scheduled, if you're so worried about offending Carvajal. A few wisecracks aren't going to do permanent damage, are they?"

"They won't help any."

"They won't hurt that much. We've got two years before Quinn has to go before the voters again. He can make five pilgrimages to Tel Aviv in that time, if he has to." Lombroso came close and put his hand on my shoulder. This near, the force of his strong, vibrant personality was overwhelming. With great warmth and intensity he said, "Are you all right these days, Lew?"

"What do you mean?"

"You worry me. All this lunacy about seeing the future. And so much dither over one lousy speech. Maybe you need some rest. I know you've been under a great strain lately, and—"

"Strain?"

"Sundara," he said. "We don't need to pretend I don't know what's going on."

"I'm not happy about Sundara, no. But if you think my wife's pseudo-religious activities have affected my judgment, my mental balance, my ability to function as a member of the mayor's staff—"

"I'm only suggesting that you're very tired. Tired men find many things to worry about, not all of them real, and worrying makes them even more tired. Break the pattern, Lew. Skip off to Canada for a couple of weeks, say. A little hunting and fishing and you'll be a new man. I have a friend who has an estate near Banff, a nice thousand-hectare spread up in the mountains, and—"

"Thanks, but I'm in better shape than you seem to think," I said. "I'm sorry I wasted your time this morning."

"Not at all a waste. It's important for us to share our difficulties, Lew. For all I know, Carvajal *does* see the future. But it's a hard notion for a rational man like me to swallow."

"Assume it's true. What do you advise?"

"Assuming it's true, I think you'd be wise not to do anything that could turn Carvajal off. Assuming it's true. Assuming it's true, it's in our best interests to milk him for further information, and therefore you ought not chance a break over something as minor as the consequences of this one speech"

I nodded. "I think so, too. You won't drop any hints to Quinn, then, about what he ought to say or not to say at that bank dedication?"

"Of course not."

He began to usher me toward the door. I was shaky and sweating and, I imagine, wild-eyed.

I couldn't shut up, either. "And you won't tell people I'm cracking up, Bob? Because I'm not. I may be on the verge of a tremendous breakthrough in consciousness, but I'm not going crazy. I really am not going crazy," I said, so vehemently that it sounded unconvincing even to me.

"I do think you could use a short vacation. But no, I won't spread any rumors of your impending commitment to the funny farm."

"Thanks, Bob."

"Thank you for coming to me"

"There was no one else."

"It'll work out," he said soothingly. "Don't worry about Quinn. I'll start checking to see if he really is getting in trouble with Mrs. Goldstein and Mr. Rosenblum. You might try some polltaking through your own department." He clasped my hand. "Get some rest, Lew. Get yourself some rest."

21 And so I engineered the fulfilling of the prophecy, though it had been in my power to thwart it. Or had it been? I had declined to put Carvajal's ice-etched unbending determinism to the test. I had accomplished what they used to call a cop-out when I was a boy. Quinn would speak at the dedication. Quinn would make his dumb jokes about Israel. Mrs. Goldstein would mutter; Mr. Rosenblum would curse. The mayor would acquire needless enemies; the *Times* would have a juicy story; we would set about the process of repairing the political damage; Carvajal would once more be vidicated. It would have been so easy to interfere, you say. Why not test the system? Call Carvajal's bluff. Verify his assertion that the future, once glimpsed, is graven as if on tablets of stone. Well, I hadn't done it. I had had my chance, and I had been afraid to take it, as though in some secret way I knew the stars in their courses would come crashing into confusion if I meddled with the course of events. So I had surrendered to the alleged inevitability of it all with hardly a struggle But had I really given in so easily? Had I ever been truly free to act? Was my surrender not also, perhaps, part of the unchangeable eternal script?

22

Everyone has the gift, Carvajal said to me. *Very few know how to use it.* And he had talked of a time when I would be able to *see* things myself. Not if, but when.

Was he planning to awaken the gift in me?

The idea terrified and thrilled me. To look into the future, to be free of the buffeting of the random and the unexpected, to move beyond the vaporous imprecisions of the stochastic method into absolute certainty—oh, yes, yes, yes, how wonderous, but how frightening! To swing open that dark door, to peer down the track of time at the wonders and mysteries lying in wait—

> *A miner was leaving his home for his work*
> *When he heard his little child scream.*
> *He went to the side of the little girl's bed.*
> *She said, Daddy, I've had such a dream.*

Frightening because I knew I might *see* something I didn't want to see, and it might drain and shatter me as Carvajal apparently had been drained and shattered by knowledge of his death. Wondrous because to *see* meant escape from the chaos of the unknown, it meant attain-

137

ment at last of that fully structured, fully determined life toward which I had yearned since abandoning my adolescent nihilism for the philosophy of causality.

> Please, Daddy, don't go to the mines today,
> For dreams have so often come true.
> My daddy, my daddy, please don't go away,
> For I never could live without you.

But if Carvajal did indeed know some way of bringing the vision to life in me, I vowed I would handle it differently, not letting it make a shriveled recluse out of me, not bowing passively to the decrees of some invisible playwright, not accepting puppethood as Carvajal had done. No, I would use the gift in an active way, I would employ it to shape and direct the flow of history, I would take advantage of my special knowledge to guide and direct and alter, insofar as I was able, the pattern of human events.

> Oh, I dreamed that the mines were all flaming with fire
> And the men all fought for their lives.
> Just then the scene changed and the mouth of the mine
> Was covered with sweethearts and wives.

According to Carvajal such shaping and directing was impossible. Impossible for him, perhaps; but would I be bound by his limitations? Even if the future is fixed and unchangeable, knowledge of it could still be put to use to cushion blows, to redirect energies, to create new patterns out of the wreckage of the old. I would try. Teach me to *see*, Carvajal, and let me try!

> Oh, Daddy, don't work in the mines today,
> For dreams have so often come true.
> My daddy, my daddy, please don't go away,
> For I never could live without you.

23

Sundara vanished at the end of June, leaving no message, and was gone for five days. I didn't notify the police. When she returned, saying nothing by way of explanation, I didn't ask where she had been. Bombay again, Tierra del Fuego, Capetown, Bangkok, they were all the same to me. I was becoming a good Transit husband. Perhaps she had spent all five days spread-eagled on the altar at some local Transit house, if they have altars, or perhaps she'd been putting in time at a Bronx bordello. Didn't know, didn't want to care. We were badly out of touch with each other now, skating side by side over thin ice and never once glancing toward each other, never once exchanging a word, just gliding on silently toward an unknown and perilous destination. Transit processes occupied her energies night and day, day and night. What do you get out of it? I wanted to ask her. What does it *mean* to you? But I didn't. One sticky July evening she came home late from doing God knows what in the city, wearing a sheer turquoise sari that clung to her moist skin with a lasciviousness that would get her a ten-year sentence for public lewdity in puritan New Delhi, and came up to me and rested her arms on my shoulders and sighed and leaned close to me, so that I felt the warmth of her body and it made me tremble, and her eyes met mine, and there was in her dark shining eyes a look of pain and loss and regret, a terrible look of aching grief. And as though I were able to read her thoughts, I could clearly hear her telling me, "Say the word, Lew, only say the word, and I'll quit them, and everything will be as it used to be for us." I know that was what her eyes were telling me. But I didn't say the word. Why did I remain silent? Because I suspected Sundara was merely playing out another meaningless Transit exercise on me, playing a game of Did-you-think-I-meant-it? Or because somewhere within me I really didn't want her to swerve from the course she had chosen?

24

Quinn sent for me. It was the day before the ceremony at the Bank of Kuwait Building.

He was standing in the middle of his office when I entered. The room was drab, drearily functional, nothing at all like Lombroso's awesome sanctum—dark awkward municipal furniture, portraits of former mayors—but today it had an eerie shimmer of brightness. Sunlight streaming through the window behind Quinn cloaked him in a dazzling golden nimbus, and he seemed to radiate strength and authority and purpose, emitting a flood of light more intense than that he was receiving. A year and a half as New York's mayor had left an imprint on him: the network of fine lines around his eyes was deeper than it had been on inaugural day, the blond hair had lost some of its sheen, his massive shoulders seemed to hunch a little, as if he were sagging under an impossible weight. During much of this edgy, humid summer he had appeared weary and irritable and there had been times when he seemed much older than his thirty-nine years. But all that was gone from him now. The old Quinn vigor had returned. His presence filled the room.

He said, "Remember about a month ago you told me new patterns were shaping up and you'd be able to give

141

me a forecast soon for the year ahead?"

"Sure. But I—"

"Wait. New factors have been shaping up, but you don't have access to all of them yet. I want to give them to you so you can work them into your synthesis, Lew."

"What sort of factors?"

"My plans for running for President."

After a long gawky pause I managed to say, "You mean running next year?"

"I don't stand a snowball's chance for next year," Quinn replied evenly. "Wouldn't you agree?"

"Yes, but—"

"No buts. The ticket for 2000 is Kane and Socorro. I don't need your skill at projection to realize that. They have enough delegates in their pockets now for a first-ballot nomination. Then they'll go up against Mortonson a year from November and get clobbered. I figure Mortonson's going to rack up the biggest landslide since Nixon in '72, no matter who runs against him."

"I think so, too."

Quinn said, "Therefore I'm talking about '04. Mortonson won't be able to run for another term and the Republicans have nobody else of his stature. Whoever grabs the New Democratic nomination that year is going to be President, right?"

"Right, Paul."

"Kane won't get a second chance. Landslide losers never do. Who else is there? Keats? He'll be past sixty. Pownell? No staying power. He'll be forgotten. Randolph? I can't see him as anything better than somebody's vice-presidential pick."

"Socorro will still be around," I pointed out.

"Socorro, yes. If he plays his cards right during next year's campaign, he'll come out looking good no matter how badly the ticket is beaten. The way Muskie did losing in '68, and Shriver losing in '72. Socorro's been very much on my mind all this summer, Lew. I've been watching him move up like a rocket ever since Leydecker died. That's why I've decided to stop being coy and start my push for the nomination this early. I've got to head off Socorro. Because if he gets the nomination in '04, he's going to win, and if he wins he'll be a two-term President, and that puts me on the sidelines until the year 2012." He gave me a dose of the classic Quinn eye contact, transfixing me until I wanted to squirm. "I'll be fifty-one years old in 2012, Lew. I don't want to have to wait that long. A potential candidate can get awfully withered if he dangles on the vine a dozen years waiting his turn. What do you think?"

"I think your projection checks out all the way," I said.

Quinn nodded. "Okay. This is the timetable that Haig and I have been working out the past couple of days. We spend the rest of '99 and the first half of next year simply laying the substructure. I make some speeches around the country, I get to know the big party leaders better, I become friendly with a lot of precinct-house small fry who are *going* to be big party leaders by the time 2004 comes around. Next year, after Kane and Socorro are nominated, I campaign nationwide for them, with special emphasis on the Northeast. I do my damnedest to deliver New York State for them. What the hell, I figure they'll take six or seven of the big industrial states anyway, and they might as well have mine, if I'm going to come on like a dynamic party leader; Mortonson will still wipe them out in the South and the farm belt. In 2001 I lay low and concentrate on getting re-elected mayor, but once that's behind me I resume national speechmaking and after the 2002 Congressional elections I announce my candidacy. That gives me all of '03 and half of '04 to sew up the delegates, and by the time the primaries come around I'll be sure of the nomination. Well?"

"I like it, Paul. I like it a lot."

"Good. You're going to be my key man. I want you to concentrate full time on isolating and projecting national political patterns, so you can draw up game plans within the larger structure I've just outlined. Leave the little local stuff alone, the New York City crap. Mardikian can handle my re-election campaign without much help. You look for the big picture, you tell me what the people out in Ohio and Hawaii and Nebraska think they want, you tell me what they're likely to want four years from now. You're going to be the man who'll make me President, Lew."

"Damned right I will," I said.

"You're going to be the eyes that see into the future for me."

"You know it, man."

We slapped palms. "Onward to 2004!" he yelled.

"Washington, here we come!" I bellowed.

It was a silly moment, but it was touching, too. History on the hoof, marching toward the White House, me in the vanguard carrying the flag and playing the drums. I was so swept by emotion that I almost started to tell Quinn to pass up the Bank of Kuwait ceremony. But then I thought I saw Carvajal's sad-eyed face hovering in the dust motes of that beam of light pouring through the mayor's window, and I caught myself. So I said nothing, and Quinn went and made his speech, and of course he jammed his foot deep into his epiglottis with a couple of elephantine quips about the Near Eastern political situation. ("I hear that last week King Abdullah and Premier Eleazar were playing poker down at the casino in Eilat, and the king bet three camels and an oil well and the premier raised him five hogs and a submarine, so the king . . ." Oh, no, it's too dumb to repeat.) Naturally Quinn's performance made every network that night, and the next day City Hall was inundated by angry telegrams. Mardikian phoned me to say the place was being picketed by B'nai B'rith, the United Jewish Appeal, the Jewish Defense League, and the whole House of David starting team. I went over there, slinking goyishly through the mob of outraged Hebrews and wanting to apologize to the entire cosmos for having by my silence permitted all this to happen. Lombroso was there with the mayor. We exchanged glances. I felt triumphant—had Carvajal not predicted the incident perfectly?—and sheepish, and frightened, too. Lombroso gave me a quick wink, which could have meant any one of a dozen things, but which I took to be a token of reassurance and forgiveness.

Quinn didn't look perturbed. He tapped the huge box of telegrams smartly with his toe and said in a wry voice, "And thus we commence our pursuit of the American voter. We aren't off to much of a start, are we, lad?"

"Don't worry," I told him, Boy Scout fervor creeping into my voice. "This is the last time anything of this sort is going to happen."

25 I phoned Carvajal. "I have to talk to you," I said.

We met along the Hudson Promenade near Tenth Street. The weather was ominous, dark and moist and warm, the sky a threatening greenish yellow, with black-edged thunderheads piled high over New Jersey and a sense of impending apocalypse pervading everything. Shafts of fierce off-color sunlight, more gray-blue than gold, burned through a filtering layer of murky clouds clustered like a crumpled blanket in mid-sky. Preposterous weather, operatic weather, a noisy overstated backdrop for our conversation.

Carvajal's eyes had an unnatural gleam. He looked taller, younger, jazzing along the promenade on the balls of his feet. Why did he seem to gain strength between each of our meetings?

"Well?" he demanded.

"I want to be able to *see*."

"*See*, then. I'm not stopping you, am I?"

"Be serious," I begged.

"I always am. How can I help you?"

"Teach me to do it."

"Did I ever tell you it could be taught?"

"You said everyone has the gift but very few know how to use it. All right. Show me how to use it."

"Using it can perhaps be learned," Carvajal said, "but it can't be taught."

"Please."

"Why so eager?"

"Quinn needs me," I told him abjectly. "I want to help him. To become President."

"So?"

"I want to help him. I need to *see*."

"But you can project trends so well, Lew!"

"Not enough. Not enough."

Thunder boomed over Hoboken. A cold damp wind out of the west stirred the clotted clouds. Nature's scene-setting was becoming grotesquely, comically excessive.

Carvajal said, "Suppose I told you to give me complete control over your life. Suppose I asked you to let me make every decision for you, to shape all your actions to my orders, to put your existence entirely into my hands, and I said that if you did that, there'd be a chance that you'd learn how to *see*. A chance. What would your reply be?"

"I'd say that it's a deal."

"*Seeing* may not be as wonderful as you think it is, you know. Right now you look upon it as the magic key to everything. What if it turns out to be nothing but a burden and an obstacle? What if it's a curse?"

"I don't think it will be."

"How can you know?"

"A power like that can be a tremendous positive force. I can't see it as anything but beneficial for me. I can see its potential negative side, sure, but still—a curse? No."

"What if it is?"

I shrugged. "I'll take that risk. Has it been a curse for you?"

Carvajal paused and looked up at me, eyes searching mine. This was the appropriate moment for lightning to crackle across the heavens, for drum rolls of terrible thunder to sound up and down the Hudson, for tempestuous rain to slash across the promenade. None of that happened. Abruptly, the clouds directly overhead parted and sweet soft yellow sunlight enveloped the dark storm-frowns. So much for nature as a setter of scene.

"Yes," Carvajal said quietly. "A curse. If anything, yes, a curse, a curse."

"I don't believe you."

"What does that matter to me?"

"Even if it's been a curse for you, I don't think it would for me."

"Very courageous, Lew. Or very foolish."

"Both. Nevertheless, I want to be able to *see*."

"Are you willing to become my disciple?"

Strange, jarring word. "What would that involve?"

"I've already told you. You give yourself to me on a no-questions-asked, no-results-guaranteed basis."

"How will that help me to *see*?"

"No questions asked," he said. "Just give yourself to me, Lew."

"Done."

The lightning came. The skies opened and a crazy drenching downpour battered us with implausible fury.

26 A day and a half later. "The worst of it," Carvajal said, "is *seeing* your own death. That's the moment when the life goes out of you, not when you actually die, but when you have to *see* it."

"Is that the curse you were talking about?"

"Yes. That's the curse. That's what killed me, Lew, long before my proper time. I was almost thirty years old, the first time I *saw* it. I've *seen* it many times since. I know the date, the hour, the place, the circumstances. I've lived through it again and again, the beginning, the middle, the end, the darkness, the silence. And once I *saw* it, life became nothing more than a meaningless puppet show for me."

"What was the worst part?" I asked. "Knowing when, knowing how?"

"Knowing that," he said.

"That you would die at all?"

"Yes."

"I don't understand. I mean, it must be disturbing, yes, to watch yourself die, to see your own finish as if on a newsreel, but there can't be any fundamental element of surprise in it, can there? I mean, death is inevitable and we all know it from the time we're little children."

"Do we?"

"Of course we do."

"Do you think you'll die, Lew?"

I blinked a couple of times. "Naturally."

"Are you absolutely convinced of that?"

"I don't get you. Are you implying I have delusions of immortality?"

Carvajal smiled serenely. "Everybody does, Lew. When you're a boy your pet goldfish dies, or your dog, and you say, Well, goldfish don't live long, dogs don't live long, and that's how you slough off your first experience of death. It doesn't apply to you. The boy next door falls off his bicycle and fractures his skull. Well, you say, accidents happen, but they don't *prove* anything; some people are more careless than others, and I'm one of the careful ones. Your grandmother dies. She was old and sick for years, you say, she let herself get too heavy, she grew up in a generation when preventive medicine was still primitive, she didn't know how to take care of her body. It won't happen to me, you say. It won't happen to me."

"My parents are dead. My sister died. I had a turtle that died. Death isn't something remote and unreal in my life. No, Carvajal, I believe in death. I accept the fact of death. I know I'm going to die."

"You don't. Not really."

"How can you say that?"

"I know how people are. I know how I used to be, before I *saw* myself die, and what I became afterward. Not many have had that experience, have been changed as I've been changed. Perhaps no one else, ever. Listen to me, Lew. Nobody genuinely and fully believes he's going to die, whatever he may think he thinks. You may accept it up here on top, but you don't accept it on the cellular level, down on the level of metabolism and mitosis. Your heart hasn't missed a beat in thirty-odd years and it knows it never will. Your body goes merrily along like a three-shift factory manufacturing corpuscles, lymph, semen, saliva, round the clock, and so far as your body knows it always will. And your brain, it perceives itself as the center of a great drama whose star is Lew Nichols, the whole universe just a giant collection of props, everything that happens happening around *you*, in relation to *you*, with *you* as the pivot and fulcrum, and if you go to somebody's wedding the name of that scene isn't *Dick and Judy Get Married,* no, it's *Lew Goes to Somebody's Wedding*, and if a politician gets elected it isn't *Paul Quinn Becomes President*, it's *Lew Experiences Paul Quinn Becoming President*, and if a star explodes the headline isn't *Betelgeuse Goes Nova* but *Lew's Universe Loses a Star*, and so on, the same for everyone, everyone the hero of the great drama of existence, Dick and Judy each in starring roles in their own heads, Paul Quinn, maybe even Betelgeuse, and each of you knows that if you were to die the whole universe would have to wink out like a switched-off light, and that isn't possible, so therefore you aren't going to die. You know you're the one exception. Holding the whole business together by your continued existence. All those others, Lew, you realize *they're* going to die; sure, they're the bit parts, the spear carriers, the script calls for them all to vanish along the way, but not you, oh, no, not you! Isn't that how it truly is, Lew, down in the basement of your soul, down in those mysterious levels you visit only now and then?"

I had to grin. "Maybe it is, after all. But—"

"It is. It's the same way for everyone. It was for me. Well, people *do* die, Lew. Some die at twenty and some die at a hundred and twenty, and it's *always* a surprise. They stand there seeing the big blackness opening up for them, and as they go into the hole they say, My God, I was wrong after all, it's really going to happen to me, even to *me!* What a shock that is, what a terrific blow to the ego, to discover that you aren't the unique exception you thought you were. But it's comforting, right up until that moment arrives, to cling to the idea that maybe you'll sneak through, maybe you'll somehow be exempt. Everybody has that scrap of comfort to live by, Lew. Everyone except me."

"You found *seeing* it as bad as that?"

"It demolished me. It stripped me of that one big illusion, Lew, that secret hope of immortality, that keeps us going. Of course, I had to keep going, thirty years or so more, because I could *see* that it wouldn't happen until I was an old man. But the knowledge put a wall around my life, a boundary, an unbreakable seal. I wasn't much more than a boy and I had already had the real summing up, the period at the end of the sentence. I couldn't count on enjoying all of eternity, the way others think they do. I had only my thirty-odd years left to go. Knowing that about yourself constricts your life, Lew. It limits your options."

"It isn't easy for me to understand why it should have that effect."

"Eventually you'll understand."

"Maybe it won't be that way for me, when I come to know."

"Ah!" Carvajal cried. "We all think we'll be the exception!"

27 He told me, the next time we met, how his
death would come to pass. He had less than a year to
live, he said. It was going to happen in the spring of 2000,
somewhere between the tenth of April and the twenty-fifth
of May; although he claimed to know the exact date even
down to the time of day, he was unwilling to be any
more specific about it than that.

"Why withhold it from me?" I asked.

"Because I don't care to be burdened with your private
tensions and anticipations," Carvajal told me bluntly. "I
don't want you showing up that day knowing it *is* the day,
and arriving full of irrelevant emotional confusion."

"Am I going to be there?" I asked, astounded.

"Certainly."

"Will you tell me where it'll happen?"

"At my apartment," he said. "You and I will be dis-
cussing something having to do with a problem troubling
you then. The doorbell will ring. I'll answer it and a man
will force his way into the house, an armed man with
red hair, who—"

"Wait a minute. You once told me that no one had ever
bothered you in that neighborhood and no one ever
would."

"No one *who lives there*," said Carvajal. "This man will be a stranger. He has been given my address by mistake—he has the wrong apartment—and expects to be picking up a consignment of drugs, something that sniffers use. When I tell him I don't have any drugs, he'll refuse to believe me; he'll think it's some kind of doublecross and will start to get violent, waving the gun around, threatening me."

"And what am I doing while all this is going on?"

"Watching it."

"Watching? Just standing there with my arms folded like a spectator?"

"Just watching," Carvajal said. "Like a spectator." There was a sharp edge to his tone. As if he were giving me an order: *You will do nothing throughout this scene. You will remain entirely out of it, off to one side, a mere onlooker.*

"I could hit him with a lamp. I could try to grab the gun."

"You won't."

"All right," I said. "What happens?"

"Somebody knocks at the door. It's one of my neighbors, who's heard the commotion and is worried about me. The gunman panics. Thinks it's the police, or maybe a rival gang. He fires three times; then he breaks a window and disappears down the fire escape. The bullets strike me in the chest, the arm, and the side of my head. I linger for a minute or so. No last words. You're not harmed at all."

"And then?"

Carvajal laughed. "And then? And then? How would I know? I've told you: I *see* as though through a periscope. The periscope reaches only as far as that moment, and no farther. Perception ends for me there."

How calm he was about it!

I said, "Is this the thing you *saw* the day you and I had lunch at the Merchants and Shippers Club?"

"Yes."

"You sat there watching yourself get gunned down, and then casually asked to look at the menu?"

"The scene was nothing new to me."

"How often have you *seen* it?" I asked.

"No idea. Twenty times, fifty, maybe a hundred. Like a recurring dream."

"A recurring nightmare."

"One gets used to it. It ceases to carry much emotional charge after the first dozen viewings or so."

"It's nothing but a movie to you? An old Cagney flick on the late-night television?"

"Something like that," said Carvajal. "The scene itself becomes trivial, a bore, stale, predictable. It's the implications that linger, that never lose their power over me, while the details themselves have become unimportant."

"You just accept it. You won't try to slam the door in the man's face when the moment comes. You won't let me hide behind the door and club him down. You won't ask the police to put you under special guard that day."

"Naturally not. What good would any of that do?"

"As an experiment—"

He pursed his lips. He looked annoyed at my stubborn return to a theme that was absurd to him. "What I *see* is what will happen. The time for experiments was fifty years ago, and the experiments failed. No, we won't interfere, Lew. We'll play our parts obediently, you and I. You know we will."

28 Under the new regime I conferred with Carvajal daily, sometimes several times a day, usually by telephone, transmitting to him the latest inside political information—strategies, data projections, anything that might seem even peripherally pertinent to the business of getting Paul Quinn into the White House. The reason for filing all this stuff in Carvajal's mind was the periscope effect: he couldn't *see* anything that his consciousness would not ultimately somehow perceive, and what he couldn't *see* he couldn't pass along to me. What I was doing, then, was phoning messages to myself out of the future—messages relayed by way of Carvajal. The things I told him today were of course worthless for this purpose, since present-me already knew them; but what I would tell him a month from now might prove to be of value to me today, and, since the information had to get into the system at some point, I began the input flow here, feeding Carvajal now the data he had *seen* months or even years ago. Over the remaining year of Carvajal's life he would become a unique repository of future political events. (In fact he already was that repository, but now I had to follow through by making certain he received the information that we both knew he was going to receive.

There are paradoxes inherent in all this but I prefer not to examine them too closely.)

And Carvajal, day by day, flowed data back to me—mainly things having to do with the long-range shaping of Quinn's destinies. These I passed along to Haig Mardikian, usually, though some fell into the domain of George Missakian—media relations—and some, having to do with financial matters, went to Lombroso, and a few I took directly to Quinn himself. My Carvajal-derived memos in a typical week included items like this:

> *Invite Commun. Devel. Commissioner Spreckels to lunch. Suggest possibil. of judgeship.*

> *Attend wedding, son of Sen. Wilkom of Mass.*

> *Tell Con Ed, confidential, no hope of okay for proposed Flatbush fusion plant.*

> *Gov.'s brother—name him to Triboro Authority. Defuse nepotism issue in advance with jokes at press conf.*

> *Call in Assembly Spkr. Feinberg for gentle arm-twisting in re NY-Mass-Conn pod-hookup bill.*

> *Position papers: libraries, drugs, interstate population transfer.*

> *Tour Garment District Historic Site with new Israeli consul-general. Include in party: Leibman, Berkowitz, Ms. Weisbard, Rabbi Dubin, also Msgr. O'Neill.*

Sometimes I understood why my future self was recommending a given course of action to Quinn, and at other times I was altogether baffled. (Why, say, tell him to veto an innocuous City Council proposal reopening a no-parking zone south of Canal Street? How would that help him become President?) Carvajal offered no aid. He was merely passing along tips he was getting from the me of eight or nine months from now. Since he'd be dead before any of these things could manifest their ultimate implications, he had no idea what effect they might

produce, and could hardly have cared less. He gave everything to me on a bland take-it-or-leave-it basis. Mine not
to reason why. Follow the script, Lew, follow the script.

I followed the script.

My vicarious political ambitions were beginning to take
on the character of a divine mission: using Carvajal's gift
and Quinn's charisma, I would be able to reshape the
world into a Better Place of unspecified ideal character. I
felt the throbbing conduits of power in my grasp. Whereas
before I had seen Quinn's presidency as a goal worth
pursuing for its own sake, now I became practically Uto-
pian in my plans for a world guided by the ability to *see*.
No longer did I think in terms of manipulation, of rede-
ployment of motivations, of political machination, except
in service of the higher end toward which I imagined
myself working.

Day after day I streamed my memos toward Quinn and
his minions. Mardikian and the mayor assumed the stuff I
was handing in was the result of my own projections, the
product of my polltakers, my computers, and my sweet
canny cerebrum. Since my record of stochastic insight
over the years had been consistently excellent, they did
as I told them. Unquestioningly. Quinn occasionally
laughed and said, "Boy, this one doesn't make much sense
to me," but I told him, "It will, it will," and he went along
with it. Lombroso, though, must have realized I was
getting a lot of these things from Carvajal. But he never
said a word about that to me—nor, I believe, to Quinn
or Mardikian.

From Carvajal I also got instructions of a more personal kind.

"It's time to get your hair cut," he told me early in
September.

"Short, you mean?"

"Off."

"Are you telling me to shave my scalp?"

"That's what I'm telling you."

"No," I said. "If there's one silly fad I detest—"

"Irrelevant. As of this month you began wearing your
hair like that. Do it tomorrow, Lew."

"I wouldn't ever have gotten a Pruss," I objected. "It's altogether out of keeping with my—"

"You did," Carvajal said simply. "How can you quarrel with that?"

But what was the use of arguing? He had *seen* me bald; hence I must go and get a Pruss. No questions asked, the man had told me when I came aboard: just follow the script, boy.

I yielded myself up unto the barber. I came out looking like an oversized Erich von Stroheim, minus monocle and stiff collar.

"How marvelous it looks!" Sundara cried. "How gorgeous!"

She ran her hands tenderly over my stubbly scalp. It was the first time in two or three months that there had been any kind of current flowing between us. She loved the haircut, absolutely adored it. Of course: getting cropped like that was a crazy Transit sort of thing for me to do. To her it was a sign that I might yet shape up.

There were other orders.

"Spend a weekend in Caracas," Carvajal said. "Charter a fishing boat. You'll catch a swordfish."

"Why?"

"Do it," he said implacably.

"I don't see the relevance of my going to—"

"Please, Lew. You're being difficult."

"Will you explain this, at least?"

"There's no explanation. You have to go to Caracas."

It was absurd. But I went to Caracas. I drank too many margaritas with some lawyers from New York who didn't know I was Quinn's right hand and put him down rather noisily, going on and on about the good old days when Gottfried kept the rabble in line. Fascinating. I hired a boat and did indeed catch a swordfish, nearly breaking both wrists in the process, and had the damned beast mounted at staggering cost. It began to occur to me that Carvajal and Sundara might be in league to drive me crazy, or maybe to drive me into the arms of the nearest Transit proctor. (Same thing?) But that was impossible. More likely Carvajal was merely giving me a crash course in following the script. Accept whatever dictate comes to you out of tomorrow: never ask questions.

I accepted the dictates.

I grew a beard. I bought nippy-dip new clothes. I picked up a sullen cow-breasted sixteen-year-old in Times Square, filled her with rum swizzles in the highest eyrie of the Hyatt Regency, rented a room there for two hours and grimly fornicated her. I spent three days up at the Columbia Medical Center as a volunteer subject for sonopuncture research, and left there with every bone buzzing. I went down to my neighborhood Numbers office and put a thousand bucks on 666, and got wiped out, because that day's winner was 667. I complained bitterly about that to Carvajal. "I don't mind doing craziness, but this is expensive craziness. Couldn't you at least have given me the right number?" He smiled obliquely and said he *had* given me the right number. I assume I was *supposed* to lose. All part of my training, it seemed. Existential masochism: the Zen approach to gambling. All right. Never ask questions. A week later he had me put a thou on 333, and I hit for a not-so-small fortune. So there were a few compensations.

Follow the script, kid. Ask no questions.

I wore my funny clothes. I got my scalp scraped regularly. I endured the itching of my beard, and after a while I stopped noticing it. I sent the mayor off lunching and dinnering with a weird assortment of eventually influential politicians. God help me, I followed the script.

Early in October Carvajal said, "Now you file for a divorce."

29 Divorce, Carvajal said, on a brisk crisp blue-skied Wednesday in October, a day of withered yellow early-falling maple leaves dancing in the sharp westerly wind, now you file for a divorce, now you arrange the termination of your marriage. Wednesday, the sixth of October, 1999, just eighty-six days left to the end of the century, unless, of course, you were the kind of purist who insisted, with logic if not emotional justice on your side, that the new century would not properly begin until the first of January, 2001. At any rate, eighty-six days left until the changing of the digit. *As the digit shifts*, Quinn had said in his most famous speech, *let us wipe clean the slate and begin afresh, remembering but not re-enacting the errors of the past*. Had marrying Sundara been one of the errors of the past? Now you file for a divorce, Carvajal told me, and he was not so much stating an imperative command as he was reporting impersonally to me on the necessary state of things to come. Thus does the unyielding, inescapable future ineluctably devour the present. For Orville and Wilbur Wright came Kitty Hawk time; for John F. Kennedy came Lee Harvey Oswald time; for Lew and Sundara Nichols now was coming divorce time, looming like an iceberg out of the months ahead, and why, why, for what end, to what purpose, *por qué, pourquoi, warum?* I still loved her.

Yet the marriage had plainly been ailing all through the summer, and euthanasia was a plausible prescription now. Whatever we had had was gone, altogether fallen into ruin; she was lost in the rhythms and rituals of Transit, wholly given over to her sacred absurdities, and I was deep into dreams of visionary powers, and though we shared an apartment and a bed we shared nothing else. What powered our relationship was the thinnest of fuels, the pale petrol of nostalgia, that and such little momentum as remembered passion can supply.

I think we made love three times that final summer. *Made love!* Preposterous euphemism for fucking, almost as bad as the most grotesque of all, *slept together.* Whatever Sundara and I made, in those three pressings of flesh to flesh, love couldn't have been the commodity; we made sweat, we made rumpled sheets, we made heavy breathing, we even made orgasms, but love? Love? The love was there, encapsulated within me and perhaps even within her, too, made long before, laid down in a cache like wine of the *premier cru,* like precious capital stored away and when our bodies grappled in the dark on those three clammy summer nights we were at that moment not making love but drawing on an existing and dwindling deposit. Living off assets.

Three times in three months. Not too many months ago we had managed a better tally than that in any given five-day span, but that was before the mysterious glassy barrier had unexpectedly descended between us. The fault was probably mine: I never reached for her now, and she, perhaps acting under some Transit commandment, was content never to reach for me. Her supple sultry body had lost none of its beauty in my eyes, nor was I festeringly jealous over some other lover, for not even the episode of the brothel license had had any effect on my desire for her, none, none at all. What she might do with others, even that, had always become as nothing the moment she was in my arms. But these days it seemed to me that sex between Sundara and me was irrelevant, inappropriate, an obsolete interchange in a demonetized currency. We had nothing to offer each other now except our bodies, and with all other levels of contact between us eroded away the body-to-body one had become worse than meaningless.

The last time we—made love, slept together, performed the act, fucked—was six days before Carvajal passed his sentence of death on the marriage. I didn't know then that it would be the last time, though I suppose I should have, if I had been half the prophet that people were paying me to be. But how could I have detected the apocalyptic overtones, the sense of a curtain descending? There weren't even ominous thunderheads in the sky. Thursday, the thirtieth of September, it was, a mild night on the cusp between summer and autumn. We were out with old friends that Thursday night, the Caldecott three-group, Tim and Beth and Corinne. Dinner at the Bubble, sky show afterwards. Tim and I had belonged to the same tennis club long ago and we had once won a mixed-doubles tournament, which was enough of a bond to have kept us in touch ever since; he was long-legged, easy-going, vastly wealthy, and entirely apolitical, which made his company a joy in these days of my City Hall responsibilities. No speculations about the whims of the electorate, no covert suggestions intended to be funneled back to Quinn, no hard-nosed analyses of current trends, just fun and games. We drank too much, we boned too much, we carried on a playful five-way flirtation that looked for a time to have me heading toward bed with any two of the Caldwell trio—most likely Tim and golden-haired Corinne—while Sundara settled in with the other. But as the evening unfolded I detected strong signals coming my way from Sundara. Surprise! Was she so boned she had forgotten I was only her husband? Was she indulging in a Transit unpredictability process? Or had it been so long since our last screw that I seemed a tempting novelty to her? I don't know. I never will. But the warmth of her sudden glance set off a light-pumping resonance between us that quickly became incandescent, and we excused ourselves from the Caldecotts with delicacy and gaiety—they are such natural aristocrats of sensibility that there were no hard feelings, no intimations of rejection, and we parted gracefully, talking of another get-together soon—and Sundara and I hurried home. Still resonating, still incandescent.

Nothing happened to snap the mood. Our clothes fell away, our bodies moved close together. Not tonight the elaborate *Kama Sutra* rituals of foreplay; she was in heat, so was I, and like animals we interpenetrated. She gave an odd little quivering sigh as I went into her, a husky sound that seemed to hit several notes at once, like a sound from one of those medieval Indian instruments that were tuned only to minor keys and produced sad twanging modal tone clusters. Perhaps she knew then that this was the final joining of our flesh. I moved against her with the assurance that I could do no wrong: if ever I followed the script it was then, no premeditation, no calculation, no separation of self from deed—myself as moving point on the face of the continuum, figure and ground merged and indistinguishable, perfectly in tune with the vibrations of the instant. I lay above her, clasping her in my arms, the classic Western position but one which we—with our shared repertoire of Oriental variations—rarely adopted. My back and hips felt strong as tempered Damascene steel, resilient as the most polymerized of plastics, and I swung inward and upward, inward and upward, inward and upward, moving with easy confident strokes, lifting her as though on jeweled ratchets to ever-higher levels of sensation and not incidentally bringing myself up there, too. For me it was a flawless screw, born of fatigue and despair and intoxication and confusion, an I-don't-have-anything-left-to-lose kind of copulation. There was no reason why it couldn't have gone on right through until morning. Sundara clung tight to me, matching my thrusts perfectly. Her knees were drawn almost to her breasts, and as I ran my hands down the satin of her skin I encountered, again and again, the cool metal of the Transit emblem strapped to her thigh—she never took it off, *never*—and even that d dn't shatter the perfection. But of course it wasn't an act of love: it was a mere athletic event, two matchless discoboli moving in tandem through the prescribed and preordained rituals of their specialty, and what did love have to do with that? There was love in me for her, yes, a desperate hungry tremble-and-scratch-and-bite kind of love, but there was no longer a way to express any of that, in or out of bed.

So we collected our Olympic gold medals, the high dive and the trampoline dance, the 300-kilo press and the fancy figure skating, the pole vault and the 400-meter hurdles, and by imperceptible nudgings and murmurings we clued each other closer to the ultimate moment, and then we were there, and for an unending interval we were dissolved into the fount of creation, and then the unending interval ended and we fell away from each other, sweaty and sticky and exhausted.

"Would you mind getting me a glass of water?" Sundara asked after a few minutes.

Which was how it ended.

Now you file for a divorce, said Carvajal six days later.

30 Give yourself to me, that was the deal, no questions asked, nothing guaranteed. No questions asked. But this time I had to ask. Carvajal was pushing me toward a step that I couldn't take without some sort of explanation.

"You promised not to ask," he said sulkily.

"Nevertheless. Give me a clue or the deal's off."

"Do you mean that?"

"I do."

He tried to stare me down. But those blank eyes of his, sometimes so fiercely unanswerable, didn't intimidate me now. My hunch function said I should go ahead, press him, demand to know the structure of events into which I was entering. Carvajal resisted. He squirmed and sweated and told me that I was setting my training back by weeks or even months with this unseemly outburst of insecurity. Have faith, he urged, follow the script, do as you're told, and all will be well.

"No," I said. "I love her, and even today divorce is no joke. I can't do it on a whim."

"Your training—"

"To hell with that. Why should I leave my wife, other than the simple fact that we haven't been getting along very well lately? Breaking up with Sundara isn't like changing my haircut, you know."

"Of course it is."

"What?"

"All events are equal in the long run," he said.

I snorted. "Don't talk garbage. Different acts have different consequences, Carvajal. Whether I wear my hair short or long can't have much effect on surrounding events. But marriages sometimes produce children, and children are unique genetic constellations, and the children that Sundara and I might produce, if we chose to produce any, would be different from children that she or I might have with other mates, and the differences— Christ, if we break up I might marry someone else and become the great-great-grandfather of the next Napoleon, and if I stay with her I might— Well, how can you say that in the long run all events are equal?"

"You grasp things very slowly," said Carvajal sadly. "What?"

"I wasn't speaking of consequences. Merely of events. All events are equal *in their probability*, Lew, by which I mean that there's total probability of any event happening that is going to happen—"

"Tautology!"

"Yes. But we deal in tautologies, you and I. I tell you, I *see* you divorcing Sundara, just as I *saw* you getting that haircut, and so those events are of equal probability."

I closed my eyes. I sat still a long time.

Eventually I said, "Tell me *why* I divorce her. Isn't there any hope of repairing the relationship? We aren't fighting. We don't have serious disagreements about money. We think alike on most things. We've lost touch with each other, yes, but that's all, just a drifting toward different spheres. Don't you think we could get back together if we both made a sincere effort?"

"Yes."

"Then why don't I try it instead of—"

"You'd have to go into Transit," he said.

I shrugged. "I think I could manage that if I had to. If the only alternative was losing Sundara."

"You couldn't. It's alien to you, Lew. It opposes everything you believe and everything you're working toward."

"But to keep Sundara—"

"You've lost her."

"Only in the future. She's still my wife."

"What's lost in the future is lost now."

"I refuse to—"

"You have to!" he cried. "It's all one, Lew, it's all one! You've come this far with me and you don't see that?"

I saw it. I knew every argument he was likely to muster, and I believed them all, and my belief wasn't something laid on from outside, like walnut paneling, but rather something intrinsic, something that had grown and spread within me over these past months. And still I resisted. Still I looked for loopholes. I was still clutching for any straw that eddied around me in the maelstrom, even as I was being sucked under.

I said, "Finish telling me. Why is it necessary and inevitable that I leave Sundara?"

"Because her destiny lies with Transit and yours lies as far from Transit as you can stay. They work toward uncertainty, you toward certainty. They try to undermine, you want to build. It's a fundamental philosophical gulf that's going to keep on getting wider and can't ever be bridged. So the two of you have to part."

"How soon?"

"You'll be living alone before the end of the year," he told me. "I've *seen* you several times in your new place."

"No woman living with me?"

"No."

"I'm not good at celibacy. I haven't had much practice."

"You'll have women, Lew. But you'll live alone."

"Sundara gets the condo?"

"Yes."

"And the paintings, the sculptures, the—"

"I don't know," Carvajal said, looking bored. "I really haven't paid any attention to details like that. You know they don't matter to me."

"I know."

He let me go. I walked about three miles uptown, seeing nothing around me, hearing nothing, thinking nothing. I was one with the void; I was a member of the vast emptiness. At the corner of Something Street and God-Knows-What Avenue I found a phone booth and dropped a token in the slot and dialed Haig Mardikian's office, and vipped my way through the shield of receptionists until Mardikian himself was on the line. "I'm getting divorced," I told him, and listened for a moment to the silent roaring of his amazement booming across the wire like the surf at Fire Island in a March storm. "I don't care about the financial angles," I said after a bit. "I just want a clean break. Give me the name of a lawyer you trust, Haig. Somebody who'll do it fast without hurting her."

31 In waking dreams I imagine a time when I am truly able to *see*. My vision pierces the murky invisible sphere that surrounds us all, and I penetrate into the realm of light. I have been asleep, I have been imprisoned, I have been blind, and now, now that the transformation has come upon me, it is like an awakening. My chains are gone; my eyes are open. About me move slow uncertain shadow-shrouded figures, blind and stumbling, their faces gray with bewilderment and uncertainty. These figures are you. And among you and about you I dance, my eyes luminous, my body ablaze with the joy of new perception. It has been like living beneath the sea, bent under a terrible pressure and held away from the tantalizing brightness by that membrane, flexible yet impenetrable, that is the interface between sea and sky; and now I have broken through it, into a place where everything glows and gleams, everything is haloed with radiance, shimmering in gold and violet and scarlet. Yes. Yes. At last I *see*.

What do I *see*?

I *see* the sweet and tranquil earth upon which our dramas are played. I *see* the sweaty struggles of the blind and deaf, buffeted as they strive by an incomprehensible fate. I *see* the years unrolling like the long uncoiling fronds of spring ferns, bright green at the tips, stretching away from me into infinity. In brilliant flashes of intermittent illumination I *see* decades sprouting into centuries and centuries becoming eons and epochs. I *see* the slow processions of the seasons, the systole and diastole of winter and summer, autumn and spring, the whole delicately interlocked rhythm of warmth and cold, of drought and rain, of sunlight and mist and darkness.

There are no limits to my vision. Here are the labyrinths of tomorrow's cities, rising and falling and rising again, New York in lunatic growth, tower piled on tower, the old foundations becoming the rubble on which the new foundations rest, layer upon layer down below like the jumbled strata of Schliemann's Troy. Through twisted streets scuttle strangers in unfamiliar clothing, speaking a jargon beyond my understanding. Machines walk about on jointed legs. Mechanical birds, twittering like creaky gates, flutter overhead. All is in flux. Look, the ocean recedes, and slippery brown beasts lie stranded and gasping on the naked sea floor! Look, the sea returns, lapping at the ancient highways that span the city's margin! Look, the sky is green! Look, the rain is black! Look, here is change, here is transformation, here are the whims of time! I *see* it all!

These are the eternal motions of the galaxies, dim and fathomless. These are the precessing equinoxes, these are the shifting sands. The sun is very warm. Words have become needle sharp. I catch quick glimpses of great entities sprouting and rising and decaying and dying. These are the boundaries of the empire of the toads. This wall marks the place where the republic of the long-legged insects begins. Man himself changes. His body is transformed many times, he becomes gross and then pure and then more gross than ever, he evolves strange organs that tremble like tuning forks from the nodes of his leathery skin, he has no eyes and is seamless from lips to scalp, he has many eyes, he is covered with eyes, he is no longer male and female but functions in the form of some intermediate sex, he is tiny, he is vast, he is liquid, he is metallic, he leaps across the starry spaces, he huddles in moist caverns, he floods the planet with legions of his own kind, he diminishes by choice to a few dozen, he shakes his fist at a red swollen sky, he sings frightening songs in a nasal drone, he gives love to monsters, he abolishes death, he basks like a mighty whale in the sea, he becomes a horde of buzzing insectlike toilers, he pitches his tent in blazing diamond-bright desert sands, he laughs with the sound of drums, he lies down with dragons, he writes poems of grass, he builds vessels of air, he becomes a god, he becomes a demon, he is everything, he is nothing.

The continents move ponderously about, like hippopotamuses doing a stately polka. The moon dips low in the sky, peering out of its own forehead like an aching white blister, and shatters with a wonderful glassy *ping*! that reverberates for years. The sun itself drifts from its moorings, for everything in the universe is in constant motion and the journeys are infinitely various. I *see* it slide into the gulf of night, and I wait for it to return, but it does not return, and a sleeve of ice glides over the black skin of the planet, and those who live at that time become things of the night, cold-loving, self-sustaining. And across the ice come hard-breathing beasts from whose nostrils fog issues; and from the ice come flowers of blue and yellow crystal; and in the sky shines a new light, I know not from where.

What do I *see*, what do I *see*?

These are the leaders of mankind, the new kings and emperors, holding their batons of office aloft and summoning fire from the mountaintops. These are the gods yet unimagined. These are the shamans and warlocks. These are the singers, these the poets, these the makers of images. These are the new rites. These are the fruits of war. Look: lovers, killers, dreamers, seers! Look: generals, priests, explorers, lawgivers! There are unknown continents to find. There are untasted apples to eat. Look! Madmen! Courtesans! Heroes! Victims! I *see* the schemes. I *see* the mistakes. I *see* the miraculous achievements, and they bring tears of pride to my eyes. Here is the daughter of your daughter's daughter. Here is the son of your sons beyond reckoning. These are nations still unknown; these are nations newly reborn. What is this language, all clicks and hisses? What is this music, all stabs and snarls? Rome will fall again. Babylon will come a second time, and lie astride the world like a great gray octopus. How wondrous are the times to come! All that you can ever imagine will befall, and more, much more, and I *see* it all.

Are these the things I *see*?

Are all doors open to me? Are all walls made into windows?

Do I look upon the murdered prince and the newborn savior, on the fires of the destroyed empire burning on the horizon, on the tomb of the lord of lords, on the hard-eyed voyagers setting forth across the golden sea that spans the belly of the transformed world? Do I survey the million million tomorrows of the race, and drink it all down, and make the future's flesh my own? The heavens falling? The stars colliding? What are these unfamiliar constellations that shape and reshape themselves as I watch? Who are these masked faces? What does this stone idol, tall as three mountains, represent? When will the cliffs that wall the sea be ground to red powder? When will the polar ice descend like inexorable night upon the fields of red flowers? Who owns these fragments? Oh, what do I *see*, what do I *see*?

All of time, all of space.

No. Of course it won't be like that. All I'll *see* is what I can send myself out of my own few scruffy tomorrows. Brief dull messages, like the vague transmissions of the tin-can telephones we built as boys: no epic splendors, no baroque apocalypses. Yet even those blurred and muffled sounds are more than I could have hoped to have when I was asleep like you, when I was one of those blind and stumbling figures moving in clumsy sluggish lurches through the kingdom of shadows that is this world.

32 Mardikian found me a lawyer. He was Jason Komurjian—another Armenian, of course, one of the partners in Mardikian's own firm, the divorce specialist, a great fullback of a man with oddly sad little eyes set close together within a massive swarthy slab of a face. He was a college classmate of Haig's, and therefore must have been about my own age, but he seemed older, much older, ageless, a patriarch who had taken upon himself the traumas of thousands of contumacious spouses. His features were youthful, his aura was ancient.

We conferred in his office on the ninety-fifth floor of the Martin Luther King Building, a dark incense-ridden office almost rivaling Bob Lombroso's for pomp and circumstance, a place as rich and heavy in ornamentation as the imperial chapel of a Byzantine cathedral. "Divorce," Komurjian said dreamily, "you wish to obtain a divorce, yes, to terminate, yes, a final parting," rotating the concept in the vast vaulted arenas of his consciousness as though it were some fine point of theology, as though we were talking about the consubstantiality of the Father and Son or the doctrine of the apostolic succession. "Yes, it should be possible to obtain that for you. You live separately now?"

"Not yet."

He looked displeased. His heavy lips sagged, his beefy face took on a deeper hue. "This must be done," he said. "Continued cohabitation endangers the plausibility of any suit for termination of matrimony. Even today, even today. Establish separate lodgings. Establish separate financial conduits. Demonstrate your purposes, my friend. Eh?" He reached for an ornate jeweled crucifix on his desk, a thing of rubies and emeralds, and played with it, running thick fingers over its sleek well-worn surface, and for a time he was lost in his own ruminations. I imagined the tones of an unseen organ, I saw a procession of bedecked and bearded priests strolling through the choirs of his mind. I could almost hear him muttering to himself in Latin, not church Latin but a lawyer Latin, a litany of platitudes. *Magna est vis consuetudinis, falsus in uno, falsus in omnibus, eadem sed aliter, res ipsa loquiter.* Huius huius huius, hunc haec hoc. He looked up, spearing me with an unexpectedly intent stare. "Grounds?"

"No, not that kind of divorce. We just want to break it up, to go our individual ways, a simple termination."

"Of course you've discussed this with Mrs. Nichols and come to a preliminary understanding."

I reddened. "Ah—not yet," I said, uneasy.

Komurjian plainly disapproved. "You must introduce the subject at some point, you realize. Presumably her reaction will be tranquil. Then her lawyer and I will meet and the thing will be done." He reached for a memo belt. "As for division of property—"

"She can have whatever she wants."

"*Whatever?*" He sounded amazed.

"I don't want a hassle with her over anything."

Komurjian spread his hands before me on the desk. He wore more rings even than Lombroso. These Levantines, these luxurious Levantines! "What if she demands everything? All the assets in common? You yield without contest?"

"She won't do that."

"Is she not of allegiance to the Transit Creed?"

Startled, I said, "How do you know that?"

"Haig and I have discussed the case, you must realize."

"I see."

"And Transit people are unpredictable."

I managed a choked laugh. "Yes. Very."

"She might whimsically ask for all the assets," Komurjian said.

"Or whimsically ask for none."

"Or none, true. One never knows. Are you instructing me to accept whatever position she takes?"

"Let's wait and see," I said. "She's basically a reasonable person, I think. It's my feeling that she won't make any unusual demand about division of property."

"And settlement of income?" the lawyer asked. "She will want no continuing payments from you?" You have a standard two-group contract, yes?"

"Yes. Termination ends all financial responsibility."

Komurjian began to hum, very quietly, almost beneath my threshold of hearing. Almost. How routine all this must seem to him, this severing of sacramental unions! "Then there should be no problems, yes? But you must announce your intentions to your wife, Mr. Nichols, before we go further."

Which I did. Sundara was now so busy with her manifold Transit activities—her process sessions, her volatility circles, her ego-decay exercises, her missionary duties, and all the rest—that close to a week passed before I was able to have a quiet word with her at home. By then I had rehearsed the whole thing in my head a thousand times, so that the lines were worn like tracks; if ever there was an instance of following the script, this would be it. But would she give me the right cues?

Almost apologetically, as though it were an intrusion on her privacy for me to request the privilege of a conversation with her, I said early one evening that I wanted to talk to her about something important, and then I told her, as I had so often heard myself telling her, that I was going to get a divorce. Saying it, I understood something of what it must be like, for Carvajal to *see*, because

I had lived this scene so often in imagination that it already felt like an event of the past to me.

Sundara regarded me thoughtfully, saying nothing, displaying neither surprise nor annoyance nor hostility nor enthusiasm nor dismay nor despair.

Her silence baffled me.

I said, eventually, "I've hired Jason Komurjian as my lawyer. One of Mardikian's partners. He'll sit down with your lawyer, when you've got one, and they'll work everything out. I want this to be a civilized parting of the ways, Sundara."

She smiled. Mona Lisa of Bombay.

"You don't have anything to say?" I asked.

"Not really."

"Is divorce such a trifle to you?"

"Divorce and marriage are aspects of the same illusion, my love."

"This world seems more real to me than it does to you, I think. That's one reason why it doesn't appear to be a good idea for us to go on living together."

She said, "Will there be a messy fight about dividing the things we own?"

"I told you I want this to be a civilized parting of the ways."

"Good. So do I."

The ease with which she was accepting all this dumbfounded me. We had been so badly out of touch with each other recently that we had never even discussed the growing failures of communication between us; but there are many marriages that go on like that for centuries, placidly drifting, no one caring to rock the boat. Now I was preparing to sink the boat, and she had no comment. Eight years of living together; suddenly I call in the lawyers; Sundara has no comment. Her imperturbability was a measure of the change Transit had worked in her, I decided.

"Do all Transit people accept great upheavals in their lives so casually?" I asked.

"Is this a great upheaval?"

"It seems like one to me."

"To me it seems only the ratifying of a decision made a long time ago."

"It's been a bad time," I admitted. "But even at the worst of it I always kept telling myself it's just a phase, it's a passing thing, every marriage goes through it, we'll get back together eventually."

As I spoke, I found myself convincing myself that all that was still true, that Sundara and I could still work out a continuing relationship like the basically reasonable human beings we were. And yet here I was asking her to hire a lawyer. I remembered Carvajal telling me, *You've lost her,* with inexorable finality in his voice. But he had been speaking of the future, not the past.

She said, "Now you think it's hopeless, is that it? What made you change your mind?"

"Well?"

"Did you change your mind?"

I said nothing.

"I don't think you really want a divorce, Lew."

"I do," I said hoarsely.

"So you say."

"I'm not asking you to read my mind, Sundara. Just to go along with the legal rigmarole we have to follow in order to be free to live our separate lives."

"You don't want a divorce, but yet you do. How strange, Lew. An attitude like that is a perfect Transit situation, you know, what we call a keying point, a situation where you hold opposing positions simultaneously and try to reconcile them. There are three possible outcomes of that. Are you interested in hearing this? One possibility is schizophrenia. One is self-deception, as when you pretend to embrace both alternatives but really don't. And the third is the condition of illumination known in Transit as——"

"Please, Sundara."

"I thought you were interested."

"I guess I'm not."

She studied me for a long moment. Then she smiled. "This divorce business is connected somehow with your gift of precognition, isn't it? You don't really want a divorce now, even though we aren't getting along very well, but you nevertheless think you *ought* to start arranging a divorce, because you've had a hunch that sometime in the near future you're going to have one, and— Isn't that right, Lew? Come on: tell me the truth. I won't be angry."

"You aren't far off the mark," I said.

"I thought not. Well, what shall we do?"

"Work out terms of a separation," I replied grimly. "Hire a lawyer, Sundara."

"And if I don't?"

"You mean you'll contest it?"

"I never said that. I simply don't want to deal through a lawyer. Let's handle it ourselves, Lew. Like civilized human beings."

"I'll have to check with Komurjian about that. That way may be civilized, but it may not be smart."

"Do you think I'll cheat you?"

"I don't think anything any more."

She walked up to me. Her eyes glowed; her body radiated a throbbing sensuality. I was helpless before her. She could have had anything from me. Leaning forward, Sundara kissed the tip of my nose and said huskily, stagily, "If you want a divorce, darling, you can have your divorce. Whatever you want. I won't stand in the way. I want you to be happy. I love you, you know." She smiled wickedly. Oh, that Transit mischief! "Whatever you want," she said.

33 I rented an apartment for myself in Manhattan, a three-room furnished job in an old, once-luxurious high rise on East Sixty-third near Second Avenue, which is an old, once-luxurious neighborhood not yet seriously into disrepair. The building's pedigree was evidenced by an assortment of security devices dating from the 1960s or thereabouts through the early 1990s, everything from police locks and hidden peepholes up to early-model filter mazes and velocity screens. The furniture was simple and timeless in style, venerable and utilitarian, couches and chairs and bed and tables and bookcases and stuff of that sort, so anonymous as to be invisible. I felt invisible, too, after I was completely moved in and the movers and the building superintendent had gone away, leaving me standing alone in my new living room like an ambassador newly arrived from nowhere to take up residence in limbo. What was this place, and how had it happened that I was living here? Whose chairs are these? Whose fingerprints on the bare blue walls?

Sundara had let me take some of the paintings and sculptures, and I set them up here and there; they had seemed magnificently integral to the lavish textures of our Staten Island condo, but here they looked awkward and unnatural, penguins in the veldt. There were no spot-lights here, no cunning arrangements of solenoids and rheostats, no carpeted pedestals: just low ceilings, dirty walls, windows without opaquers. Yet I felt no self-pity, finding myself here, only confusion, emptiness, dislocation. I spent the first day unpacking, organizing, setting up the lares and penates, working slowly and inefficiently, pausing often to think about nothing in particular. I didn't go out, not even for groceries; instead I phoned a hundred-dollar order to Gristede's market on the corner by way of initial stocking of the larder. Dinner was a solitary tasteless business of miscellaneous synthetic glop, absentmindedly prepared and hastily shoveled down. I slept alone, and, to my surprise, I slept very well. In the morning I phoned Carvajal and told him what had been happening.

He grunted his approval and said, "You have a view of Second Avenue from your bedroom window?"

"Yes. And Sixty-third Street from the living room. Why?"

"Light blue walls?"

"Yes."

"A dark couch?"

"Yes. Why do you want to know all this?"

"I'm just checking," he said. "To make certain you found the right place."

"You mean, that I found the one you've been *seeing?*"

"That's right."

"Was there any doubt?" I asked. "Have you stopped trusting the things you *see?*"

"Not for a moment. But do you?"

"I trust you, I trust you. What color is my bathroom sink?"

"I don't know," Carvajal said. "I've never bothered to notice. But your refrigerator is light brown."

"Okay, already. I'm impressed."

"I hope so. Are you ready to take notes?"

I found a scratchpad. "Go ahead," I said.

"Thursday, October twenty-first. Quinn will fly to Louisiana next week for a meeting with Governor Thibodaux. Afterward Quinn issues a statement declaring his support for the Plaquemines Project. When he gets back to New York he fires Housing Commissioner Ricciardi and gives the job to Charles Lewisohn. Ricciardi is named to the Racing Authority. And then—"

I took it all down, shaking my head as usual, hearing Quinn mutter, *What's Thibodaux to me? Why should I give a crap about the Plaquemines Dam? I thought dams were obsolete anyway. And Ricciardi's been doing a reasonably good job, considering his limited intelligence; won't it offend the Italians if I kick him upstairs like that?* Et cetera, et cetera. More and more frequently these days I had been coming to Quinn with bizarre stratagems, inexplicable and implausible, for now the pipeline from Carvajal was flowing freely out of the immediate future, carrying advice for me to relay to Quinn on how best to maneuver and manipulate; Quinn went along with everything I suggested, but sometimes I was hard put to make him do the things I asked him to do. One of these days he'd turn down an idea outright and would not be budged; what would happen then to Carvajal's unalterable future?

I was at City Hall the customary time the next day— it felt a little odd taking a cab downtown via Second Avenue instead of podding over from Staten Island—and by half past nine I had my latest batch of memos ready for the mayor. I sent them in. A little after ten my intercom bleeped and a voice said that Deputy Mayor Mardikian wanted to see me.

There was going to be trouble. I felt it intuitively as I went down the hall, and I saw it all over Mardikian's face as I entered his office. He looked uncomfortable—edgy, off center, tense. His eyes were too bright and he was chewing at the corner of his lip. My newest memoranda were spread out in a diamond-shaped pattern on his desk. Where was the smooth, slick, lacquer-finish Mardikian? Gone. Gone. And this rattled, jangled man before me was in his place.

He said, hardly looking up at me, "Lew what the hell is this garbage about Ricciardi?"

"It's advisable to remove him from his current job."

"I know it's advisable. You just advised us. *Why* is it advisable?"

"Long-range dynamics dictate it," I said, trying to bluff. "I can't give you any convincing and concrete reason, but my feeling is that it's unwise to keep a man in that job who's so closely identified with the Italian-American community here, especially the real estate interests within that community. Lewisohn's a good neutral non-abrasive figure who might be safer in that slot next year as we approach the mayoralty election, and—"

"Quit it, Lew."

"What?"

"Knock it off. You aren't telling me a thing. You're just giving me a lot of noise. Quinn thinks Ricciardi's been doing decent work and he's upset about your memo, and when I ask you for supportive data you just shrug and say it's a hunch. Now also—"

"My hunches have always—"

"Wait," Mardikian said. "This Louisiana thing. Christ! Thibodaux is the antithesis of everything Quinn has been trying to stand for. Why in *hell* should the mayor haul his ass all the way down to Baton Rouge to embrace an antediluvian bigot and espouse a useless and controversial and ecologically risky dam-building project? Quinn's got everything to lose and nothing visible to gain from that, unless you think it'll help him get the redneck vote in 2004 and you think the redneck vote is going to be vital to his chances, which God help us all if it is. Well?"

"I can't explain it, Haig."

"You can't explain it? You can't explain it? You give the mayor a highly explicit instruction like this, or like the Ricciardi thing, something that obviously has to have been the product of a whole lot of complicated thinking, and you don't know why? If you don't know why, how are we supposed to? Where's the rational basis for our actions? You want the mayor to be wandering around like a sleepwalker, like some sort of zombie, just doing as you say and not knowing why? Come on, kid! A hunch is a hunch, but we've hired you to make rational comprehensible projections, not to be a soothsayer."

Quietly I said, after a long wobbly pause, "Haig, I've been going through a lot of bad stuff lately, and I don't have much reserve of energy. I don't want to have a heavy hassle with you now. I'm just asking you to take it on faith that there's logic in the things I propose."

"I can't."

"Please?"

"Look, I realize that having your marriage fall apart has really ripped you up, Lew, but that's exactly why I have to challenge what you've handed in today. For months now you've been giving us these weird trips to do, and sometimes you justify them convincingly and sometimes you don't, sometimes you give us the most shamelessly cockeyed reasons for some course of action, and without exception Quinn has ultimately gone along with all your advice, frequently against his own better judgment. And I have to admit that so far everything has worked out surprisingly well. But now, but now—" He looked up, and his eyes drilled into mine. "Frankly, Lew, we're starting to have some doubts about your stability. We don't know if we ought to trust your suggestions as blindly as we have in the past."

"Jesus!" I cried. "You think that breaking up with Sundara has destroyed my sanity?"

"I think it's taken a lot out of you," Mardikian said, speaking more gently. "You yourself used the phrase about not having much reserve of energy. Frankly, Lew, we think you're under a strain, we think you're fatigued, weary, groggy, that you've overtaxed yourself seriously, that you can use a rest. And we—"

"Who's *we?*"

"Quinn. Lombroso. Me."

"What has Lombroso been saying about me?"

"Mainly that he's been trying to get you to take a vacation since last August."

"What else?"

Mardikian looked puzzled. "What do you mean, what else? What do you think he'd say? Christ, Lew, you're sounding awfully paranoid all of a sudden. Bob's your friend, remember? He's on your side. We're all on your side. He told you to go up to so-and-so's hunting lodge, but you wouldn't. He's worried about you. We all are. Now we'd like to put it a little more strongly. We feel you *need* a rest, Lew, and we want you to take one. City Hall won't fall apart if you aren't around for a few weeks."

"Okay. I'll go on vacation. I could use one, sure. But one favor, first."

"Go on."

"The Thibodaux thing and the Ricciardi thing. I want you to put them through and have Quinn do them."

"If you'll give me some plausible justification."

"I can't, Haig." Suddenly I was sweating all over. "Nothing that would sound convincing. But it's important that the mayor go along with those recommendations."

"Why?"

"It is. Very important."

"To you or to Quinn?"

It was a shrewd shot, and it hit me hard. *To me*, I thought, *to me, to Carvajal, to the whole pattern of faith and belief I've been constructing.* Had the moment of truth come at last? Had I handed Quinn instructions that he would refuse to follow? And what then? The paradoxes sprouting from such a negative decision dizzied me. I felt sick.

"Important to everybody," I said. "Please. As a favor. I haven't given him any bad advice up to now, have I?"

"He's hostile to this. He needs to know something of the projective structure behind these suggestions."

Almost panicky, I said, "Don't push me too hard, Haig. I'm right at the brink. But I'm not crazy. Exhausted, maybe, yes, but not crazy, and the stuff I handed in this morning makes sense, it *will* make sense, it'll be perfectly apparent in three months, five, six, whenever. Look at me. Look me right in the eye. I'll take that vacation. I appreciate the fact that you're all worried about me. But I want this one favor from you, Haig. Will you go in there and tell Quinn to follow those memos? For my sake. For the sake of all the years we've known each other. I tell you, those memos are kosher." I halted. I was babbling,

I knew, and the more I said, the less likely it was that
Haig would risk taking me seriously. Did he already see
me as a dangerously unstable lunatic? Were the men in
the white coats waiting in the corridor? What chance was
there, actually, that anybody would pay heed to this
morning's memos? I felt pillars tumbling, the sky falling.

Then Mardikian said, astonishingly, smiling warmly,
"All right, Lew. It's nutty, but I'll do it. Just this once.
You get yourself off to Hawaii or somewhere and sit
on the beach for a couple of weeks. And I'll go in there
and talk Quinn into firing Ricciardi and visiting Louisiana
and all the rest. I think it's crazy advice, but I'll gamble
on your track record." He left his desk and came around
to me, towering above me, and, abruptly, clumsily, he
pulled me to him and gave me a hug. "You worry me,
kid," he muttered.

34 I took a vacation. Not the beaches of Hawaii —too crowded, too hectic, too far away—and not the hunting lodge in Canada, for the snows of late autumn would already be descending there; I went off to golden California, Carlos Socorro's California, to magnificent Big Sur, where another friend of Lombroso's conveniently managed to own an isolated redwood cottage on an acre of clifftop overlooking the ocean. For ten restless days I lived in rustic solitude, with the densely wooded slopes of the Santa Lucia Mountains, dark and mysterious and ferny, to my back, and the broad breast of the Pacific before me, five hundred feet below. It was, they had assured me, the finest time of the year in Big Sur, the idyllic season that separates the summer's fogs from the winter's rains, and indeed it was so, with warm sunlit days and cool starry nights and an astonishing purple and gold sunset every evening. I hiked in the silent redwood groves, I swam in chilly, swift mountain streams, I scrambled down rocks thick with cascading glossy-leaved succulents to the beach and the turbulent surf. I watched cormorants and gulls at their dinners, and, one morning, a comical sea otter, swimming belly-up fifty meters off shore as he munched on a crab. I read no newspapers. I made no telephone calls. I wrote no memoranda.

But peace eluded me. I thought too much about Sundara, wondering in a blank, baffled way how I had come to lose her; I fretted about dreary political matters that any sane man would have banished from his mind in such stunning surroundings; I invented complex entropic catastrophes that might occur if Quinn failed to go to Louisiana. Living in paradise, I contrived to be twitchy and tense and ill at ease.

Yet slowly I allowed myself to feel refreshed. Slowly the magic of the lush coastline, miraculously preserved throughout a century in which almost everything else had been spoiled, worked itself on my stale and tangled soul.

Possibly I *saw* for the first time while I was in Big Sur.

I'm not sure. Months of proximity to Carvajal hadn't yet produced any definite results. The future sent me no messages that I could read. I knew now the tricks Carvajal used to induce the state, I knew the symptoms of an oncoming vision, I felt certain that before much longer I'd be *seeing*, but I had had no certain visionary experience, and the harder I tried to attain one, of course, the more distant my goal appeared. But there was one odd moment late in my stay in Big Sur. I had been to the beach, and now, toward the end of the afternoon, I was climbing swiftly up the steep trail to the cottage, getting tired fast, breathing hard, enjoying the heady dizziness that was coming over me as I deliberately pushed heart and lungs to their limits. Reaching a sharp switchback, I paused for a moment, turning to look back and down, and the glare of the dipping sun reverberating off the surface of the sea hit me and dazzled me, so that I swayed and shivered and had to clutch at a bush to keep from falling. And in that moment it seemed to me—it seemed, it was only an illusory sensation, a brief subliminal flicker —that I was staring through the golden fire of the sunlight into a time not yet arrived, that I beheld a vast rectangular green banner rippling above a mighty concrete plaza, and the face of Paul Quinn looked at me out of the center of the banner, a powerful face, a commanding face, and the plaza was full of people, thousands of them jammed together, hundreds of thousands, waving their arms, shouting wildly, saluting the banner, a mob, an immense collective entity lost in hysteria, in Quinn-worship. It could just as easily have been 1934, Nuremberg, a different face on the banner, weird hyperthyroid eyes and stiff black mustache, and what they were shouting could just as easily have been *Sieg! Heil! Seig! Heil!* I gasped and fell to my knees, stricken by dizziness, fear, amazement, awe, I know not what, and I moaned and put my hands to my face, and then the vision was gone, then the afternoon breeze swept banner and mob from my throbbing brain, and nothing lay before me but the endless Pacific.

Did I *see?* Had the veil of time parted for me? Was Quinn the coming *führer*, was he tomorrow's *duce?* Or had my weary mind conspired with my weary body to spawn a quick paranoid flash, crazy imaginings and nothing more? I didn't know. I still don't. I have my theory, and my theory is that I *saw*, but never have I *seen* that banner again, never have I heard the terrible resonating shouts of that ecstatic mob, and until the day of the banner is actually upon us I will not know the truth.

Eventually, deciding that I had sequestered myself in the woods long enough to re-establish my standing at City Hall as a stable and trustworthy adviser, I drove up to Monterey, hopped the coastal pod to San Francisco, and flew home to New York, to my dusty, untended flat on Sixty-third Street. Not much had changed. The days were shorter, now that November had come, and autumn's haze had yielded to the first sharp blasts of the onrushing winter, slicing crosswise through the city from river to river. The mayor, *mirabile dictu*, had been to Louisiana and, to the displeasure of the *New York Times'* editorial writers, had advocated construction of the dubious Plaquemines Dam, had been photographed embracing Governor Thibodaux: Quinn looked sourly determined, smiling the way a man might smile who had been hired to hug a cactus.

Next I went out to Brooklyn to visit Carvajal.

It was a month since I had seen Carvajal, but he

looked very much more than a month older—sallow, shrunken, eyes dim and watery, a tremor in his hands. He hadn't seemed so wasted and worn since our first meeting, in Bob Lombroso's office, back in March; all the strength he had gained in the spring and summer now was gone from him, all the sudden vitality which perhaps he had drawn from his relationship with me. Not perhaps: surely. For, minute by minute, as we sat and talked, color returned to him, the gleam of energy reappeared in his features.

I told him what had happened on the hillside in Big Sur. He may have smiled. "Possibly a beginning," he said softly. "Eventually it has to start. Why not there?"

"If I did *see*, though, what did the vision mean? Quinn with banners? Quinn exciting a mob?"

"How would I know?" Carvajal asked.

"You haven't ever *seen* anything like that?"

"Quinn's true time is after mine," he reminded me. His eyes reproached me mildly. Yes: this man had less than six months to live, and knew it, down to the hour, to the moment. He said, "Possibly you can remember how old Quinn seemed to be, in your vision. The color of the hair, the lines in the face . . ."

I tried to remember. Quinn was only thirty-nine now. How old was the man whose face had filled that great banner? I had recognized him instantly as Quinn, so the changes couldn't have been great. Jowlier than the present Quinn? The blond hair graying at the temples? The lines of that iron grin more deeply incised? I didn't know. I hadn't noticed. Only a fantasy, perhaps. Hallucination born of fatigue. I apologized to Carvajal; I promised to do better the next time, if I were to be granted a next time. He assured me there would be. I would *see*, he said firmly, growing more animated. He was more vigorous the longer we were together. I would *see*, no doubt of that.

He said, "Time for business. New instructions for Quinn."

There was only one thing to convey this time: the mayor was supposed to start shopping around for a new police commissioner, because Commissioner Sudakis was shortly going to resign. That startled me. Sudakis had been one of Quinn's best appointments—effective and popular, the closest thing to a hero the New York Police Department had had in a couple of generations, a solid, reliable, incorruptible, personally courageous man. In his first year and a half as head of the department he had come to seem a fixture; it was as if he had always been in charge, always would be. He had done a beautiful job transforming the Gestapo that the police had become under the late Mayor Gottfried into a peacemaking force once again, and the job was not yet done: only a couple of months ago I had heard Sudakis tell the mayor he would need another year and a half to finish the cleanup. Sudakis about to quit? It didn't ring true.

"Quinn won't believe it," I said. "He'll laugh in my face."

Carvajal shrugged. "Sudakis will no longer be police commissioner after the first of the year. The mayor ought to have a capable replacement ready."

"Maybe so. But it's all so damned implausible. Sudakis sits there like the Rock of Gibraltar. I can't go in and tell the mayor he's about to quit, even if he is. There was so much static over the Thibodaux and Ricciardi businesses that Mardikian insisted I take a rest cure. If I go in there with something as wild as this, they might have me put away."

Carvajal stared at me imperturbably, implacably.

I said, "At least give me some supporting data. *Why* does Sudakis plan to quit?"

"I don't know."

"Would I get any clues if I approached Sudakis myself?"

"I don't know."

"You don't know. You don't know. And you don't care, do you? All you know is that he's planning to leave. The rest is trivial to you."

"I don't even know that, Lew. Only that he *will* leave. Sudakis may not know it himself yet."

"Oh, fine. Fine! I tell the mayor, the mayor sends for

Sudakis, Sudakis denies everything, because as of now it isn't so."

"Reality is always conserved," said Carvajal. "Sudakis will resign. It will happen very suddenly."

"Must I be the one to tell Quinn that? What if I don't say anything? If reality is truly conserved, Sudakis will leave no matter what I do. Isn't that so? Isn't it?"

"Do you want the mayor to be caught unprepared when it happens?"

"Better that than to have the mayor think I'm crazy."

"Are you afraid to warn Quinn about the resignation?"

"Yes."

"What do you think would happen to you?"

"I'll be put in an embarrassing position," I said. "I'll be asked to justify something that makes no sense to me. I'll have to fall back on saying it's a hunch, only a hunch, and if Sudakis denies he's going to quit I'll lose influence with Quinn. I might even lose my job. Is that what you want?"

"I have no desires whatever," said Carvajal distantly.

"Besides, which, Quinn won't let Sudakis quit."

"Are you sure?"

"Positive. He needs him too much. He won't accept his resignation. No matter what Sudakis says, he'll stay on the job, and what does that do to the conservation of reality?"

"Sudakis won't stay," Carvajal said indifferently.

I went away and thought about it.

My objections to recommending that Quinn start looking for a successor to Sudakis struck me as logical, reasonable, plausible, and unarguable. I was unwilling to crawl into so exposed a position so soon after my return, when I was still vulnerable to Mardikian's skepticism about my stability. On the other hand, if some unforeseen turn of events *would* force Sudakis to quit, I'd have been derelict in my duties if I had failed to give the mayor the warning. In a city forever on the edge of chaos, even a few days' confusion about lines of authority in the Police Department could bring matters close to anarchy in the streets, and one thing Quinn really didn't need as a potential presidential candidate was a resurgence, however brief, of the lawlessness that had roiled the city so often before the repressive Gottfried administration and in the time of the feeble Mayor DiLaurenzio. And on the third hand, I had never before refused to be the vehicle of one of Carvajal's directives, and it troubled me to defy him now. Imperceptibly Carvajal's notions of reality conservation had become part of me; imperceptibly I had accepted his philosophy to an extent that left me fearful of tampering with the inevitable uncoiling of the inevitable. Feeling a bit like someone who was climbing aboard an ice floe heading downstream in the Niagara River, I found myself resolving to bring the Sudakis story to Quinn, misgivings or no.

But I let a week slide by, hoping the situation would somehow resolve itself without my interference, and then I let most of another week go past; and so I might have allowed the rest of the year to slip away, but I knew I was deluding myself. So I drew up a memo and sent it in to Mardikian.

"I'm not going to show this to Quinn," he told me two hours later.

"You have to," I said without much conviction.

"You know what'll happen if I do? He'll have your ass, Lew. I had to do half a day of fancy dancing over Ricciardi and the Louisiana trip, and the things Quinn said about you then weren't very complimentary. He's afraid you're cracking up."

"All of you think that. Well, I'm not. I had a nice sweet vacation in California and I've never felt better in my life. And come next January this town is going to need a new police commissioner."

"No, Lew."

"No?"

Mardikian grunted heavily. He was tolerating me, humoring me; but he was sick of me and my predictions, I knew. He said, "After I got your memo I called in Sudakis and told him there's a rumor going around that he's thinking of quitting. I didn't attribute it. I let him think I got it from one of the boys in the press corps.

You should have seen his face, Lew. You'd have thought I'd called his mother a Turk. He swore by seventy saints and fifty angels that the only way he'd leave his job was if the mayor fired him. I can usually tell when a man's putting me on, and Sudakis was as sincere as anybody I've ever seen."

"All the same, Haig, he's going to quit in a month or two."

"How can that be?"

"Unexpected circumstances do arise."

"Such as?"

"Anything. Reasons of health. A sudden scandal in the department. A megabuck job offer from San Francisco. I don't know what the exact reason will be. I'm just telling you—"

"Lew, how can you possibly know what Sudakis is going to do in January when not even Sudakis does?"

"I know," I insisted.

"How can you?"

"It's a hunch."

"A hunch. A hunch. You keep saying that. It's one hunch too many, Lew. Your skill has to do with interpretation of trends, not with individual predictive instances, right, but more and more you've been coming in with these isolated shots, these crystal-ball stunts, these—"

"Haig, have any of them been wrong?"

"I'm not sure."

"None. Not a one. A lot of them haven't proved out yet, one way or the other, but there isn't one that's been contradicted by later developments, no recommended course of action that has definitely been shown to be unwise, no—"

"All the same, Lew, I told you the last time, we don't believe in soothsayers around here. Stick to broad projections of visible trends, will you?"

"I'm only looking out for Quinn's welfare."

"Sure. But I think you ought to start looking out more for your own."

"What does that mean?" I asked.

"That unless your work here takes on, well, a less

unconventional tone, the mayor may have to terminate your services."

"Crap. He needs me, Haig."

"He's starting not to think so. He's starting to think you may even be a liability."

"He doesn't realize how much I've done for him, then. He's a thousand kilometers closer to the White House than he would ever have been without me. Listen, Haig, whether or not you and Quinn think I'm crazy, this city is going to wake up without a police commissioner one day in January, and the mayor ought to begin a personnel search this afternoon, and I want you to let him know that."

"I won't. For your own protection," Mardikian said. "Don't be obstinate."

"Obstinate? *Obstinate?* I'm trying to save your neck."

"What would it hurt if Quinn did quietly start looking for a new commissioner? If Sudakis doesn't quit, Quinn could drop the whole thing and nobody'd need to know. Do I have to be right all the time? I happen to be right about Sudakis, but even if I'm not, what of it? It's a potentially useful bit of information I'm offering, something important if true, and—"

Mardikian said, "Nobody says you have to be a hundred percent right, and of course there'd be no harm in opening a quiet contingency search for a new police commissioner. The harm I'm trying to avoid is to you. Quinn as much as told me that if you show up with one more way-out bit of black-magic prophecy he'd transfer you to the Department of Sanitation or worse, and he will, Lew, he will. Maybe you've had a tremendous run of luck, pulling stuff like this out of the air, but—"

"It isn't luck, Haig," I told him quietly.

"What?"

"I'm not using stochastic processes at all. I'm not operating by guesswork. I *see*, is what I'm saying. I'm able to look into the future and hear conversations, read headlines, observe events, I can dredge all sorts of data out of time to come." It was only a small lie, displacing Carvajal's powers to myself. Operationally the results were the same, whichever one of us was doing the *seeing*. "That's why I can't always give supporting data to explain my memos," I said. "I look into January, I *see* Sudakis resigning, and that's all, I don't know why, I don't yet perceive the surrounding structure of cause and effect, only the event itself. It's different from projection of trends, it's something else entirely, wilder, a lot less plausible, but more reliable, a hundred percent reliable, one hundred percent! Because I can *see* what's going to happen."

Mardikian was silent a very long time.

He said, finally, in a hoarse, cottony voice, "Lew, are you serious?"

"Extremely."

"If I go and get Quinn, will you tell him exactly what you just told me? Exactly?"

"Yes."

"Wait here," he said.

I waited. I tried not to think about anything. Keeping mind a blank, let the stochasticity flow: had I blundered, had I overplayed my hand? I didn't believe so. I believed the time had come for me to reveal something of what I was really up to. For the sake of plausibility I hadn't bothered to mention Carvajal's role in the process, but otherwise I had held nothing back, and I felt a great release from tension, I felt a warm flood of relief surging in me, now that I had come out at last from behind my cover.

After what may have been fifteen minutes Mardikian returned. The mayor was with him. They took a few steps into the office and halted side by side near the door, an oddly mismatched pair, Mardikian dark and absurdly tall, Quinn fairhaired, short, thick-bodied. They looked terribly solemn.

Mardikian said, "Tell the mayor what you told me, Lew."

Blithely I repeated my confession of second sight, using, as far as was possible, the same phrases. Quinn listened expressionlessly. When I finished, he said, "How long have you been working for me, Lew?"

"Since the beginning of '96."

"Four years, almost. And how long is it since you've had a direct pipeline into the future?"

"Not long. Only since last spring. You remember, when I urged you to get that oil-gellation bill through the City Council, just before those tankers broke up off Texas and California? It was about then. I wasn't just guessing. And then, the other things, the ones that sometimes seemed so weird—"

"Like having a crystal ball," Quinn said wonderingly.

"Yes. Yes. You remember, Paul, the day you told me you had decided to make a run for the White House in '04, what you said to me? You told me, You're going to be the eyes that see into the future for me. You didn't know how right you were!"

Quinn laughed. It wasn't a cheerful laugh.

He said, "I thought if you just went off to rest for a couple of weeks, Lew, it would help you get yourself together. But now I see the problem runs much deeper than that."

"What?"

"You've been a good friend and a valuable adviser for four years. I won't underestimate the value of the help you've provided. Maybe you were getting your ideas from close intuitive analysis of trends, or maybe from computers, or maybe a genie was whispering things in your ear, but wherever you got it, you were giving me useful advice. But I can't risk keeping you on the staff after what I've heard. If word gets around that Paul Quinn's key decisions are made for him by a guru, by a seer, by some kind of clairvoyant Rasputin, that I'm really nothing but a puppet twitching in the dark, I'm done for, I'm dead. We'll put you on full-time leave, effective today, with your salary continuing through to the end of the fiscal year, all right? That'll give you better than seven months to rebuild your old private consulting business before you're dropped from the municipal payroll. With your divorce and everything, you're probably in a tight financial position, and I don't want to make it any worse. And let's make a deal, you and me: I won't make any public statements about the reasons for your resignation, and you won't make any open claims about the alleged origin of the advice you were giving me. Fair enough?"

"You're firing me?" I muttered.

"I'm sorry, Lew."

"I can make you President, Paul!"

"I'll have to get there on my own, I guess."

"You think I'm crazy, don't you?" I said.

"That's a harsh word."

"But you do, right? You think you've been getting advice from a dangerous lunatic, and it doesn't matter that the lunatic's advice was always right, you have to get rid of him now, because it would look bad, yes, it would look very bad if people started thinking you had a witch doctor on your staff, and so—"

"Please, Lew," Quinn said. "Don't make this any harder for me." He crossed the room and caught my limp, cold hand in his fierce grip. His face was close to mine. Here it came: the famed Quinn Treatment, once more, one last time. Urgently he said, "Believe me, I'm going to miss you around here. As a friend, as an adviser. I may be making a big mistake. And it's painful to have to do this. But you're right: I can't take the risk, Lew. I can't take the risk."

35 I cleaned out my desk after lunch and went home, went to what passed for home for me, and wandered around the shabby half-empty rooms the rest of the afternoon, trying to comprehend what had happened to me. Fired? Yes, fired. I had taken off my mask, and they hadn't liked what was underneath. I had stopped pretending to science and had admitted sorcery, I had told Mardikian the true truth, and now no more would I go to City Hall and sit among the mighty, and no longer would I shape and guide the destinies of the charismatic Paul Quinn, and when he took the oath of office in Washington come January five years hence I would watch the scene on television from afar, the forgotten man, the shunned man, the leper of the administration. I felt too forlorn even to cry. Wifeless, jobless, purposeless, I roamed my dreary flat for hours, and, wearying of that, stood idly by a window for an hour or more, watching the sky turn leaden, watching the unexpected flakes of the season's first snowfall begin to descend, watching cold night spread over Manhattan.

Then anger displaced despair and, furious, I phoned Carvajal.

"Quinn knows," I said. "About the Sudakis resignation.

I gave the memo to Mardikian and he conferred with the mayor."

"Yes?"

"And they fired me. They think I'm crazy. Mardikian checked with Sudakis, who said he didn't have any intention of quitting, and Mardikian said he and the mayor were worried about my wild crystal-ball predictions, they wanted me to go back to straight projective stuff, so I told them about *seeing*. I didn't mention you. I said I was able to do it, and that was where I was getting stuff like the Thibodaux trip and the Sudakis resignation, and Mardikian made me repeat everything to Quinn, and Quinn said it was too dangerous for him to keep a lunatic like me on his staff. He put it more gently than that, though. I'm on leave until June thirtieth, and then I get cut from the city payroll."

"I see," said Carvajal. He didn't sound upset and he didn't sound sympathetic.

"You knew this would happen."

"Did I?"

"You must have. Don't play games with me, Carvajal. Did you know I'd get thrown out if I told the mayor that Sudakis was going to quit in January?"

Carvajal said nothing.

"Did you know or didn't you?"

I was shouting.

"I knew," he said.

"You knew. Of course you knew. You know everything. But you didn't tell me."

"You didn't ask," he replied innocently.

"It didn't occur to me to ask. God knows why, but it didn't. Couldn't you have warned me? Couldn't you have said, Keep a tight lip, you're in worse trouble than you suspect, you're going to get tossed out on your ass if you aren't careful?"

"How can you ask such a question this late in the game, Lew?"

"You were willing to sit back calmly and let my career be destroyed?"

"Think carefully," Carvajal said. "I knew you'd be

dismissed, yes. Just as I know Sudakis will resign. But what could I do about it? To me your dismissal has already happened, remember. It isn't subject to prevention."

"Oh, Jesus! Conservation of reality again?"

"Of course. Really, Lew, do you think I'd warn you against anything that might seem to be in your power to change? How futile that would be! How foolish! We don't change things, do we?"

"No, we don't," I said bitterly. "We stand off to one side and politely let them happen. If necessary we *help* them happen. Even if it involves the destruction of a career, even if it involves the ruination of an attempt to stabilize the political fortunes of this miserable misgoverned country by guiding into the presidency a man who— Oh, Jesus, Carvajal, you led me right into this, didn't you? You set me up for the whole thing. And you don't give a damn. Isn't that so? You simply don't give a damn!"

"There are worse things than losing a job, Lew."

"But everything I was building, everything I was trying to shape— How in God's name am I going to help Quinn now? What am I going to do? You've broken me!"

"What has happened is what had to happen," he said.

"Damn you and your pious acceptance!"

"I thought you had come to share that acceptance."

"I don't share anything," I told him. "I was out of my mind ever to get involved with you, Carvajal. Because of you I've lost Sundara, I've lost my place at Quinn's side, I've lost my health and my reason, I've lost everything that mattered to me, and for what? *For what?* For one stinking squint into the future that may have been nothing but a quick fatigue high? For a head full of morbid fatalistic philosophy and half-baked theories about the flow of time? Christ! I wish I'd never heard of you! You know what you are, Carvajal? You're a kind of vampire, some sort of bloodsucker, pulling energy and vitality out of me, using me to support your strength as you drift along toward the end of your own useless, sterile, motiveless, pointless life."

Carvajal didn't seem at all moved. "I'm sorry to hear you so disturbed, Lew," he said mildly.

"What else are you concealing from me? Come on, give me all the bad news. Do I slip on the ice at Christmas and break my back? Do I use up my savings and get shot holding up a bank? Am I going to become a sniffer addict next? Come on, tell me what's heading toward me now!"

"Please, Lew."

"Tell me!"

"You ought to try to calm down."

"Tell me!"

"I'm holding nothing back. You won't have an eventful winter. It's going to be a time of transition for you, of meditation and inner change, without any dramatic external events. And then—and then—I can't tell you any more, Lew. You know I can't *see* beyond this coming spring."

Those last few words hit me like a knee in the belly. Of course. Of course! Carvajal was going to die. A man who would do nothing to prevent his own death wasn't going to interfere while someone else, even his only friend, marched serenely on toward catastrophe. He might even nudge that friend down the slippery slope if he felt a nudge was appropriate. It was naïve of me to have thought Carvajal would ever have done anything to protect me from harm once he had *seen* the harm coming. The man was bad news. And the man had set me up for disaster.

I said, "Any deal that may have existed between us is off. I'm afraid of you. I don't want anything more to do with you, Carvajal. You won't hear from me again."

He was silent. Perhaps he was laughing quietly. Almost certainly he was laughing quietly.

His silence sapped the melodramatic force from my little parting speech.

"Goodbye," I said, feeling silly, and hung up with a crash.

36 Now winter closed upon the city. Some years no snow comes until January or even February; but we had a white Thanksgiving, and in the early weeks of December there was blizzard after blizzard, until it seemed that all life in New York would be crushed in the grip of a new ice age. The city has sophisticated snow-removal equipment, heating cables buried in the streets, sanitation trucks with melt-tanks, an armada of scoops and catchments and scrapers and skimmers, but no gadg-etry could cope with a season that dropped ten centi-meters of snow on Wednesday, a dozen more on Friday, fifteen on Monday, half a meter on Saturday. Occasionally we had a thaw between storms, allowing the top of the accumulated pack to soften and slush to drip into the gutters, but then came the cold again, the killing cold, and what had melted turned quickly to knife-edged ice. All activities halted in the frozen city. A weird silence prevailed. I stayed indoors; so did anyone else who had no powerful reason for going out. The year 1999, the whole twentieth century, seemed to be taking leave in frigid stealth.

In this bleak time I had virtually no contact with any-one except Bob Lombroso. The financier phoned five or six days after my dismissal to express his regrets. "But why," he wanted to know, "did you ever decide to tell Mardikian the real story?"

"I felt I had no choice. He and Quinn had stopped taking me seriously."

"And they'd take you more seriously if you claimed to be able to see the future?"

"I gambled. I lost."

"For a man who's always had such a superb sixth sense of intuition, Lew, you handled that situation in a strikingly dumb way."

"I know. I know. I suppose I thought Mardikian had a more resilient imagination. Maybe I overestimated Quinn, too."

"Haig didn't get where he is today by having a resilient imagination," Lombroso said. "As for the mayor, he's playing for big stakes and he doesn't feel like taking any unnecessary risks."

"I'm a necessary risk, Bob. I can help him."

"If you have any notion of persuading him to take you back, forget it. Quinn's terrified of you."

"Terrified?"

"Well, maybe that's too strong a word. But you make him profoundly uncomfortable. He half suspects that you might actually be able to do the things you claim. I think that's what scares him."

"That he may have fired an authentic seer?"

"No, that authentic seers exist at all. He said—and this is absolutely confidential, Lew, it'll do me harm if he finds out you've heard this—he said that the idea that people might really be capable of seeing the future oppresses him like a hand around his throat. That it makes him feel paranoid, that it limits his options, that it makes the horizon close in around him. Those are his phrases. He hates the entire concept of determinism; he believes he's a man who's always been the shaper of his own destinies, and he feels a kind of existential terror when faced with somebody who maintains that the future is a fixed record, a book that can be opened and read. Because that turns him into a sort of puppet following a preordained pattern. It takes a lot to push Paul Quinn into paranoia, but I think you've succeeded. And what bothers him particularly is that he hired you, he made you a member of his inner team, he kept you close by him for four years, without realizing what a threat you were to him."

"I've never been a threat to him, Bob."

"He sees it differently."

"He's wrong. For one thing, the future *hasn't* been an open book to me all the years I've been with him. I worked by means of stochastic processes until quite recently, until I got entangled with Carvajal. You know that."

"But Quinn doesn't."

"What of it? It's absurd for him to feel threatened by me. Look, my feelings about Quinn have always been a mingling of awe and admiration and respect and, well, love. Love. Even now. I still think he's a great human being and a great political leader, and I want to see him become President, and though I wish he hadn't panicked over me I don't resent it at all. I can see how from his viewpoint it might have seemed necessary to get rid of me. But I *still* want to do all I can for him."

"He won't take you back, Lew."

"Okay. I accept that. But I can still work for him without his knowing it."

"How?"

"Through you," I said. "I can pass suggestions along to you and you can convey them to Quinn as though you've thought of them yourself."

"If I come to him with the sort of things you've been bringing him," Lombroso said, "he'll get rid of me as fast as he got rid of you. Maybe faster."

"They won't be the same sort, Bob. For one thing, I know now what's too risky to tell him. For another, I don't have my source any more. I've broken with Carvajal. You know, he never warned me I was going to get fired? Sudakis' future he tells me about, but not my own. I think he *wanted* me to get fired. Carvajal's been nothing but grief to me, and I'm not going back for more of the same. But I still have my own intuitive processes to offer, my stochastic knack. I can analyze trends and generalize strategies, and I can relay my insights to you, can't I? Can't I? We'll fix it so Quinn and Mardikian never find out that you and I are in contact. You can't just let me go to waste, Bob. Not while there's still a job to do for Quinn. Well?"

"We can try," said Lombroso warily. "I suppose we can give it a try, yes. All right. I'll be your mouthpiece, Lew. Provided you allow me the option of deciding what I want to pass along to Quinn and what I don't. It's my neck on the block now, remember, not yours."

"Sure," I told him.

If I couldn't serve Quinn myself, I could do it by proxy. For the first time since my dismissal I felt alive and hopeful. It didn't even snow that night.

37 But the proxy arrangement didn't work out. We tried, and we failed. I diligently sat down with the newspapers and caught up with current developments— one week out of touch and I had lost track of half a dozen emerging patterns—and then I made the perilous frosty journey across town to the Lew Nichols Associates office, still a going concern though ticking but feebly, and ran off some projections on my machinery. I transmitted the results to Bob Lombroso by courier, not wanting to chance the telephone. What I gave him was no big deal, a couple of piffling suggestions about city labor policy. During the next few days I generated a few more equally tame ideas. Then Lombroso called and said, "You might as well stop. Mardikian shot us down."

"What happened?"

"I've been feeding your stuff in, you know, a bit at a time. Then last night I had dinner with Haig and when we reached the dessert he suddenly asked me if you and I were keeping in touch."

"And you told him the truth?"

"I tried not to tell him anything," Lombroso said. "I was cagey, but I guess not cagey enough. Haig's pretty sharp, you know. He saw right through me. He said,

You're getting this stuff from Lew, aren't you? And I shrugged and he laughed and said, I know you are. It's got his touch all over it. I didn't admit anything. Haig just assumed—and his assumptions were correct. Very amiably he told me to cut it out, that I'd be jeopardizing my own position with Quinn if the mayor started to suspect what was going on."

"Then Quinn doesn't know yet?"

"Apparently not. And Mardikian isn't planning to tip him off. But I can't take any chances. If Quinn gets wise to me, I'm through. He goes into absolute paranoia whenever anyone mentions the name of Lew Nichols around him."

"It's that bad, is it?"

"It's that bad."

"So I've become the enemy now," I said.

"I'm afraid you have. I'm sorry, Lew."

"So am I," I said, sighing.

"I won't be calling you. If you need to get in touch with me, do it by way of my Wall Street office."

"Okay. I don't want to get you in trouble, Bob."

"I'm sorry," he said again.

"Okay."

"If I could do anything for you—"

"Okay. Okay. Okay."

38　　There was a foul storm two days before Christmas, a mean reptilian blizzard, fierce brutal winds and sub-Arctic temperatures and a heavy fall of dry, hard, rough snow. It was the sort of storm that would depress a Minnesotan and make an Eskimo cry. All day long my windows shivered in their venerable frames as cascades of wind-driven snow pounded them like clusters of pebbles, and I shivered with them, thinking that we still had all the misery of January and February to come, and snow not implausible in March either. I went to bed early and woke up early into a dazzling sunny morning. Cold sunny days are common after snowstorms as clear dry air moves in, but there was something odd about the quality of the light, which was not the harsh brittle lemon hue of a winter day but rather the sweet mellow gold of spring; and, turning the radio on, I heard the announcer talking about the dramatic shift in the weather. Apparently some vagrant air mass out of the Carolinas had moved north during the night and the temperature had risen to improbable late-April warmth.

And April remained with us. Day after day the unseasonable heat caressed the winter-weary city. Of course everything was a mess at first as the great hummocks of

recent snow softened and melted and ran in furious
rivers along the gutters; but by the middle of the holiday
week the worst of the slush was gone, and Manhattan, dry
and trim, took on an unfamiliar well-scrubbed look. Lilacs
and forsythias rashly began to break their buds, months
too soon. A wave of giddiness swept New York: topcoats
and snow robes disappeared, the streets were crowded
with smiling buoyant people in light tunics and jerkins,
throngs of nude and semi-nude sunbathers, pale but eager,
sprawled on the sunny embankments of Central Park,
every fountain in midtown had its full complement of
musicians and jugglers and dancers. The carnival atmo-
sphere intensified as the old year ticked away and the
startling weather lingered, for this was 1999 and what
was ebbing was not only a year but an entire millennium.
(Those who insisted that the twenty-first century and the
third millennium would not properly begin until January
1, 2001, were regarded as spoilsports and pedants.) The
coming of April in December unhinged everyone. The
unnatural mildness of the weather following so soon on
the unnatural cold, the mysterious brightness of the sun
hanging low on the southern horizon, the weird soft
springlike texture of the air, gave a bizarre apocalyptic
flavor to these days, so that anything seemed possible and
it would not have been a surprise to behold strange comets
in the night sky, or violent shifts in the constellations. I
imagine it was something like that in Rome just before
the arrival of the Goths, or in Paris on the verge of the
Terror. It was a joyous but obscurely disturbing and
frightening week; we relished the miraculous warmth, but
we took it also as an omen, a portent, of some somber
confrontation yet to come. As the final day of December
approached there was an odd, perceptible heightening of
tension. The giddy mood was still with us, but there was
a sharp edge to it. What we felt was the desperate gaiety
of tightrope walkers dancing over a fathomless abyss.
There were those who said, taking a cruel pleasure in
the grim prediction, that New Year's Eve would be
blighted by sudden vast snow, by tidal waves or tornadoes,
despite the weather bureau's forecast of continued balm-

iness. But the day was bright and sweet, like the seven days preceding it. By noon, we learned, it was already the warmest December 31 since such records had been kept in New York City, and the mercury continued to climb all afternoon, so that we passed from pseudo-April into a perplexing imitation of June.

During this whole time I had kept to myself, shrouded in murky confusions and, I suppose, self-pity. I called no one—not Lombroso nor Sundara nor Mardikian nor Carvajal nor any of the other shreds and fragments of my former existence. I did go out for a few hours each day to roam the streets—who could resist that sun?—but I spoke to nobody and I discouraged people from speaking to me, and by evening I was home, alone, to read a bit, drink some brandy, listen to music without really listening, go early to bed. My isolation seemed to deprive me of all stochastic grace: I lived entirely in the past, like an animal, with no notion of what might happen next, no hunches, none of the old sense of patterns gathering and meshing.

On New Year's Eve I felt a need to be outdoors. To barricade myself in solitude on such a night was intolerable, the eve of, among other things, my thirty-fourth birthday. I thought of phoning friends, but no, the social energies had deserted me: I would slink solitary and unknown through the byways of Manhattan, like the Caliph Haroun al-Raschid touring Baghdad. But I dressed in my nippy-dip peacock best, summer clothes of scarlet and gold with glistening underthreads, and I trimmed my beard and scraped my scalp, and I went out jauntily to see the century into its tomb.

Darkness had come by late afternoon—this was still the depth of winter, no matter what the thermometer told us —and the lights of the city glittered. Though it was only seven o'clock, the partying evidently was beginning early; I heard singing, distant laughter, the sounds of chanting, the far-off crash of breaking glass. I had a meager dinner in a small automated restaurant on Third Avenue and walked aimlessly westward and southward.

Ordinarily one didn't stroll like this in Manhattan after

dark. But tonight the streets were as busy as they were by day, pedestrians everywhere, laughing, peering into shopwindows, waving to strangers, jostling one another playfully, and I felt safe. Was this truly New York, the city of closed faces and wary eyes, the city of knives that gleamed on dark sullen streets? Yes, yes, yes, New York, but a New York transformed, a millennial New York, New York on the night of the climactic Saturnalia.

Saturnalia, yes, that was what it was, a lunatic revel, a frenzy of ecstatic spirits. Every drug in the psychedelic pharmacopoeia was being peddled on streetcorners, and sales seemed brisk. No one walked a straight line. Sirens wailed everywhere as the gaiety mounted in pitch. I took no drugs myself except the ancient one, alcohol, which I took most copiously, stopping in tavern after tavern, a beer here, a shot of awful brandy there, some tequila, some rum, a martini, even dark rich sherry. I was dizzy but not demolished: somehow I stayed upright and more or less coherent, and my mind functioned with what seemed like its customary lucidity, observing, recording.

There were definite increments of wildness from hour to hour. In the bars nudity was still uncommon by nine, but by half past there was bare sweaty flesh everywhere, jiggling breasts, waggling buttocks, clap hands and kick, everyone join in a circle. It was half past nine before I saw anyone screwing in the streets, but outdoor fornication was widespread by ten. An undercurrent of violence had been present all evening—smashing of windows, shooting out of streetlamps—but it picked up strength rapidly after ten: there were fistfights, some genial, some murderous, and at the corner of Fifty-seventh and Fifth there was a mob battle going on, a hundred men and women clubbing at each other in what looked like a random way, and motorists were having noisy disputes everywhere, and it seemed to me that some drivers were deliberately ramming their cars into others for the sheer destructive fun of it. Were there murders? Most certainly. Rapes? By the thousand. Mutilations and other monstrosities? I have no doubt.

And where were the police? I saw them, now and

then, some trying desperately to hold back the tide of disorder, others giving in and joining it, policemen with flushed faces and glazed eyes happily wading into fights and escalating them to savage warfare, policemen buying drugs from the corner peddlers, policemen stripped to the waist groping naked girls in bars, policemen raucously smashing windshields with their nightsticks. The general craziness was contagious. After a week of apocalyptic build-up, a week of grotesque tension, no one could hold too tightly to his sanity.

Midnight found me in Times Square. The old custom, long since abandoned by a city in decay: thousands, hundreds of thousands, crammed shoulder to shoulder between Forty-sixth and Forty-second Streets, singing, shouting, kissing, swaying. Suddenly the hour struck. Startling searchlights speared the sky. The summits of office towers turned radiant with brilliant floodlights. The year 2000! The year 2000! And my birthday had come! Happy birthday! Happy, happy, happy me!

I was drunk. I was out of my mind. The universal hysteria raged in me. I found my hands grasping someone's breasts, and squeezed, and jammed my mouth against a mouth, and felt a hot moist body pressed tight to mine. The crowd surged and we were swept apart, and I moved on the human tide, hugging, laughing, fighting to catch my breath, leaping, falling, stumbling, nearly going down beneath a thousand pairs of feet.

"There's a fire!" someone yelled, and indeed flames were dancing high on a building to the west along Forty-fourth Street. Such a lovely orange hue—we began to cheer and applaud. We are all Nero tonight, I thought, and was swept onward, southward. I could no longer see the flames but the smell of smoke was spreading through the area. Bells tolled. More sirens. Chaos, chaos, chaos.

And then I felt a sensation as of a fist pounding the back of my head, and dropped to my knees in an open space, dazed, and covered my face with my hands to ward off the next blow, but there was no next blow, only a flood of visions. Visions. A baffling torrent of images roared through my mind. I saw myself old and frayed, coughing in a hospital bed with a shining spidery lattice of medical machinery all about me; I saw myself swimming in a clear mountain pool; I saw myself battered and heaved by surf on some angry tropical shore. I peered into the mysterious interior of some vast incomprehensible crystalline mechanism. I stood at the edge of a field of lava, watching molten matter bubble and pop as on the earth's first morning. Colors assailed me. Voices whispered to me, speaking in fragments, in pulverized bits of words and tag ends of phrases. This is a trip, I told myself, a trip, a trip, a very bad trip, but even the worst trip ends eventually, and I crouched, trembling, trying not to resist, letting the nightmare sweep through me and play itself out. It may have gone on for hours; it may have lasted only a minute. In one moment of clarity I said to myself, This is *seeing*, this is how it begins, like a fever, like a madness. I remember telling myself that.

I remember vomiting, too, casting forth the evening's mixture of liquors in quick heavy tremors, and huddling afterward near my own stinking pool, weak, shaking, unable to rise. And then came thunder, like the anger of Zeus, majestic and unanswerable. There was a great stillness after that one terrifying thunderclap. All over the city the Saturnalia was halting as New Yorkers stopped, stiffened, turned their eyes in wonder and awe to the skies. What now? Thunder on a winter night? Would the earth open and swallow us all? Would the sea rise and make an Atlantic of our playground? There came a second clap of thunder minutes after the first, but no lightning, and then, after another pause, a third, and then came rain, gentle at first, torrential in a few moments, a warm spring rain to welcome us to the year 2000. I rose uncertainly to my feet and, having remained chastely clothed all evening, stripped now, naked on Broadway at Forty-first Street, feet flat on the pavement, head upturned, letting the downpour wash the sweat and tears and weariness from me, letting it sluice my mouth to rinse me of the foul taste of vomit. It was a wondrous moment. But quickly I felt chilled. April was over; December was returning. My sex shriveled and my shoulders sagged. Shivering, I fumbled for my sodden clothes, and, sober now, drenched, miserable, timid, imagining brigands and cutpurses lurking in every alley, I began the long slow shuffle across town. The temperature seemed to plummet five degrees for every ten blocks I traversed; by the time I reached the East Side I felt I was freezing, and as I crossed Fifty-seventh Street I noticed the rain had turned to snow, and the snow was sticking, making a fine powdery dusting that covered streets and automobiles and the slumped bodies of the unconscious and the dead. It was snowing with full wintry malevolence when I reached my apartment. The time was five in the morning, January 1, A.D. 2000. I dropped my clothing on the floor and fell naked into bed, quivering, sore, and I pressed my knees to my chest and huddled there, half expecting to die before dawn. Fourteen hours passed before I awoke.

39 What a morning after! For me, for you, for all of New York! Not until night was beginning to fall, that first of January, was the full impact of the previous night's wild events apparent, how many hundreds of citizens had perished in violence or in foolish misadventure or of mere exposure, how many shops had been looted, how many public monuments vandalized, how many wallets lifted, how many unwilling bodies violated. Had any city known a night like that since the sack of Byzantium? The populace had gone berserk, and no one had tried to restrain the fury, no one, not even the police. The first scattered reports had it that most of the officers of the law had joined the fun, and, as detailed investigations proceeded throughout the day, it turned out that that had in fact been the case: in the contagion of the moment the men in blue had often led rather than contained the chaos. On the late news came word that Police Commissioner Sudakis, taking personal responsibility for the debacle, had resigned. I saw him on the screen, face rigid, eyes reddened, his fury barely under control; he spoke raggedly of the shame he felt, the disgrace; he talked of the breakdown of morality, even of the decline of urban civilization; he looked like a man who had had

216

no sleep for a week, a pitiful shattered embarrassment of a man, mumbling and coughing, and I prayed silently for the television people to have done with him and go elsewhere. Sudakis' resignation was my own vindication, but I could take little pleasure in it. At last the scene shifted; we saw the rubble of a five-block area in Brooklyn that had been allowed to burn by absentminded firemen. Yes, yes, Sudakis has resigned. Of course. Reality is conserved; Carvajal's infallibility is once more confirmed. Who could have anticipated such a turn of events? Not I, not Mayor Quinn, not even Sudakis; but Carvajal had.

I waited a few days, while the city slowly returned to normal; then I phoned Lombroso at his Wall Street office. He wasn't there, of course. I told the answering machine to program a return call at his earliest convenience. All high city officials were with the mayor at Gracie Mansion virtually on a round-the-clock basis. Fires in every borough had left thousands homeless; the hospitals were stacked three tiers deep with victims of violence and accident; damage claims against the city, mainly for failure to provide proper police protection, were already in the billions and mounting hourly. Then, too, there was the damage to the city's public image to deal with. Since entering office Quinn had painstakingly tried to restore the reputation New York had had in the middle of the twentieth century as the nation's most exciting, vital, stimulating city, the true capital of the planet and the center of all that was interesting, a city that was thrilling yet safe for visitors. All that had been ruined in one orgiastic night more in keeping with the nation's familiar view of New York as a brutal, insane, ferocious, filthy zoo. So I heard nothing from Lombroso until the middle of January, when things were fairly quiet again, and by the time he called I had given up hearing from him at all.

He told me what was going on at City Hall: the mayor, worried about the effects of the riot on his presidential hopes, was preparing a sheaf of drastic, almost Gottfriedesque, measures to maintain public order. The police shakeup would be accelerated, drug traffic would be restricted almost as severely as it had been before the liberalizations of the 1980s, an early-warning system would be put into effect to head off civic disturbances involving more than two dozen persons, et cetera, et cetera. It sounded wrongheaded to me, a rash, panicky response to a unique event, but my advice was no longer welcome and I kept my thoughts to myself.

"What about Sudakis?" I asked.

"He's definitely out. Quinn refused his resignation and spent three full days trying to persuade him to stay, but Sudakis regards himself as permanently discredited here by the stuff his men did that night. He's taken some small-town job in western Pennsylvania and he's already gone."

"I don't mean that. I mean, has the accuracy of my prediction about Sudakis had any effect on Quinn's attitude toward me?"

"Yes," Lombroso said. "Definitely."

"Is he reconsidering?"

"He thinks you're a sorcerer. He thinks you may have sold your soul to the devil. Literally. Literally. Underneath all the sophistication, he's still an Irish Catholic, don't forget. In times of stress it surfaces in him. Around City Hall you've become the Antichrist, Lew."

"Has he gone so crazy that he can't see it might be useful to have somebody around who can tip him to things like the Sudakis resignation?"

"No hope, Lew. Forget about working for Quinn. Put it absolutely out of your mind. Don't think about him, don't write letters to him, don't try to call him, don't have anything to do with him. You might look into the idea of leaving the city, in fact."

"Jesus. Why?"

"For your own good."

"What's that supposed to mean? Bob, are you trying to tell me I'm in *danger* from Quinn?"

"I'm not trying to tell you anything," he said, sounding nervous.

"Whatever you are doing, I'm not having any. I won't believe Quinn's as afraid of me as you think, and I completely refuse to believe he might take some sort of action against me. It isn't credible. I know the man. I was practically his alter ego for four years. I—"

"Listen, Lew," Lombroso said, "I've got to get off the line. You can't imagine how much work is stacking up here."

"All right. Thanks for returning my call."

"And—Lew—"

"Yes?"

"It might be a good idea for you not to call me. Not even at the Wall Street number. Except in case of some dire emergency, of course. My own position with Quinn has been a little delicate ever since we tried to work that proxy deal, and now—and now—well, you understand, don't you? I'm sure you understand."

40 I understood. I have spared Lombroso the perils of further telephone calls from me. Eleven months, nearly, have passed since the day of that conversation, and in that time I haven't spoken to him at all, not a word to the man who was my closest friend during my years in the Quinn administration. Nor have I had any contact, direct or otherwise, with Quinn himself.

41 In February the visions began. There had been one harbinger on the cliff at Big Sur and another in Times Square on New Year's Eve, but now they became a routine part of my daily life. *None can pierce the vast black veil uncertain*, the poet said, *Because there is no light behind the curtain*. Oh, but the light, the light, the light, the light is there! And it lit my winter days. At first the visions came over me no more often than once every twenty-four hours, and they came unasked, like epileptic fits, usually in the late afternoon or just before midnight, signaling themselves with a glow at the back of my skull, a warmth, a tickling that would not go away. But soon I understood the techniques for invoking them, and I could summon them at will. Even then I was able to *see* at most once a day, with a prolonged period of recuperation required afterward. Within a few weeks, though, I became capable of entering the *seeing* state more readily —two or even three times a day—as if the power were a muscle that thrived with use. Eventually the interval of recuperation became minimal. Now I can turn the gift on every fifteen minutes if I feel like it. Once, experimentally, toward the early part of March, I tried it—on-off, on-off—constantly for several hours, tiring myself but not diminishing the intensity of what I *saw*.

If I don't evoke the visions at least once a day they come to me anyway, breaking through of their own accord, pouring unbidden into my mind.

42

I *see* a small red-shingled house on a country lane. The trees are in full leaf, dark green; it must be late summer. I stand by the front gate. My hair is still short and stubbly but growing in; this scene must lie not very far in the future, probably this very year. Two young men are with me, one dark-haired and slight, the other a burly red-haired one. I have no idea who they are, but the self I *see* is relaxed and easy with them, as if they are intimate companions. So they are close friends that I am yet to meet. I *see* myself taking a key from my pocket. "Let me show you the place," I say. "I think it's about what we need as the headquarters for the Center."

Snow is falling. The automobiles in the streets are bullet-shaped, snub nosed, very small, very strange to me. Overhead a kind of helicopter soars. Three paddlelike projections dangle from it, and there are loudspeakers, apparently, at the tip of each paddle. From the three speakers in unison comes a wistful bleating sound, high-pitched and gentle, emitted for a period of perhaps two seconds spaced by five-second spans of silence. The rhythm is perfectly steady, each mild bleep arriving on

schedule and cutting effortlessly through the dense swirls
of descending flakes. The helicopter flies slowly up Fifth
Avenue at an altitude of less than 500 meters, and as it
makes its bleating way northward the snow melts below
its path, clearing a zone exactly as wide as the avenue.

Sundara and I meet for cocktails at a glittering lounge
hanging like the gardens of Nebuchadnezzar from the
summit of some gigantic tower looming over Los Angeles.
I assume it's Los Angeles because I can make out the
feathery shapes of palm trees lining the streets far beneath
the window, and the architecture of the surrounding buildings is distinctly Southern Californian, and through the
twilight haze there is a hint of a vast ocean not far to
the west and mountains to the north. I have no idea
what I'm doing in California nor how I come to be seeing
Sundara there; it's plausible that she has returned to
her native city to live and I, visiting on business, have
promoted a reunion. We have both changed. Her hair is
streaked now with white, and her face seems leaner,
less voluptuous; her eyes sparkle as before, but the gleam
in them is the glint of hard-won knowledge, and not just
playfulness. I am long-haired, graying, dressed with chaste
ferocity in an unadorned black tunic; I look about forty-
five, and I strike myself as crisp, taut, impressive, a
commanding executive type, so self-possessed that I awe
myself. Are there signs about my eyes of that tragic
exhaustion, that burned-out devastation that had marked
Carvajal after so many years of *seeing?* I don't think so;
but perhaps my second sight is not yet intense enough
to register such subjective details. Sundara wears no
wedding ring, nor are there any of the insignia of Transit
visible about her. My watching self longs to ask a thousand questions. I want to know whether there has been
a reconciliation, whether we see each other often, whether
we are lovers, whether perhaps we are even living together again. But I have no voice, I am unable to speak
through the lips of my future self, it is altogether impossible for me to direct or modify his actions; I can
merely observe. He and Sundara order drinks; they clink

glasses; they smile; they exchange trivial chatter about the sunset, the weather, the decor of the cocktail lounge. Then the scene slips away and I have learned nothing.

Soldiers move through the canyons of New York, five abreast, looking warily to all sides. I watch them from an upper-story window. They wear bizarre uniforms, green with red piping, gaudy yellow and red berets, ruffles at their shoulders. They are armed with weapons that look a little like crossbows—sturdy metal tubes about a meter in length, widening to a fan at the outer end and bristling with lateral whiskers of bright wire coil —which they carry with the wide ends balanced across their left forearms. The self who watches them is a man of at least sixty, white-haired, gaunt, with deep vertical lines scored in his cheeks; he is recognizably myself, and yet he is almost wholly strange to me. In the street a figure erupts from a building and rushes wildly toward the soldiers, shouting slogans, waving his arms. One very young soldier jerks his right arm up and a cone of green light emerges quietly from his weapon; the onrushing figure halts, incandescent, and disappears. Disappears.

The self I *see* is still youthful, but older than I am now. Say, forty: then this would be about the year 2006. He lies on a rumpled bed next to an attractive young woman with long black hair; they are both naked, sweaty, disheveled; obviously they have been making love. He asks, "Did you hear the President's speech last night?"

"Why should I waste my time listening to that murderous fascist bastard?" she replies.

A party is going on. Shrill unfamiliar music, strange golden wine poured freely from double-spouted bottles. The air is dense with blue fumes. I hold court at one corner of the crowded room, talking urgently with a plump freckle-faced young woman and one of the young men who had been with me at that red-shingled house. But my voice is covered by the raucous music and I perceive only shreds and scraps of what I am saying; I pick up words like *miscalculation* and *overload* and *demonstration* and *alternative distribution*, but they are embedded in gibberish and it is all ultimately unintelligible. The clothing styles are odd, loose irregular garments decked with patches and strips of mismatched fabrics. In the middle of the room about twenty of the guests are dancing with weird intensity, milling in a ragged circle, slashing the air fiercely with elbows and knees. They are nude; they have coated their bodies entirely with a glossy purple dye; they are altogether hairless, both men and women totally depilated from head to foot, so that but for their jiggling genitals and bobbing breasts they might easily pass for plastic mannequins jolted into a twitching, spasmodic counterfeit of life.

A humid summer night. A dull booming sound, another, another. Fireworks explode against the blackness of the sky over the Hudson's Jersey shore. Skyrockets litter the heavens with Chinese fire, red, yellow, green, blue, dazzling streaks and starbursts, cycle upon cycle of flaming beauty accompanied by terrifying hisses and pops and roars and bangs, climax after climax, and then, just as one assumes the splendor now will die away into silence and darkness, there comes an amazing final pyrotechnical frenzy, culminating in a grand double set piece: an American flag spectacularly quivering above us with every star discernible, and, exploding out of the center of Old Glory's field, the image of a man's face, limned in startling realistic flesh tones. The face is the face of Paul Quinn.

I am aboard a great airplane, a plan whose wings seem to stretch from China to Peru, and through the porthole beside me I see a vast gray-blue sea on whose bosom the reflected sun shines in a furious glaring brightness. I am strapped down, awaiting landing, and now I can make out our destination: an enormous hexagonal platform rising steeply from the sea, an artificial island as symmetrical in its angles as a snowflake, a concrete island encrusted with squat red-brick buildings and split down its middle by the long white arrow of an airstrip, an island that is entirely alone in this immense sea with thousands of kilometers of emptiness bordering each of its six sides.

Manhattan. Autumn, chilly, the sky dark, the windows overhead glowing. Before me a colossal tower rising just east of the venerable Fifth Avenue library. "The tallest in the world," someone says behind me, one tourist to another, twanging Western accent. Indeed it must be. The tower fills the sky. "It's all government offices," the Westerner goes on. "Can you catch it? Two hundred floors high, and all government offices. With a palace for Quinn right at the top, so they say. For whenever he comes to town. A goddamned palace, like for a king."

What I particularly fear as these visions crowd upon me is my first confrontation with the scene of my own death. Will I be destroyed by it, I wonder, as Carvajal was destroyed—all drive and purpose sucked from me by one glimpse of my last moments? I wait, wondering when it will come, dreading it and eager for it, wanting to absorb the terrifying knowledge and be done with it, and when it does come it's an anticlimax, a comic letdown. What I *see* is a faded, weary old man in a hospital bed, gaunt and worn, perhaps seventy-five years old, maybe eighty, even ninety. He is surrounded by a bright cocoon of life-support apparatus; needled arms arch and weave about him like the tails of scorpions, filling him with enzymes, hormones, decongestants, stimulants, whatever. I've seen him before, briefly, that drunken night in Times Square when I crouched dazzled and astounded, tripping out on a torrent of voices and images, but now the vision continues a little further than that other time, so that I perceive this future me not merely as a sick old man, but as a dying old man on his way out, sliding away, sliding away, the whole vast wonderful lattice of medical equipment unable any longer to sustain the feeble beat of life. I can feel the pulse ebbing in him. Quietly, quietly, he is going. Into the darkness. Into the peace.

He is very still. Not yet dead, else my perceptions of him would cease. But almost. Almost. And now. No more data. Peace and silence. A good death, yes.

Is that all? Is he truly dead, out there fifty or sixty years from now, or has the vision merely been interrupted? I can't be sure. If only I could *see* beyond that moment of quietus, just a glimpse past the curtain, to watch the routines of death, the expressionless orderlies placidly disconnecting the life-support system, the sheet pulled up over the face, the cadaver wheeled off to the morgue. But there is no way to pursue the image. The picture show ends with the last flicker of light. Yet I am certain that this is it. I am relieved and almost a bit disappointed. So little? Just to fade away at a great old age? Nothing to dread in that. I think of Carvajal, crazy-eyed from having seen himself die too often. But I'm not Carvajal. How can such knowledge harm me? I admit the inevitability of my death; the details are mere footnotes. The scene recurs, a few weeks later, and then again, and again. Always the same. The hospital, the spidery maze of life-support stuff, the sliding, the darkness, the peace. So there is nothing to fear from *seeing*. I've seen the worst, and it hasn't harmed me.

But then all is cast into doubt and my newfound confidence is shattered. I *see* myself again in that great plane, and we are swooping toward the hexagonal artificial island. A cabin attendant rushes up the aisle, distraught, alarmed, and behind her comes a bellying oily burst of black smoke. Fire on board! The plane's wings dip wildly. There are screams. Unintelligible cries over the public-address system. Muffled, incoherent instructions. Pressure nails my body to my seat; we are plunging toward the ocean. Down, down, and we hit, an incredible cracking impact, the ship is ripped apart; still strapped in, I plummet face first into the cold dark depths. The sea swallows me and I know no more.

The soldiers move in sinister columns through the

streets. They pause outside the building where I live; they confer; then a detachment bursts into the house. I hear them on the stairs. No use trying to hide. They throw open the door, shouting my name. I greet them, hands raised. I smile and tell them I'll go peacefully. But then —who knows why?—one of them, a very young one, in fact, only a boy, swings suddenly around, aiming his crossbowlike weapon at me. I have time only to gasp. Then the green radiance comes, and darkness afterward.

"This is the one!" someone yells, raising a club high above my head and bringing it down with terrible force.

Sundara and I watch nightfall engulf the Pacific. The lights of Santa Monica sparkle before us. Tentatively, timidly, I cover her hand with mine. And in that moment I feel a stabbing pain in my chest. I crumple, I topple, I kick frantically, knocking the table over, I pound my fists against the thick carpet, I struggle to hold on to life. There is the taste of blood in my mouth. I fight to live, and I lose.

I stand on a parapet eighty stories above Broadway. With a quick, easy motion I push myself outward into the cool spring air. I float, I make graceful swimming gestures with my arms, I dive serenely toward the pavement.

"Look out!" a woman close beside me cries. "He's got a bomb!"

The surf is rough today. Gray waves rise and crash, rise and crash. Yet I wade out, I force my way through the breakers, I swim with lunatic dedication toward the horizon, cleaving the bleak sea as though out to set an endurance record, swimming on and on despite the throbbing in my temples and the pounding at the base of my throat, and the sea grows more tempestuous, its surface heaving and swelling even out here, so far from short. The water hits me in the face and I go under, choking, and battle my way to the surface, and I am hit again, again, again . . .

"This is the one!" someone yells.

I *see* myself again in that great plane, and we are swooping toward the hexagonal artificial island.

"Look out!" a woman close beside me cries.

The soldiers move in sinister columns through the streets. They pause outside the building where I live.

The surf is rough today. Gray waves rise and crash, rise and crash. Yet I wade out, I force my way through the breakers, I swim with lunatic dedication toward the horizon.

"This is the one!" someone yells.

Sundara and I watch nightfall engulf the Pacific. The lights of Santa Monica sparkle before us.

I stand on a parapet eighty stories above Broadway. With a quick, easy motion I push myself outward into the cool spring air.

"This is the one!" someone yells.

And so. Death, again and again, coming to me in many forms. The scenes recurring, unvarying, contradicting and nullifying one another. Which is the true vision? What of that old man fading peacefully in his hospital bed? What am I to believe? I am dizzied with an overload of data; I stumble about in a schizophrenic fever, *seeing* more than I can comprehend, integrating nothing, and constantly my pulsating brain drenches me with scenes and images. I am coming apart. I huddle on the floor next to my bed, trembling, waiting for new confusions to seize me. How shall I perish next? The torturer's rack?

A plague of botulism? A knife in a dark alleyway? What does all this mean? What's happening to me? I need help. Desperate, terrified, I rush to see Carvajal.

43 It was months since I had last seen him, half a year, from late November to late April, and he had evidently been through some changes. He looked smaller, almost doll-like, a miniature of his old self, all surplus pared away, the skin drawn back tightly over his cheekbones, his color a peculiar off-yellow, as though he were turning into an elderly Japanese, one of those desiccated little ancients in blue suits and bowties that can sometimes be seen sitting calmly beside the tickers in downtown brokerage houses. There was an unfamiliar Oriental calmness about Carvajal, too, an eerie Buddha-tranquillity that seemed to say he had reached a place beyond all storms, a peace that was, happily, contagious: moments after I arrived, full of panic and bewilderment, I felt the charge of tension leaving me. Graciously he seated me in his dismal living room, graciously he brought me the traditional glass of water.

He waited for me to speak.

How to begin? What to say? I decided to vault completely over our last conversation, putting it away, making no reference to my anger, to my accusations, to my repudiation of him. "I've been *seeing*," I blurted.

"Yes?" Quizzical, unsurprised, faintly bored.

"Disturbing things."

"Oh?"

Carvajal studied me incuriously, waiting, waiting. How placid he was, how self-contained! Like something carved from ivory, beautiful, glossy, immobile.

"Weird scenes. Melodramatic, chaotic, contradictory, bizarre. I don't know what's clairvoyance and what's schizophrenia."

"Contradictory?" he asked.

"Sometimes. I can't trust what I *see*."

"What sort of things?"

"Quinn, for one. He recurs almost daily. Images of Quinn as a tyrant, a dictator, some sort of monster, manipulating the entire nation, not so much a President as a generalissimo. His face is all over the future. Quinn this, Quinn that, everyone talking about him, everyone afraid of him. It can't be real."

"Whatever you *see* is real."

"No. That's not the real Quinn. That's a paranoid fantasy. I *know* Paul Quinn."

"Do you?" Carvajal asked, his voice reaching me from a distance of fifty thousand light-years.

"Look, I was dedicated to that man. In a real sense I loved that man. And loved what he stood for. Why do I get these visions of him as a dictator? *Why have I become afraid of him?* He isn't like that. I know he isn't."

"Whatever you *see* is real," Carvajal repeated.

"Then there's a Quinn dictatorship coming in this country?"

Carvajal shrugged. "Perhaps. Very likely. How would I know?"

"How would I? How can I believe what I *see*?"

Carvajal smiled and held up one hand, palm toward me. "Believe," he urged in the weary, mocking tone of some old Mexican priest advising a troubled boy to have faith in the goodness of the angels and the charity of the Virgin. "Have no doubts. Believe."

"I can't. There are too many contradictions." I shook my head fiercely. "It isn't just the Quinn visions. I've been *seeing* my own death, too."

"Yes, one must expect that."

"Many times. In many different ways. A plane crash. A suicide. A heart attack. A drowning. And more."

"You find it strange, eh?"

"Strange? I find it absurd. Which one is the reality?"

"They all are."

"That's crazy!"

"There are many levels of reality, Lew."

"They can't all be real. That violates everything you've told me about one fixed and unalterable future."

"There's one future that *must* occur," Carvajal said. "There are many that do not. In the early stages of the *seeing* experience the mind is unfocused, and reality becomes contaminated with hallucination, and the spirit is bombarded with extraneous data."

"But—"

"Perhaps there are many time lines," Carvajal said. "One true one, and many potential ones, abortive lines, lines that have their existence only in the gray borderlands of probability. Sometimes information from those time lines crowds in on one if one's mind is open enough, if it is vulnerable enough. I've experienced that."

"You never said a word about it."

"I didn't want to confuse you, Lew."

"But what do I do? What good is any of the information I'm receiving? How do I distinguish the real visions from the imaginary ones?"

"Be patient. Things will clarify."

"How soon?"

"When you *see* yourself die," he said, "have you ever seen the same scene more than once?"

"Yes."

"Which one?"

"I've had one at least twice."

"But one more than any of the others?"

"Yes," I said. "The first one. Myself as an old man in a hospital, with a lot of intricate medical equipment surrounding my bed. That one comes frequently."

"With special intensity?"

I nodded.

"Trust it," Carvajal said. "The others are phantoms. They'll stop bothering you before long. The imaginary ones have a feverish, insubstantial feel to them. They waver and blur at the edges. If you look at them closely, your gaze pierces them and you behold the blankness beyond. Soon they vanish. It's been thirty years, Lew, since such things have troubled me."

"And the Quinn visions? Are they phantoms out of some other time line, too? Have I helped to set a monster loose in this country or am I just suffering from bad dreams?"

"There's no way I can answer that for you. You'll simply have to wait and see, and learn to refine your vision, and look again, and weigh the evidence."

"You can't give me any suggestions more precise than that?"

"No," he said. "It isn't possible to—"

The doorbell rang.

"Excuse me," Carvajal said.

He left the room. I closed my eyes and let the surf of some unknown tropical sea wash across my mind, a warm salty bath erasing all memory and all pain, making the rough places smooth. I perceived past, present, and future now as equally unreal: wisps of fog, shafts of blurred pastel light, far-off laughter, furry voices speaking in fragmentary sentences. Somewhere a play was being produced, but I was no longer on stage, nor was I in the audience. Time lay suspended. Perhaps, eventually, I began to *see*. I think Quinn's blunt earnest features hovered before me, bathed in garish green and blue spotlights, and I might have *seen* the old man in the hospital and the armed men moving through the streets; and there were glimpses of worlds beyond worlds, of the empires still unborn, of the dance of the continents, of the sluggish creatures that crawl over the great planet-girdling shell of ice at the end of time. Then I heard voices from the hallway, a man shouting, Carvajal patiently explaining, denying. Something about drugs, a doublecross, angry accusations. What? What? I struggled up out of the fog that bound me. There was Carvajal,

by the door, confronted by a short freckle-faced man
with wild blue eyes and unkempt flame-red hair. The
stranger was clutching a gun, an old clumsy one, a blue-
black cannon of a gun, swirling it excitedly from side
to side. The shipment, he kept yelling, where's the shipment, what are you trying to pull? And Carvajal shrugged
and smiled and shook his head and said over and over,
mildly, This is a mistake, it's simply an error. Carvajal
looked radiant. It was as though all his life had been
bent and shaped toward this moment of grace, this
epiphany, this confused and comic doorway dialogue.

I stepped forward, ready to play my part. I devised
lines for myself. I would say, *Easy, fellow, stop waving
that gun around. You've come to the wrong place. We've
got no drugs here.* I saw myself moving confidently toward the intruder, still talking. *Why don't you cool down,
put the gun away, phone the boss and get things straight-
ened out? Because otherwise you'll find yourself in heavy
trouble, and*—Still talking, looming over the little freckle-
faced gunman, calmly reaching for the gun, twisting it
out of his hand, pressing him against the wall—

Wrong script. The real script called for me to do
nothing. I knew that. I did nothing.

The gunman looked at me, at Carvajal, at me again.
He hadn't been expecting me to emerge from the living
room and he wasn't sure how to react. Then came a
knock at the outside door. A man's voice from the
corridor asking Carvajal if everything was okay in there.
The gunman's eyes flashed in fear and bewilderment. He
jerked away from Carvajal, pulling in on himself. There
was a shot—almost peripherally, incidentally. Carvajal
began to fall but supported himself against the wall. The
gunman sprinted past me, toward the living room. Paused
there, trembling, in a half crouch. He fired again. A third
shot. Then swung suddenly toward the window. The
sound of breaking glass. I had been standing frozen, but
now at last I started to move. Too late; the intruder
was out the window, down the fire escape, disappearing
into the street.

I turned toward Carvajal. He had fallen and lay near

the entrance to the living room, motionless, silent, eyes open, still breathing. His shirt was bloody down the front; a second patch of blood was spreading along his left arm; there was a third wound, oddly precise and small, at the side of his head, just above the cheekbone. I ran to him and held him and saw his eyes glaze, and it seemed to me he laughed right at the end, a small soft chuckle, but that may be scriptwriting of my own, a little neat stage direction. So. So. Done at last. How calm he had been, how accepting, how glad to be over with it. The scene so long rehearsed, now finally played.

44

Carvajal died on April 22, 2000. I write this in early December, with the true beginning of the twenty-first century and the start of the new millennium just a few weeks away. The coming of the millennium will find me at this unprepossessing house in this unspecified town in northern New Jersey, directing the activities, still barely under way, of the Center for Stochastic Processes. We have been here since August, when Carvajal's will cleared probate with me as sole heir to his millions.

Here at the Center, of course, we don't dabble much in stochastic processes. The place is deceptively named; we are not stochastic here but rather post-stochastic, going on beyond the manipulation of probabilities into the certainties of second sight. But I thought it wise not to be too candid about that. What we're doing is a species of witchcraft, more or less, and one of the great lessons of the all-but-concluded twentieth century is that if you want to practice witchcraft, you'd better do it under some other name. *Stochastic* has a pleasant pseudo-scientific resonance to it that provides the right texture for a disguise, evoking as it does an image of platoons of pale young researchers feeding data into vast computers.

There are four of us so far. There'll be more. We

build gradually here. I find new followers as I need them. I know the name of the next one already, and I know how I'll persuade him to join us, and at the right moment he'll come to us, just as these first three came. Six months ago they were strangers to me; today they are my brothers.

What we build here is a society, a sodality, a community, a priesthood, if you will, a band of *seers*. We are extending and refining the capabilities of our vision, eliminating ambiguities, sharpening perception. Carvajal was right: everyone has the gift. It can be awakened in anyone. In you. In you. And so we'll reach out, each of us offering a hand to another. Quietly spreading the post-stochastic gospel, quietly multiplying the numbers of those who *see*. It'll be slow. There'll be danger, there'll be persecution. Hard times are coming, and not only for us. We still must pass through the era of Quinn, an era that seems as familiar to me as any in history, though it hasn't yet begun: the election that will anoint him is still four years in the future. But I *see* past it, to the upheavals that follow, the turmoil, the pain. Never mind that. We'll outlast the Quinn regime, as we outlasted Assurbanipal, Attila, Genghis Khan, Napoleon. Already the clouds of vision part and we *see* beyond the coming darkness to the time of healing.

What we build here is a community dedicated to the abolition of uncertainty, the absolute elimination of doubt. Ultimately we will lead mankind into a universe in which nothing is random, nothing is unknown, all is predictable on every level from the microcosmic to the macrocosmic, from the twitching of an electron to the journeys of the galactic nebulae. We'll teach humanity to taste the sweet comfort of the foreordained. And in that way we'll become as gods.

Gods? Yes.

Listen, did Jesus know fear when Pilate's centurions came for him? Did he whimper about dying, did he lament the shortening of his ministry? No, no, he went calmly, showing neither fear nor bitterness nor surprise, following the script, playing his appointed role, serenely aware that what was happening to him was part of a predetermined and necessary and inevitable Plan. And what of Isis, the young Isis, loving her brother Osiris, knowing even as a child everything that was in store, that Osiris must be torn apart, that she would seek his sundered body in the mud of the Nile, that through her he would be restored, that from their loins would spring the potent Horus? Isis lived with sorrow, yes, and Isis lived with the foreknowledge of terrible loss, *and she knew these things from the beginning,* for she was a god. And she acted as she had to act. Gods are not granted the power of choice; it is the price and the wonder of their godhead. And gods do not know fear or self-pity or doubt, because they are gods and may not choose any path but the true one. Very well. We shall be as gods, all of us. I have come through the time of doubt, I have endured and survived the onslaught of confusions and terrors, I have moved into a realm beyond those things, but not into a paralysis such as afflicted Carvajal; I am in another place, and I can bring you to it. We will *see,* we will understand, we will comprehend the inevitability of the inevitable, we will accept every turn of the script gladly and without regret. There will be no surprises; therefore there will be no pain. We will live in beauty, knowing that we are aspects of the one great Plan.

About forty years ago a French scientist and philosopher named Jacques Monod wrote, "Man knows at last that he is alone in the indifferent immensity of the universe, whence he has emerged by chance."

I believed that once. You may believe it now.

But examine Monod's statement in the light of a remark that Albert Einstein once made. "God does not throw dice," Einstein said.

One of those statements is wrong. I think I know which one.